Praise for the Keepsake Cove Mysteries

A Vintage Death

"Another deftly crafted and skillfully presented mystery by a master of the genre."

—*Midwest Book Review*

"A satisfying mystery ... Suggest for fans of other mysteries set in cute tourist areas, such as Lorna Barrett's Booktown mysteries."

—*Library Journal*

A Fatal Collection

"Hughes kicks off her new Keepsake Cove series with a charming locale."

—*Kirkus Reviews*

Also by Mary Ellen Hughes

Keepsake Cove Mysteries
(Midnight Ink)
A Fatal Collection
A Vintage Death

Maggie Olenski Mysteries
(Avalon Books)
Resort to Murder
A Taste of Death

Craft Corner Mysteries
(Penguin Group)
Wreath of Deception
String of Lies
Paper-Thin Alibi

Pickled and Preserved Mysteries
(Penguin Group)
The Pickled Piper
License to Dill
Scene of the Brine

A Curio Killing

— A KEEPSAKE COVE MYSTERY —

MARY ELLEN HUGHES

MIDNIGHT INK
WOODBURY, MINNESOTA

FIRST EDITION
First Printing, 2019

Book format by Samantha Penn
Cover design by Shannon McKuhen
Cover Illustration by Mary Ann Lasher-Dodge

Midnight Ink, an imprint of Llewellyn Worldwide Ltd.

Library of Congress Cataloging-in-Publication Data
Names: Hughes, Mary Ellen, author.
Title: A curio killing : a Keepsake Cove mystery / Mary Ellen Hughes.
Description: First Edition. | Woodbury, Minnesota : Midnight Ink, [2019] |
    Series: A Keepsake Cove mystery ; #3
Identifiers: LCCN 2019013882 (print) | LCCN 2019015568 (ebook) | ISBN
    9780738755502 () | ISBN 9780738752266 (alk. paper)
Subjects: LCSH: Murder—Investigation—Fiction. | GSAFD: Mystery fiction.
Classification: LCC PS3558.U3745 (ebook) | LCC PS3558.U3745 C87 2019 (print)
    | DDC 813/.54—dc23
LC record available at https://lccn.loc.gov/2019013882

Midnight Ink
Llewellyn Worldwide Ltd.
2143 Wooddale Drive
Woodbury, MN 55125-2989
www.midnightinkbooks.com

Printed in the United States of America

For Therese Lemanski Luedtke.
Still miss you.

One

"They're setting up the tents!" Delia Hamilton leaned through the doorway of *House of Melody*, Callie Reed's collectible music box shop. Callie, who'd just ended a phone call, lit up. She'd been looking forward to the Keepsake Cove Spring Festival for weeks, and now her long wait through wintery snows and chilly March drizzles was coming to an end. The festival, along with the area's dogwoods and azaleas, was beginning to bud and bloom.

This would be Callie's first Keepsake Cove Spring Festival. She'd inherited her Aunt Melodie's shop and the amazing fairy-tale cottage behind it just eleven months earlier and had gone through a lot in that time, including less-than-pleasant happenings that involved murder. But there had been plenty of good times, too. This, she was sure, was going to be one of them.

"Have you heard from your friend?" she asked. Delia, who owned the shop next door, had told Callie about her childhood friend Jill Burns. Jill moonlighted as a costume photographer, and Delia had talked that up to the festival planners as a fun addition to the music, food, and games. Families and individuals, she'd declared, love photos of themselves dressed as historical figures or comic strip characters to post on Instagram or Facebook. The organizers had agreed.

"She's on her way. I'm so glad she was available," Delia said. "I can't wait to see her. It's been ages."

"I can't wait to see her costumes." Tabitha, Callie's part-time assistant, emerged from the back office. "I'm dying to have my photo taken in something exotic."

Callie stared at Tabitha, unsure if she was joking. The young woman's regular wardrobe was nearly always a costume of one sort or another, put together from thrift-shop pieces and Tabitha's creative imagination. Just that morning she'd arrived dressed in a vintage gray-blue suit with a pair of wire-framed eyeglasses, her chestnut hair pulled back severely in a bun. At Callie's puzzled look, she'd patiently explained that she was Diana Prince, Wonder Woman's alter ego. Callie had nodded, happy only that her assistant hadn't chosen the much briefer Wonder Woman costume, which would certainly startle many of her music box customers.

Longtime *House of Melody* customers, though, had gotten used to Tabitha's habit and apparently enjoyed guessing her character of the day. So it wasn't hard for Callie to go along with it, especially since she was extremely grateful for Tabitha's knowledgeable help at the shop from day one.

"Tabitha," Delia said, "I'm sure Jill couldn't top anything you already do. But I know she'd love to meet you."

"Who'd love to meet her?" a male voice asked. Brian Greer appeared behind Delia, having crossed the street from his business, a breakfast-and-lunch eatery know as the Keepsake Café. He'd been stopping by *House of Melody* more and more often lately during the less-busy mid-afternoon time. Over the last several months, he and Callie had gradually progressed from friends to something-more-than-friends. The unhurried nature of the connection was just fine with Callie. At the age of twenty-nine, after moving to Keepsake Cove, she'd broken off a longtime but downward-spiraling relationship, so she felt a definite need to take things slowly—something she was very grateful that Brian understood.

"My friend Jill, the costume photographer," Delia explained, moving into the shop to allow Brian entrance. With the warmer weather, Delia had resumed her favorite attire of a loose tee over a long, flower-printed maxi skirt, all of which flowed nicely and flattered her rounder frame. Brian was in his usual: jeans and a roll-sleeved plaid shirt. He'd left his green apron behind at the café, which he owned and operated mostly by himself. When asked, he often described himself as chief cook and bottle washer.

"I think you'd look great as Abraham Lincoln," Tabitha said to Brian. "Or maybe Mr. Spock."

"I'll stick with Mr. Greer, thanks. Can't have a long beard getting in my way in the kitchen. Or long pointy ears falling into the soup. I expect to be kept hopping with all the hungry tourists coming to the festival."

"Then maybe you should be the March Hare," Callie suggested, and waited for the groan that quickly came.

"Well," Brian said, "that character did do a lot of rushing around, didn't he?"

"And he always thought it was tea time," Delia said.

"And was, um, a bit mad," Tabitha added.

"There you go," Brian said, grinning. "Perfect."

"Will Annie be helping you with the rushing part?" Callie asked. Brian's sister, who lived in the area, occasionally pitched in at the café.

"She will. But I've promised her plenty of time to enjoy the festival with Mike and the boys. They're really looking forward to it."

"So am I," Callie said.

"Do you enjoy dancing?" Delia asked her. "I understand there'll be a dance floor set up under one of the tents near the bandstand."

"I'm terrible at most kinds, but I like line dancing. That can be a lot of fun." Callie didn't add how she'd happened to learn it, which was during the gigs of various country-western bands that her ex-boyfriend, Hank, had played with. Brian knew about that relationship, of course, but there was no point bringing it up unnecessarily.

"I don't know if you'll get an opportunity to line dance," Delia said. "It's not very big in Maryland."

"Oh, I don't know," Tabitha said. "There's spots here on the Eastern Shore that go in for it. I'll bet there'll be calls for it."

Callie smiled at that but saw Brian's face take on a slightly pained look. She decided she'd coax him to dance if the opportunity came up but wouldn't push him too hard out of his comfort zone.

"Well, I'd better get back to my shop," Delia said. She took off, moments before a customer walked into *House of Melody* and Tabitha stepped up to wait on her. When an older couple appeared to be heading for the shop as well, Brian told Callie he'd get out of her way.

"I've got a few things to do at the café anyway. I'll see you later." He held the door for the couple, then made a final wave to Callie.

Just my luck, Callie thought. Her shop had been quiet as a tomb for the last hour. But when she was enjoying a little face-time with her friends, things picked up. As the older couple began to browse, she watched Brian cross back to the Keepsake Café, sorry to see him go.

They'd both been extra busy the past few weeks with preparations for the festival. Brian had even stepped in to handle publicity when the original volunteer, Pearl Poepelman of *Pearl's Bangles and Beads*, needed to attend to a family emergency. The Keepsake Cove Shop Owners' Association had excused Callie from direct involvement in the planning since she'd done her bit handling the Cove's fall celebration, coordinating the street decorations as well as the Halloween book event for suspense author Lyssa Hammond. That event had turned out to be a lot more than she'd bargained for.

Nevertheless, she still had plenty to do to ready her music box shop for the influx of new customers expected to flood the streets of Keepsake Cove during the spring festival. But that, of course, was the whole point of the celebration—to bring people to the area, some of whom might not yet have discovered this quaint section of the town of Mapleton.

Each of the shops in the Cove featured a unique type of collectible item. Next door to *House of Melody*, Delia's *Shake It Up!* offered a huge variety of collectible salt and pepper shakers. On the other side, Karl Eggers's *Car-lectibles* carried classic and collectible model cars. Then there was Bill and Laurie Hart's *Kids at Heart* vintage toy shop, Orlena Martin's *Treasured Boxes*, and many, many more. Keepsake Cove was a collector's dream, and more than one shopper had been hooked after a single visit to the area.

Tabitha's customer at last decided on her purchase, a novelty piece with a ballerina figure who twirled inside a globe as the *Nutcracker's* "Waltz of the Flowers" played. Callie heard the woman tell Tabitha that her eight-year-old niece was performing in her first ballet and that the music box would be a perfect gift for her.

As that customer left, the older woman who'd been browsing with her husband asked about a particular music box from the higher-end selections. It happened to be one of Callie's current favorites, a black-enameled jewelry box with a lovely red rose design on its lid.

"The box itself was handcrafted in Italy," Callie said, lifting the lid to display the velvet lined compartments inside. "The mechanism is by Reuge, an old and very well-regarded Swiss firm." She wound the key at the back and the first several notes of one of Schumann's Romances played.

"It's beautiful," the white-haired woman said.

"It's a bit pricey," her concerned husband responded.

"It is," she agreed. "But still beautiful." She gazed at it longingly for several moments before adding, "I'll have to sleep on it."

"Of course," Callie said. "If you like, I could put it aside for forty-eight hours."

"Would you?" The woman gave her name and contact information. "Thank you so much," she said, glancing back at the music box as they made their way out.

"She'll be back," Tabitha said once the door had closed.

"Think so?"

"Uh-huh. She had that look in her eye. I've seen it before. She loved it from the start, but you made the husband a little more comfortable with the cost by throwing in the specifics."

"I might be catching up with you as far as having that kind of information in my head. When I think about how clueless I was that first day ..."

"It took me a while. There's a lot of music boxes to learn about. You had to step in pretty quick after Mel died."

Died was the gentle way of putting it, Callie thought. *Murdered* was the reality—a reality she'd gradually uncovered while still coping with the huge change that the loss of Aunt Melodie had made in her life.

She glanced up at her Grandpa Reed's polished wood music box, locked protectively in its Plexiglas case on the shelf behind the counter. Had Aunt Mel truly been sending her messages through it? Ap-

6

provals or warnings tended to ring out on their own, when no one was near enough to the music box to touch it. Callie could never be sure, but the timing of the sounds was definitely unsettling enough to keep her wondering.

"She's been quiet, lately, hasn't she?" Tabitha asked, apparently reading Callie's thoughts. Tabitha was the only one she'd discussed this topic with, and her assistant was one hundred percent convinced it was Mel's doing.

"Keepsake Cove itself has been quiet," Callie said. "Since October," she added, alluding to the two murders that had occurred at that time. "Let's hope it stays that way."

"I'm with you on that!" Tabitha glanced at the clock. "Oops, time for me to take off. I've got some beading to get to." Tabitha operated a budding beaded-jewelry business out of her home, supplementing her income with part-time work at *House of Melody* until her jewelry-making could support her. Much as Callie wished her assistant the best, she knew she'd be very sorry to lose Tabitha when the time came.

"See you tomorrow," she said as the younger woman grabbed her vintage clutch bag from behind the counter and hurried off on her chunky-heeled, Diana Prince–like shoes. How does she find those things? Callie wondered for perhaps the hundredth time, then turned to find a shelf replacement for the recently sold ballerina globe.

As she puttered around the shop, her thoughts moved between music boxes and the Spring Festival, which would officially open the next day. Would the hoped-for crowds turn out? The weather looked to be gorgeous. But there were so many competing events around the area. It was as though Maryland, neighboring Virginia, and DC all came alive once spring arrived, with horse races, boat shows, art fairs, and more. How much could the average person take in?

She picked up one of her novelty music boxes, which had been moved out of place. It had a guitar design on its lid, and Callie lifted it to hear the first few notes of "Achy Breaky Heart." Her toe started tapping and she rewound the key to hear it again, doing a few steps along with the music.

She was in the middle of a third run-through when the shop door opened and a very familiar, rich baritone voice said, "You still got it, babe."

Callie whirled around in shock.

There, in his denims, cowboy hat, and snakeskin boots stood Hank, grinning from ear to ear, obviously convinced that her shock at the sight of him came from pure delight.

Two

"Hank!" Callie sputtered. "What are you doing here?"

"Yeah, I'm a day early. The band doesn't play until tomorrow night. But this gives me more time to look around." Hank moved in for a hug that Callie was too surprised to resist, though she made an effort to keep it brief.

"So this is it, huh?" he asked, casting a broad look around. "Your aunt's place." He picked up a small music box, glanced at it, and put it down.

"The band is playing *here*?"

"Yeah! I texted you about that, didn't I? Damn, maybe I forgot. Meant to, though."

Astounded at seeing her ex, Callie was still unsure how to react. Hank looked much the same as when she'd last seen him, just as tall and slim, his dark brown hair curling below his cowboy hat. It was his rich, baritone voice that always got to her. But his confession that he'd "meant to" do yet another thing brought back all the reasons she'd decided to end their relationship. She pulled herself together and cleared her throat.

"No, you didn't let me know. It would have been nice, but it doesn't matter all that much. So you'll be performing at our festival?"

"Right! Bobby got us the gig. Two nights, and I get to be here with you."

"Not with me, Hank. Just here at the Cove. But I'm glad things are working out." She knew Hank had joined a new band shortly after she'd moved to Keepsake Cove. The manager, Bobby Linville, had offered him the spot at a time when Hank's career was stagnant, and he'd jumped at the opportunity. Callie had long known Hank had the talent; doing the work and getting the right breaks were what had always been elusive. Playing at Keepsake Cove's Spring Festival wasn't exactly what you'd call a big break, but it would help pay the bills.

"Hey, come on, babe. You know how I hate motels, and you've got your aunt's place and all—"

"No Hank. No. No way. Nada. Uh-uh."

"But—"

Callie crossed her arms and stood firm. Such wheedling might have worked in the past, but those days were over.

Hank read the look on her face and gave up, turning away and looking down at her music boxes. He spotted the one Callie had been dancing to. "Hey, I like that one!" he said, picking it up. "Looks like one of my first guitars on top, there. Remember it? No, you probably don't think of those days anymore, right?" *Was that supposed to make me feel bad?* He listened to the tune for a minute, grinning, and then asked, "How much?"

It wasn't one of her top-of-the-line music boxes, but it was definitely priced higher than her quick-sale, touristy ones because of its quality design and construction. "Who-eee!" Hank said as he found the price tag. Then, to Callie's surprise, he said, "I'll take it."

"Hank, you don't have to—"

"No, I want it. It's nice. I like it." He carried it over to the counter and pulled out his wallet.

What was he up to? Callie couldn't help wondering. Hank didn't normally go in for things like music boxes, preferring to funnel most of his cash into career-related items: guitars, performance clothing, and such. This, for him, was a big stretch.

"You're sure you want to spend—?" Callie stopped herself, not wanting to actually say that it might be a bit pricey for him.

Hank grinned, picking up her drift anyway. "Things are goin' good. Bobby's booked us solid. Plus"—he paused dramatically—"he's got a record deal for us in the works."

"Really! That's fantastic! So joining up with him was a good move, huh?"

"Looks like," Hank agreed, nodding. "I wasn't so sure at first, remember? Bobby's had his ups and downs, mostly due to his drinking problem. But he's got himself back on track and that's all in the past. Things are lookin' pretty fine, babe."

"I'm happy for you, Hank," Callie said, and she really was. Although she and Hank were better off apart—make that *much* better off—she continued to wish him well. "I hope the record deal turns into all you've always hoped for."

"Could be," he said, nodding, a deeply pleased smile on his face. "Could be." His phone dinged and he pulled it out of a shirt pocket to read the text. "It's from Bobby," he said. Seeing Callie's eyebrows shoot up, he grinned but shook his head. "Not about the deal. Just wants help checking the equipment. You gonna come to the show?"

"Tomorrow night?"

"Eight o'clock. Prime time. Someone *else* is the warm-up act."

Callie smiled, remembering all the times Hank's band had been the lower-ranked and lesser-paid opening act. Again, Keepsake Cove wasn't exactly Nashville, but she was glad he was feeling good about it. "I'll be there." She handed his credit card back and passed over the packed-up music box, noticing its weight despite the compact size. "Be good to it," she said with a smile. "See you tomorrow."

Hank winked, touched his hat brim in a salute, and headed out. Callie watched as he walked past her shop windows, then glanced down at her copy of the receipt. Not too long ago she would have wondered if Hank's payment would go through. Happily—for both of them—it didn't seem to be a concern anymore.

But Hank being in Keepsake Cove so unexpectedly was a bit staggering. How was she going to deal with it? How had it come about without her knowing? That last question answered itself fairly quickly: she hadn't been on any planning committees. But who was? Callie picked up her phone to find out.

"Duane Fletcher headed the entertainment committee," Delia informed her. "I knew the band's name but not who the members were. Even so, I might not have recognized Hank's name. I'm sorry."

"Nothing to apologize for. Duane either. Come to think of it, if Duane had actually asked how I felt about booking Hank's band, I wouldn't have stood in his way. I'm just feeling a bit blindsided. But that's nobody's fault, except maybe Hank's. *He* could have let me know."

"How awkward will it be?"

"Well, I told Hank I'd come to his show, which is fine. But I expected to go with Brian. I don't know how he'll feel about it."

"Brian's a sensible guy. He knows that relationship is all in the past, right?"

"He should. I've told him so, more than once."

"Then just get everything out in the open and over with. The sooner the better, I'd say."

"You're right, of course, Delia. Thanks. Has your friend arrived yet, by the way?"

"Jill texted that she'll be here by seven. She told me not to fix dinner since she couldn't guarantee when she'd arrive, so we'll be going out. Want to join us?"

"I'm sure you'll have a lot of catching up to do. I'll wait till tomorrow to meet her."

Delia didn't argue, only promised to bring Jill over. After they hung up, Callie glanced across the street at the Keepsake Café. Though it was closed, she could see some of the lights on, which meant Brian was busy in the back. She pressed his number on her speed dial.

"Hey!" he said, picking up.

"Hey, yourself. I'll be closing up in half an hour. Want to head over to Dino's for something to eat?" Brian had a café's worth of food at his fingertips, but it was dinner food that they needed. Plus, Callie knew he enjoyed getting away from his stove once in a while. "My treat," she added as further enticement.

"We'll see about that, but yeah, it sounds great."

Since the weather was great, they decided to walk the few blocks to the diner in the commercial part of Mapleton rather than driving there in Brian's refurbished 1967 Chevy Impala. Callie figured that along the way, she could get the news out about Hank's presence at the festival, quickly resolve any questions, and free up the rest of the evening for pleasant relaxation.

She glanced up at Grandpa Reed's music box. Had she heard a tiny ping come from it? Probably not. After all, what could possibly be a worry with such a simple plan?

Three

Callie waited for Brian in front of *House of Melody* after closing up the shop and making a quick trip back to her cottage to feed Jagger, the large gray cat she'd inherited along with everything else of Aunt Mel's. Besides fluffing her blond hair and adding a bit of color to her cheeks and lips, she'd changed from her skirt and blouse into jeans, a tee, and a light hoodie. Dino's Diner was not a dress-up kind of place by any means, though it had reliably good comfort food. Her stomach rumbled at the thought of it, and she was glad to see Brian appear soon and jog across the street toward her.

"Nice night," he said, taking her hand as they turned to start their walk.

"It is." Callie answered, liking the feel of her hand in his much larger one. She also liked that he smelled lightly of Irish Spring, which blended nicely that evening with the scents of newly cut grass and the many spring blooms in the air. She'd left her hoodie unzipped and pushed the sleeves up, knowing the still-bright sunshine would keep her warm on the walk over. The trip back, after the sun set, would be a different story, though not by much.

They walked in comfortable silence for a while, glancing into the Dickensian-style shop windows filled with colorful collectibles. *Pearl's Bangles and Beads* displayed its rows of vintage necklaces and bracelets. Next to it, Dorothy Ashby's collectible sewing shop was filled with beautiful thimbles and sewing baskets, and beyond that was a new shop totally devoted to John Wayne memorabilia. Callie had a feeling Hank had stopped in at that one.

They crossed a street, and Callie cleared her throat. It was time to bring that ex-boyfriend up.

"I had a surprise visitor this afternoon."

Brian looked over at her.

"Totally unexpected," she added. "It was Hank. Turns out his band is booked for the festival."

"Oh. Wow. That *is* a surprise."

Callie couldn't tell from his tone exactly how Brian felt about the news. "Turns out Duane Fletcher handled the entertainment arrangements," she said. "I'm sure he was simply looking for *good but affordable.*"

"And are they?"

"They're probably good, though this is a new band for Hank so I've never heard it. All I know is that he's pretty happy to be in it, and that says a lot. I have no idea about the affordability part."

"We'll find out eventually," Brian said. "When Duane gives his treasurer's report. That is, unless Laurie Hart's already demanded an accounting."

Callie smiled, first at Brian's reference to Laurie's ongoing squinty-eyed view of Duane's handling of the Keepsake Cove Shop Owners' Association's money. But also at his apparent focus on the festival budget rather than Hank's presence. *Apparent.* She probed further.

"So, as I said, Hank surprised me when he showed up at the shop this afternoon. I don't expect to see much more of him, though I do want to hear the new band."

"Sure. Me too."

"Really?"

Brian grinned at her. "Of course. And I'll be pinned to your side every minute, watching him like a hawk with a dark, warning scowl on my face. Isn't that the general routine?"

Callie laughed. "Pretty much. Let me see the scowl, though."

Brian pulled his brows together, jutted his jaw, and made grunting noises.

"Good. Just the right Neanderthal touch. Can you keep it up while line dancing?"

"Uh-uh. That's where I draw the line. Not the scowling. The dancing. Definitely not my thing."

"Okay, I'll let you off the hook on that one." Callie smiled to herself, happy with the message she'd received that Brian could be adult about the situation. Well, except for the Neanderthal business.

They arrived at Dino's and waited their turn to be seated. Within moments, a hostess was leading them through the large restaurant. As they followed, Callie heard her name called out and looked to the left to see Delia waving and beckoning.

"I'll just run over and say hello," she said to Brian, who nodded and continued on to claim their table.

"Hi!" Callie greeted Delia, then turned to the thin, dark-haired woman sitting across from her. "You must be Jill. I'm Callie Reed. Delia's been so excited about you coming."

"Callie's my next-door neighbor," Delia added. "My *wonderful* next-door neighbor, I should say."

Jill smiled. "Glad to meet you, wonderful-neighbor Callie. It was so great of Delia to get me a spot in the festival. And to put me up, too." Jill was forty-something, near Delia's age since they'd been classmates, but Callie thought she looked older—possibly from the few streaks of gray running through her pulled-back hair, but also from the shadows under her eyes and a general look of tension. Those hinted at a tougher life. "I expect we'll see a lot of each other in the next few days," Jill said.

"I hope so," Callie said. "But it'll probably be in fits and starts. I think we'll both be kept pretty busy."

"Gosh, I sure hope we're busy," Jill said. "I could really use the extra cash."

"You'll be a big hit at the festival," Delia assured her. "I'll steer plenty of people in your direction."

"I will, too," Callie said, then glanced back to see that a waitress had come up to their window table. "I'd better go. So nice to meet you, Jill. Best of luck!" She hurried off and slipped into the chair opposite Brian. As he gave his order to the waitress, she glanced over the menu, though she'd already half-decided on the broiled fish platter. Now that she lived on the Eastern Shore and was surrounded on three sides by water, the abundance of super-fresh seafood had heightened her taste for the dish.

"That's Delia's friend," she told Brian after their waitress took off. "The one who'll be doing the costume photography at the festival."

"Ah. So she made it." Brian reached for a breadstick and broke off an end.

"She seems anxious about getting enough business. I hope it works out for her."

"That's always the unpredictable part with these things. Could go either way. At least she didn't have to invest in supplies, since she must already have the camera and the costumes."

Callie heard the unspoken concern that was always a part of Brian's budgeting—estimating the right amount of food to have on hand for his café, especially during special events. At least her music boxes, like Jill's costumes, weren't perishable. "Yes, if it doesn't turn out well for her, all she's lost are her travel costs and, of course, her time. What *that* means to her, of course, we don't know."

Their food arrived, and they turned to it and to other subjects. Callie glanced over at Delia's table occasionally and saw her chatting away with Jill, apparently having a great time catching up.

She was glad for that. Delia lived alone in her cottage, just as Callie did, and though she had many friends in Keepsake Cove, Callie occasionally sensed loneliness in her. There had been that unfortunate disappointment with Duane Fletcher last summer. Duane could be quite charming and personable when he chose, and Delia, like many others, had been drawn in by it—and her feelings were of the romantic kind. But that had cooled quickly when a petty side to Duane showed itself during Laurie Hart's challenge to his association bookkeeping. Delia had seemed fine since then, but Callie liked seeing her better than fine, as she was now.

They'd finished their meals, and Brian had leaned back to enjoy his coffee, when Callie saw a strange look cross his face.

"What ...?" she started to ask, when that familiar baritone voice once again rang out behind her.

"Babe!"

Oh, Lord. Callie turned slowly. "Hank."

"Hey, spotted you through the window. What a coincidence!" Cowboy hat, boots, denims, and all, Hank loped across the diner toward her. "Bobby said, 'Where do you want to eat?' and I said, 'Oh, just pick any place, I don't care,' and he picks the place you're at! Who'd a' guessed!"

Before she knew it, Hank had pulled her to her feet and engulfed her in a hug. His shoulder blocked her from seeing Brian and nearly prevented her from drawing air. He released her and waved at the man a few steps behind to hurry over. "Callie, this is Bobby Linville."

Bobby, forty-something with thinning hair and a noticeable paunch beneath his open sports jacket, caught up, and before Callie could get out a word, claimed to have been looking forward to meeting her ever since finalizing the band's gig at Keepsake Cove. "Hank here talks about you all the time!"

A cough from Brian turned their heads in his direction.

"Hey, man," Hank said, seeming to notice Brian for the first time. "Sorry about that. We interrupting?"

"Not at all. Brian Greer." Brian had stood and held out his hand.

"We were just finishing dinner," Callie said as Hank and Bobby reached over to shake hands, noting Brian's more-than-polite demeanor and grateful for it. "So we're leaving soon. But we'll both see you at the festival. Tomorrow, right?"

Hank looked back and forth between Brian and Callie. "Yeah, tomorrow. You're gonna love the new music. Oh, hey!" he said, spotting movement outside. "There's the rest of the band comin' now. We've been settin' up and rehearsin' for hours. Everyone's starved." He turned to Bobby. "Let's go grab us a table, huh?"

"Right." But as Hank turned to go, Bobby reached into the bag he'd been carrying and pulled out a thick batch of papers. "Got these printed up just today," he said to Callie. "You can put these in your store window. Music boxes, right? Good connection, music and all, you know. Hand them out to your customers. Tell them how you and

19

Hank go way back. They'll love it!" He pressed them into Callie's hands with a wink, nodded at Brian, and headed off after Hank.

Callie looked over at Brian sheepishly and sank into her chair. "Sorry."

Brian's lips twitched. "Maybe he'd like you to wander through the Cove, too, passing those out."

"I'm sure he would." Callie looked toward Bobby as he worked his way through the restaurant. He was stopping at tables and handing out his fliers to surprised diners. Then she glanced at Delia and Jill's table. They were out of Bobby's path, but Delia was watching with some curiosity. Jill, however was a different story. Her face showed… well, Callie couldn't say for sure, not knowing the woman well. Was it simply disapproval? No, it appeared much stronger. Callie thought that what she was seeing on Jill's face was shock and pure disgust.

Four

*T*he festival was set to open at ten that morning, but Callie could already see more people on the street than usual as she raised the shade at *House of Melody*. The Keepsake Café was definitely busy, which boded well for merchants like her, since Brian's patrons generally headed off to shop after eating.

A few shop owners had set up booths on the festival grounds, especially those with more portable wares like Pearl and her vintage jewelry or Howard Graham and his collectible Christmas ornaments. Even Delia had hired someone to handle a booth for *Shake It Up!* merchandise while she tended to the shop itself. But Callie's music boxes didn't transport very easily, and so she had elected to wait—and hope—for festival goers to come to her.

With that thought in mind, she expected it to be a customer when the door dinged as she was stooped behind the counter. To her surprise, it was Duane Fletcher who walked in. His shop, *Glorious Glass*, was several blocks away, so this was a rare occurrence. Many shopkeepers took walking breaks during the day, especially when the weather was good. But Duane was not one for regular exercise, as the extra pounds on his five-foot-six frame attested. Callie assumed he'd parked his car somewhere nearby.

"Good morning," Duane called. He glanced around. "Good, you're alone. I took a chance to come over and apologize."

"Apologize?"

"I've learned about the uncomfortable situation I put you in. Please believe me, I had no idea."

"Oh! You mean about Hank?"

"If I could cancel their contract, I would. But at this point—"

"No, I'd never ask for that! Even if you had time to get another band. It's fine, Duane. Really."

His expression cleared. "You're sure?"

"Absolutely. Hank walking into my shop yesterday was definitely a surprise, but it's no big deal. I'm actually looking forward to hearing the band."

"They came well recommended."

"That's the important thing. How did you learn about my, um, situation?" As far as Callie knew, Delia and Brian were the only ones aware of it, and she couldn't picture either of them gossiping about it.

"The band's manager, Bobby Linville, brought it up when he called to tell me they'd arrived. He seemed to think I would want to play up Hank's connection to Keepsake Cove when I introduced the band."

"There is no connection!"

"Don't worry. As soon as I figured out what he was talking about, I put an end to it." Duane chuckled. "I told him it would be favoritism to single out one shop in the Cove, and that was against the by-laws of the association."

Callie grinned. "Sounds reasonable." She picked up the pack of flyers Bobby had given her. "Speaking of favoritism, he was passing these out at Dino's last night."

Duane took one and looked it over. It featured a black-and-white photo of Hank's band, the Badlanders, and listed the dates and times of their performances over the weekend.

"You'd think this was a Badlanders concert," he groused, "instead of the Keepsake Cove Spring Festival. We do have other performers on the schedule!"

"But they're not managed by Bobby Linville. Don't worry. I'll keep your official festival poster in my window and the festival flyers handy. I won't do anything with these unless someone specifically asks about the Badlanders."

"Great. Okay, so we're good? I didn't want you to think I'd purposely put you on the spot."

"We're good, Duane. And best of luck with all your entertainers. Hope everyone stays healthy and ... wait, that's *bad* luck, isn't it? I should say 'break a leg,' right?"

"Not to me, but I'll pass it on to the musicians, magicians, and the rest. Thanks. I'd better get going."

Callie watched as Duane hurried out, thinking it had been considerate of him to come by to say what he did. Did it make up for the hassle he'd stirred up last year for the Harts when he and Laurie Hart crossed swords? No, since he'd never apologized, only justified it when confronted. But he and Callie hadn't had any issues—so far. She was fine with keeping on good terms with him as a fellow shop owner, and she appreciated the positive things he did for the association. But she didn't see the two of them getting beyond smiles and polite words.

Business picked up in her shop soon after that, and continued steady for the rest of the day. Callie was delighted, but also longed to get to the festival herself. Customers shared tidbits of their experiences, and she heard occasional strains of music wafting down the few blocks from the park. Not country music, yet. Duane had brought in amateur performers to take the stage during the early part of the day. So far, the chorus from the local high school had sung—and probably brought in many proud family members—and a banjo group from the senior center had performed. She itched to experience everything firsthand, not simply hear about it from a distance.

Delia popped in late in the afternoon. "My booth handler at the festival says Jill's doing pretty well. The crowd's been building, and she's set up next to the ice cream stand. A great spot to catch the attention of families."

"I'm glad." Typical of Delia to be more concerned about how her friend was doing than how her own business at the festival was going. "She seemed anxious to do well."

Delia nodded, frowning. "When I invited her, it was because I thought it might be a fun thing for her, as well as a chance for us to catch up. Extra income, of course, is always nice, but I didn't realize how important it might be to her. I haven't pried, but I think she may have been struggling more in the last few years than I realized."

"Then I'm doubly glad the festival is working for her. I'll see if I can convince Brian to get a costume photo taken tonight."

"Are you closing up the shop to go?"

"No, Tabitha will be back to keep it open until eight. She's at the festival right now. I appreciate her putting in the extra time, and since she couldn't afford the booth fee for her beaded jewelry, I suggested she set up a display here for these two days as extra compensation."

"Oooh, I'll have to look it over," Delia said. As she looked through the window and saw customers walking into her shop, she added, "See you later!" and headed out.

24

Callie had debated bringing up Jill's surprisingly negative reaction to Bobby Linville's promotional activities at the diner the previous night, but then decided it was both none of her business and probably explainable in a dozen different ways. For all she knew, Jill might simply have had a sudden attack of heartburn, or even been thinking about something else altogether.

When her assistant arrived at six, Callie was able to report that two of Tabitha's necklace and bracelet sets had sold. "And both women took your business card. I think they'll be looking for more from you."

Tabitha glowed at that, her cheeks nearly matching the pink in her flower-printed dress, which, while perfectly nice, was unremarkable. She'd apparently decided to go "simple" that day, something that Callie hadn't asked for but was glad to see, given that many first-time customers would be coming in. The festival was distraction enough. Best not to add more.

Callie headed out the back door of the shop and followed the brick path to her little house to get ready for the evening. The sight of her red-painted cottage never failed to make her smile, with its steep-pitched roof and sage green front door. The roses twining through the white trellis over the door had started to open, adding their color and sweet perfume.

Jagger, as usual, waited inside the door, and she picked him up to cuddle. "Sorry to have to leave you alone again," she said, rubbing his fur and feeling the rumble of his purrs. "I'll make it up to you, don't worry."

Jagger didn't seem overly worried, as he soon wiggled himself down and led her to his food bowl in the kitchen. As she wound her way through the rooms, filling Jagger's bowl and then running upstairs for a shower, Callie's feelings of gratitude for the amazing gift her Aunt Mel had bestowed on her returned. The cottage, small as it was, had been so beautifully restored and decorated that she hadn't dreamed of changing a thing. From the Wedgewood blue and white living room to the airy lightness of her bedroom, every detail was perfect and a daily reminder of a special aunt.

She stared into her closet, wondering what to wear. It was tempting to reach for jeans, a plaid shirt, and a vest, a western look that tallied with her hopes of line dancing. But would it imply more than she intended? She wanted to enjoy the festival with Brian, not send signals of any sort to Hank. She pulled out dark stretch pants and topped it with a long, teal blue sweater, one that Brian had once complimented. Overthinking? Maybe, but she felt more comfortable with that choice.

They'd agreed to each grab a bite to eat on their own to save time and avoid the long lines at the festival. As Callie did so, Jagger lingered nearby, grooming himself. By the time she'd tidied up, she heard Brian's knock at the door and picked up her purse to go.

Strains of music grew louder as they neared the park.

"That must be the warm-up band," Callie said.

"Sounds pretty good."

"It does. 'A little bit country, a little bit rock 'n roll,' would you say?"

"Hmm. Where have I heard that before?"

"You mean it's not original? Darn. Oh, there's Laurie Hart." Callie waved and Laurie paused to let them catch up, looking festive in a red and white striped tee tucked into a navy skirt. At the Harts' vintage toy shop, Laurie spent most of her time in the back room sprucing up newly acquired, often dusty or scratched items, and therefore dressed mostly in sweats or denims. This was a nice change for her. Callie liked the thirty-something woman and was glad to run into her.

"Bill holding down the fort?" Brian asked, and Laurie nodded.

"We've been doing pretty good business all day. It's starting to slow down, but he said he'd keep it open a little longer and meet me later."

They ran into more fellow shopkeepers along the way, all looking pleased with how things were going. Funding for the festival had come from all the business owners, via the association, and were significant, but it was apparently paying off.

Once they entered the festival grounds, everyone headed in their own direction. Callie led Brian to the ice cream stand, partly to see how Delia's friend Jill was doing at her adjacent station. There were lines for both, it turned out, and as they waited their turn, Callie had plenty of time to watch Jill at work.

"Mmm, I like that *Gone With the Wind* dress," she said, seeing Jill hold it up for a teen.

"Cactus ice cream? Yuck," Brian responded, studying the menu board.

"It's actually cactus pear," a woman with stylishly cut dark hair turned to say. "And very good." It was Krystal Cobb, the Keepsake Cove Shop Owners' Association president. Always elegantly dressed, she'd toned things down for the occasion, but she still managed to work in her trademark sparkle with a sequin-dotted tee over designer jeans, which went well with the silver flecks in her chic bob. "Give it a try," she urged.

"I'm more of a chocolate chip kind of guy," Brian said with a smile. "Taking a break from your official duties?"

"No duties to speak of," Krystal said. "The committees have all done their jobs well. I'm a lady of leisure today." She moved up to the counter as the tall man in front of her stepped away, handing a cone to the little boy beside him.

Having made her flavor choice, Callie glanced around at the milling throng, glad to see both the high numbers and the smiling faces.

Then she spotted Bobby Linville weaving his way through the crowd in their direction.

"Uh-oh," she said quietly to Brian. "I might be in for a grilling on how many Badlanders flyers I handed out today." She saw that Bobby had already spotted her, so it was too late to turn away. Bracing herself, she waited as he approached. Then a look of surprise crossed his face as he suddenly stopped. He turned on his heel and rapidly walked in the opposite direction, disappearing quickly in the crowd.

"What was that all about?"

Brian shrugged. "Remembered something he was supposed to do?"

"It looked to me as though he didn't like what he saw. That doesn't make sense, though. It's an ice cream stand."

"Lactose intolerant?" Brian said, which made Callie smile.

"I'm going to browse through the booths," Krystal said, having gotten her cone. "What about you?"

"Not sure," Callie said, as Brian stepped up to order. "We might get a costume photo."

"See you around," Krystal said and took off.

As Callie waited beside Brian, she heard an angry voice to her right. Jill was apparently upset. It sounded like some kind of damage had been done to a costume. Unfortunately, the berating continued much too long.

Brian had also glanced over at the photographer, and he and Callie looked at each other.

"Let's walk around for a while," Callie suggested.

He nodded, and they headed off, though Callie was sorry to see other potential customers step out of Jill's line and drift away as well.

Five

$\mathcal{A}$ magician had taken the stage, and Callie watched his act with Brian as they licked their ice cream. The performance was entertaining, though more so for the children in the crowd who shrieked with glee over the rabbit appearing from inside the man's cape and drinking glasses that seemed to float in the air.

"I think he must do a lot of birthday parties," Brian said in Callie's ear.

The parents seemed just as happy as their children, and most knew more grown-up entertainment would be coming soon. As they left to browse, passing a young boy getting a Batman mask painted on his face, Callie caught sight of Bobby again. He was at the back of the narrow alleyway between Delia's collectible salt and pepper shaker booth and a vintage comic book booth and appeared to be downing a drink from a pocket-sized flask. *Uh-oh.* Hank had said Bobby's drinking problem was in the past. That didn't seem to be the case.

But then Delia's assistant, a sweet woman named Mary Lou Casey, noticed them and waved them over. By the time they'd listened to her excited listing of what she'd sold that day for Delia, Bobby was gone.

Within minutes, Duane's voice could be heard over the loudspeaker introducing the Badlanders. Callie grabbed Brian's hand and hurried toward the stage.

The band, which started out with a lively, foot-stomping song, sounded great. Callie could see that the Badlanders was a big step up from Hank's last band, and his face showed exhilaration at being part of it. The crowd obviously agreed, with much whooping, clapping in time, and cheers at the end.

Hank had a solo in the second song, and Callie felt the familiar thrill at the sound of his rich baritone, though that was the limit of the emotion. She saw him spot her and give a grin and wink, which, thankfully, didn't cause any heads to turn in her direction. She didn't know what Brian was thinking, but she took his arm and leaned closer just to let him know her own thoughts.

Delia had been right about a dance floor being set up. It was under the canopy next to the bandstand. After the third song, a band member pointed it out and invited line dancers to head over. Callie's eyes lit up. She looked questioningly at Brian, who shook his head.

"You go," he said. "I'll enjoy just watching."

Callie needed no urging, hurrying over to join the growing line. Laurie and Bill were already there, and soon Tabitha ran up, breathless from her sprint to the park after closing up *House of Melody*. They all shuffled around a bit, bumping into one another, until somebody stepped forward to lead. Gradually everyone got in sync, heels tapping and fingers snapping. Callie loved it.

She saw that Brian was indeed watching, and though she knew she was no candidate for *Dancing with the Stars*, he appeared impressed. She did one more dance, then left to rejoin him.

"That was fun," she said, slightly out of breath.

"Fun to see, too."

"Really?"

Brian smiled. "Yes, really."

"Ready to try it?"

"Oh darn. Looks like they've changed back to regular songs. Maybe next time."

"I might hold you to that."

The song ended and Hank took the microphone and waited for the applause to die down.

"Thanks, everyone. You're a great crowd. The guys and I are real pleased to be playin' here in Keepsake Cove. And we have a special number comin' up, just for you. This song was written by that guy right over there with the fiddle, Randy Brewer, with a little help from yours truly. It's called *Missin' You*, and"—he paused for effect—"it's in the works for a big recording contract. When it comes out, you all can say you heard it first! Here we go with *Missin' You*."

The crowd clapped, but Callie winced as Hank looked pointedly at her before turning back to the band and starting to play. She stayed to listen for a polite amount of time, then turned to Brian.

"What would you think of getting a photo taken about now?"

"Sure!" His enthusiasm for the idea had definitely increased several notches. Callie suspected that at this point he would have agreed to a Bugs Bunny face painting. Anything to move on.

They discreetly eased out of the crowd and headed toward Jill's area. They saw her slumped on her bench, head in hands. Callie tried to sound upbeat as she called out "Hey, Jill," unsure if she was seeing dejection or simply fatigue from the long day.

"Hi!" Jill responded, jumping up from her seat. "Did you just come from the bandstand? They sound pretty good!" Her bright smile was sudden and seemed forced.

"They're great, but I guess they drew everybody away, huh?"

"Oh, no surprise. We all expected that. Most of the booths have closed, and I was going to pack up pretty soon." Her bright smile drooped. "Actually, my business dropped before the music started. My own fault. I got pretty ticked off when one of my dresses got torn, and I sounded off about it."

"That's a shame. Is it fixable?"

Jill nodded. "Easily. Which is why I should have kept my big mouth shut. I scared away the customers who were waiting and probably a lot more who heard about it."

"I'm sorry."

"My own stupid fault. But I've been on edge, lately. And seeing— well, never mind. No excuses."

"Would you mind if we got a photo?" Brian asked. "Or are you done for the night?"

Jill perked up. "Not at all! What do you like?" She drew them to her row of costumes hanging on a line. "Historical? Movie characters? Vampires?"

They fingered through the choices, Callie appreciating Brian being so great after what might have been a tooth-grinding time back at the bandstand. Whatever costume made him the least miserable would be fine with her. She expected him to lean toward something bland, like the chef and baker outfits, and was surprised when he pulled out an elaborate Henry VIII costume.

"Really?"

Brian shrugged. "I like historical stuff."

"Okay. But do I have to be Anne Boleyn?"

"You could be Queen Elizabeth," Jill said, holding up a sparkly gown with a high neck ruff.

They slipped into their outfits, Brian getting a fake beard as well as a fake-fur-trimmed cape. Jill pulled Callie's dress to fit with strings that tied at the back, then set plastic crowns on their heads and posed them for the photo. Since it was digital, they had two freshly printed color copies in minutes.

Callie giggled at the sight of herself, her upturned freckled nose and lank blond hair not exactly working for an Elizabethan look. But Brian's wide-legged, elbow-cocked stance mimicked King Henry's familiar pose well despite his being half the king's size, width-wise.

"All you need is an enormous drumstick to chew on," she commented.

He laughed. "I'd settle for a hot dog. What about you?"

They settled their bill first, and Callie was glad to see that their posing had apparently caught the eye of another couple, who were now choosing their own costumes.

Callie and Brian got their hot dogs and wandered through the grounds as they munched, eventually finding themselves back at the bandstand area. It was currently quiet, the band apparently on a break, but the crowd had mostly remained, some going only as far as the nearest concession stand, which said a lot.

Callie was glad for it but had no intention of putting Brian through act two, so she began to veer away. But a raised voice coming from the rear and side of the bandstand area stopped her. It was Hank's. She could see him in the shadows, apparently upset with Bobby Linville. With Hank's back to her, she couldn't catch much of the rant beyond a few curse words, which told her Hank was furious about something. He didn't use words like that casually. Did it have to do with Bobby's drinking? Another band member came over to calm things down.

"C'mon, man, we got another set to play! We can handle this later." He managed to pull Hank away, leaving Bobby standing there alone.

Callie and Brian moved on, neither eager to be noticed.

Six

hough Callie had enjoyed the festival for the most part, thinking about it the next morning brought uneasy feelings. In the midst of all the excitement and fun—the music, the line dancing, the crowds of happy people milling around—there had been an undercurrent of something wrong.

She knew that no event, especially one of that size, could be expected to be one hundred percent perfect and upbeat. And some of her unease came from remembering Hank shooting flirty looks at her from the stage, with Brian beside her. But there was more.

She was thinking about that when someone tapped on her front door. Callie made an educated guess about who it would be, and wasn't terribly surprised to find Delia standing there. With Keepsake Cove shops closed on Sundays until noon, the mornings were opportunities for neighborly visits.

"Jill got in late last night," Delia said, "so I thought I'd leave the place to her for a while so she can sleep in. Mind if I bum a cup of coffee from you?"

Delia's cottage was as modestly sized as her own, so Callie understood the need to vacate to avoid disturbing a guest. She waved her friend in and led the way to the kitchen. She'd recently treated herself to a single-serve coffee maker (mini-sized to match her surroundings) and so had a variety of flavors to offer. Delia chose hazelnut, and Callie pushed the buttons to get the system going. As the coffee started to flow, she looked around her kitchen. The best offer she could come up with was, "Like some toast?"

Delia smiled knowingly. Obviously aware of how Callie's supplies tended to run out, she reached into her tote bag to pull out a plastic container of homemade cinnamon buns.

"Wow!" Callie said. "Just like that magician at the festival. Only better." She made her own dark Colombian coffee and then followed Delia into the living room, where Jagger dozed lazily on one of the chairs.

"So, how late did Jill get back last night?" Callie sank into the second chair and took a bite from her bun, savoring its cinnamony sweetness.

"Not sure. I waited up to about eleven thirty but had to turn in. I woke when I heard her on the steps but I didn't look at the clock."

"Brian and I left around ten thirty. Hank's band was still performing, but we'd had enough. Jill must have drawn some last-minute customers. Good for her."

"I hope so."

Mentioning the band made Callie think of the angry scene between Hank and Bobby. She frowned.

"Something wrong?" Delia asked.

Callie shrugged. "Nothing that has anything to do with me, but it looks like Hank's new band, which sounded really good, might have a management problem."

"That guy who was passing out his flyers at the diner?"

"Right. Bobby Linville. Hank was singing his praises a couple of days ago, but he didn't seem too happy with him last night. But again, nothing to do with me. They'll have to work it out."

"From the little I know of it," Delia said, "making a living in the music business doesn't seem like the easiest thing in the world."

"You got that right. Most people get in for the love of it. But they still have to eat." How many times had Hank mooched off of her— the one who earned the steady paycheck while his gigs were sporadic. She hadn't minded at the beginning, convinced it was short term. But after a while, being the person in the relationship who put in forty hours a week at a job while the other did maybe six and disdained doing something—anything!—that earned money during the other thirty or so hours to pay his bills put a definite strain on things.

"A few in the business," she said, "make it really big. *Very* few. The rest plug away, hoping for that big break." Callie looked down at her coffee thoughtfully. "Hank sounded like his big break, or at least a good step toward it, was on the verge of happening."

"Wonderful!" Delia said.

And it might finally get him out of my hair, Callie could have added but didn't.

Delia's phone dinged and she glanced at it. "Ah, my guest has awakened. I'd better help her put together some breakfast. Heading back to the festival this afternoon?"

"Nope. Minding the store. You?"

"I think I'll switch with Mary Lou," Delia said. "I'd like to spend an hour or two at the festival. Maybe get to hear the band!"

Callie followed her to the door, and when they paused to exchange a few more words, Delia's phone dinged again. "Looks like there's a coffee emergency at my house. See you later!"

❧

Callie opened her shop at noon, then stepped outside for a moment to enjoy the warm, late April sunshine. She saw Pearl Poepelman doing the same a couple of stores down, outside of *Pearl's Bangles and Beads,* and waved to the older woman. "Another good day for the festival," Pearl called, and Callie nodded. She could already see more people on the street than usual and she looked forward to brisk business.

She'd gone back inside and to her office to check on a few orders when she heard her shop door open. Then a voice called out, "Hey, is there any place around here where I can get a decent music box?"

Callie grinned. She knew that voice. Hurrying out, she found Lyssa Hammond standing there, her spiked red hair set off nicely by a bright blue cotton tunic over yoga pants that flattered her chunkier frame.

"You're in town!" Callie cried, delighted to see her friend.

Lyssa had bought a second home in the area after coming to Keepsake Cove for the Halloween-themed book event Callie had arranged for the fall celebration. After getting to know Callie and her friends while pitching in to solve the two murders, Lyssa had decided to invest in a place that would bring her back to the Eastern Shore regularly.

"I hit 'send' on my latest book last night after rewriting the blankety-blank ending at least twenty times," Lyssa said. "The instant it went through, I packed my bags to head across the bay. What's going on with all the throngs of people? You're not having another book thingy, are you?"

"You're in luck. It's the Keepsake Cove Spring Festival."

"Oooh," Lyssa said, not sounding all that thrilled.

"It's fun!" Callie insisted. "Granted, it's heavy on kid-type things. But it brings people to the Cove. And there's some draw for the grown-ups."

"Such as?"

"There's lots of food. And music." Callie grimaced. "Provided by my ex-boyfriend, unfortunately. But it's good! Then there's—"

"Hold on. Your ex? The country music guy? He's here?"

House of Melody's door opened, admitting two people and effectively silencing Lyssa. She smiled and stepped out of their way. Callie recognized the couple who'd put the black enameled music box on hold the other day. "We came to claim that beautiful box," the woman said, her eyes dancing.

As Callie welcomed them back, Lyssa signaled that she'd run over to Brian's café for a quick bite. Callie nodded, sure her friend would be back to get the scoop on Hank, and then went to get the lovely music box. She was pleased that the pair had returned to buy it. Tabitha had been right.

As she packed up the box, Callie listened to the couple's involved tale of what had gone into their decision to buy the expensive piece, which, among other things, they felt sure would become a family heirloom. As they carried it off, Callie was glad to see the delighted look on, at least, the woman's face. Her husband looked happy as well; mainly happy for his wife, but that was a good thing, too.

During the process, she'd heard sirens heading in the direction of the festival area. That concerned her, though she told herself it could be anything, even a false alarm. But it wasn't long until she heard a second set of sirens heading the same way. That was more worrisome, but the arrival of more customers distracted her, and since none of them knew anything about the emergency, most chattered about music boxes, gifts, and their plans for the rest of their day. So it wasn't until Lyssa came back with a serious look on her face that Callie got the bad news.

"They've found a body somewhere on the festival grounds."

Callie winced. "Who?"

"I don't know. Haven't got any details yet." She looked at Callie for a long moment. "You know, I had plans for my little getaway here. Fun things like finding a rug for my living room and putting in a garden."

"Yes?"

"But I have a feeling none of that's going to get done."

"Lyssa, don't be silly—" Callie started to say, but Lyssa interrupted her.

"I mean it. Think about it. Keepsake Cove, dead body. Sound familiar?" She twisted her mouth into a wry smile. "Fasten your seat belt, Callie. Another bumpy ride is coming up!"

Seven

*W*ith Lyssa knowing nothing beyond the fact that there was a body, Callie immediately texted Hank but got no response. She thought of the flyers Bobby Linville had given her and looked behind the counter where she'd stashed them. Was there a phone number for the Badlanders somewhere on it? No. Nothing.

"Look," Lyssa said, "it might be a while before anything more comes out. You know how it goes: identifying, notifying next of kin, all that kind of stuff."

Callie wasn't next of kin to the person she was most concerned about, nor had she wanted to be for quite a while. But that didn't mean she wouldn't care. Why wasn't Hank answering her text?

"Tell you what," Lyssa said. "I'll head over there and see what I can find out."

"Would you? I'd go, but Tabitha won't be in today."

"No problem. Just don't get your hopes up. I mean, about me getting much info. But I'll do my best. Keep texting. He's probably just busy or something."

Callie nodded, though she knew how Hank kept his phone glued to him and jumped to check every ding or vibration. She watched Lyssa head down the street and then busied herself with the shop, polishing every music box and shelf to a shine. Now that she could have used the distraction of a customer or two, nobody showed up, possibly drawn to the activity on the festival grounds. Or frightened away. That last option was most likely. Anyone who'd arrived for a day of entertainment was probably not going to hang around when they saw patrol cars and CSI vans gathered with lights flashing. She probably could have closed up and left with Lyssa. Business would be dead the rest of the day. *Dead.* She winced at the word.

Who was it? Lyssa hadn't heard if the body was that of a man or woman. The death could have been natural. Or accidental. But it seemed to have been discovered hours later—wouldn't a natural death have been reported right away? Or the person reported as missing? Too many questions. No answers. Why didn't Lyssa call? Or Hank?

Callie was on the verge of locking up the shop to run down the street to the festival grounds when her phone rang. She snatched at it. It was Lyssa.

"Okay," she said. "The good news is it's not Hank."

Callie let out a huge breath.

"The bad news is it's his manager. Name's Linville. His body was found next to the bandstand."

"Bobby! Ohmygosh! What happened to him?"

"I don't know. We'll probably have to wait on that."

"Is Hank there?"

"I asked around. The entire band is apparently talking with the police right now."

"Right. Of course. But … that sounds like it was a murder." Callie thought of the murder last fall of the man who owned the B&B where

Lyssa had been staying. The owner's estranged wife, fellow shop owner Dorothy Ashby, had been taken in for questioning almost immediately.

"It could be undetermined at this point," Lyssa said. "But from what a police source for one of my books once told me, they go ahead and gather all the info they can until the Medical Examiner pronounces one way or the other."

Callie had been relieved to hear that Hank was alive. But would that be replaced with a new worry? No, she told herself. No way could Hank be involved in the death of Bobby Linville, however that death had come about. For all his faults, Hank was not a violent person. The argument she'd overheard at the festival came back to her, but she dismissed it. It was an anomaly and most likely over Bobby's drinking. Which was upsetting but didn't rise to the level of committing murder. Though on second thought, Bobby's lapse probably shouldn't have been nearly as upsetting to Hank as it appeared to be, period. Why had he been so mad? Callie shook her head. That was a question for another time.

"I think this put an end to your festival," Lyssa said. "The only crowd left are gawkers like me. A lot of the booths are closing down."

"That's too bad. There was a lot of effort and money put into it. But I guess it can't be helped."

"Hey, I'm heading back to my place. I don't think there's anything more to learn around here, and there's a couple of things I need to take care of. I'll check with you later, okay?"

"Sure." Callie was grateful for what Lyssa had found out but wished her friend could have come back to the shop. She didn't think either her music boxes or her right arm could take any more polishing. Thankfully, Delia soon popped in. She confirmed that the festival was officially closed because of the ongoing police activity.

"Jill called to tell me," she said. "She sounded so down. I feel terrible about bringing her all the way here only for this to happen."

"Nobody could have foreseen this," Callie said.

"I know, but still …"

"Lyssa's been over there. Did Jill tell you it was Hank's band manager, Bobby Linville?"

"No! Really? Oh, wow. That's terrible. What happened to him?" When Callie explained it was all she knew, Delia said, "Well, I'm sorry for him, but at the same time it's a relief to know it isn't someone I know." Her face brightened then. "So Lyssa's in town?"

"She'll probably be around tomorrow."

"It'll be great to see her. Well, I'd better get over to the grounds and help Mary Lou pack everything up." Delia wrinkled her nose. "I don't know where I'll put all those extra salt and pepper sets I stocked up on. Guess I'll figure something out."

Callie realized that dealing with unsold inventory would probably be the case for a lot of the Keepsake Cove shop owners who'd taken booths. Then there were the concessionaires, the entertainers, and festival people like Jill. The losses would be considerable when they were totaled up. She thought of her other next-door neighbor, Karl Eggers, and was glad he hadn't taken a booth for his collectible cars. As he was cantankerous to begin with, a setback like that for Karl would mean having to walk on eggs around him for months. Callie laughed weakly. Like that would be a change?

She puttered around a bit more, worked at her bills for a while, and then gave up. The silence of her shop was getting to her. The festival was closed, and Keepsake Cove itself had effectively been closed, too. A peek out her door showed empty streets. Not at all what anyone had been looking forward to. She closed her register, locked her door, and pulled down her shade. If nothing else, she knew when to call it a day.

Later that evening, after still not having heard from Hank and increasingly uneasy about it, Callie decided to occupy herself in a way that didn't involve frenetic cleaning. Delia's morning visit had underlined the emptiness of her cupboards, so refilling them seemed like a good idea. That plus the fact that the Mapleton supermarket would be crowded tomorrow, since Monday was the weekly off-day for Keepsake Cove shopkeepers. Beating the hordes by a few hours would mean breezing through her shopping.

Callie felt quite smug as she pushed her loaded cart to the empty checkout counter, its clerk waiting there idly. She'd decided to try Delia's super-sensible practice of cooking up large batches of meals at once to freeze. "It's a huge convenience when you just want to pull something out in a hurry after a long day," Delia had said.

Tomorrow would be the day she'd finally do that, Callie decided. Surely she would have heard from Hank by then that Bobby's death was due to some sort of accident. Maybe something caused by his drinking? Hank and the other band members would pack up and move on to their next gig, and she would have the day to get at least one part of her life back in order.

The thought was satisfying, and particularly so as she unpacked her bags of fresh vegetables and meats that would soon be transformed into soups, sauces, and stews, and fresh fruits that could be blended into tasty smoothies, and more. Her recipes were lined up and ready to be executed. Not having heard back from Hank was an ongoing concern, but Callie could think of a dozen reasons for it that sent it away. Tomorrow he would text, or call, or drop in on his way out of town, and all would be settled.

Or so she convinced herself.

Eight

Callie rose early the next day and immediately checked her phone. No message from Hank. Well, he'd never been a rise and shine kind of guy. She'd hear from him later.

After a quick shower, she pulled on a T-shirt and pair of jeans and headed down to her kitchen. The sight of her overflowing cupboards, plus the jam-packed refrigerator, wasn't as exciting as it had been the night before, but trusting Delia's assurance that the rewards would be tenfold, Callie braced herself for a day of chopping, simmering, and blending.

But first, a cup of coffee.

She fixed a strong brew of her favorite Colombian and carried it outside to enjoy the pleasant morning air. Light perfume wafted from the roses Aunt Mel had set twining through the trellis overhead, and she breathed it in deeply, turning then to stroll along the line of sprouting flowers that edged the front of the cottage. Callie hadn't touched a thing in the garden beyond keeping it tidy, and she hoped the perennials would return regularly for years as one more reminder of a wonderful aunt.

She was halfway through her coffee when she heard voices coming from the shop area and stopped to listen. She thought she recognized Duane Fletcher's but wasn't sure about the others. Curiosity drew her down the footpath between her property and Karl's until she reached the street. There she found Duane facing several shop owners. From the tone of their voices and looks on their faces, this was not a friendly gathering.

Howard Graham, who ran *Christmas Collectibles*, was shaking a finger in Duane's direction. "I paid for two full days for my booth. I want half of that back!" Not normally an assertive person, Howard was apparently able to rise to the occasion when it came to money, though his high-pitched voice wobbled just a bit at the end.

"We all paid the same, Howard," Pearl Poepelman said, her vintage necklaces draping her ample bosom even on an off-day. "But he's right, Duane. We're owed refunds."

"It's not that simple," Duane protested.

"Of course it is," Karl Eggers countered. Tall and burly, Karl's thick brows were pulled together in his habitual glower, a full, dark beard adding to the fearsome look. "You write a check and it's done!"

Why was Karl part of this? He hadn't taken a booth. Callie suddenly wondered if the sounds of the argument had pulled at him like Pavlov's dog and a dinner bell.

"Right!" Howard cried. "Just write us our checks."

Callie saw Delia step out of her closed shop to see what was going on. Then Brian came out of his café. Laurie Hart, Duane's perpetual antagonist, could be seen heading over. Well, that wasn't going to calm things.

"Look," Duane said, "a lot of the association money, including the booth fees, went into costs that we'll never get back. Do you think the town leased us the grounds for nothing? Or that the stage, the dance floor, and those tents were set up for free? Then the bands had to be paid ahead of time, and they weren't cheap." Then he noticed Callie and turned to say pointedly to her, "We wouldn't be in this jam in the first place if someone hadn't pushed me to hire their boyfriend's band. Then the manager goes and drops dead!"

What? She'd had nothing to do with Duane hiring the Badlanders, and Duane knew it! Callie opened her mouth to protest but Laurie beat her to it.

"Don't go trying to shift the blame onto somebody else, Duane Fletcher. This was your responsibility. You should have planned ahead for something coming up that could cancel things. A bad storm or whatever!"

"But it wasn't a storm. It was a murder," a quiet voice said from the back. Everyone turned at that stunning statement to see who'd made it. It was Lyle Moody, a Keepsake Cove newcomer and owner of the John Wayne memorabilia shop. Leather-faced and lanky, Moody's looks fit his shop's theme, as did his fringed vest, jeans, and boots. But it was his statement that caught the group's attention.

"Murder!" Howard cried, his already-pale face blanching two shades paler.

Lyle nodded. "Yup. Just heard it on the news."

Oh, no. Callie pulled her phone from a pocket to check. No message. Brian had come to her side, and he looked questioningly at her. She shook her head. But as she did, the phone rang. It was an unfamiliar number but she quickly answered.

"Hey, babe, it's me," Hank said.

Callie turned away from the others. "Hank. Where are you?"

"Well, that's the thing. I'm, uh, kinda locked up. They think I killed Bobby. Which I didn't! Babe, I need you. You gotta get me outa here!"

Callie quickly stepped away from the group, pulling Brian with her. "It's Hank," she whispered. "He's been arrested for the murder! He wants me to help, but what can I do?"

"Does he have a lawyer?"

"Hank, do you have a lawyer?" Callie asked.

"No, I don't have a lawyer," he said, his tone blatantly sarcastic; a bad choice, Callie thought, considering the circumstances. "How'm I gonna have a lawyer in a place I never been to before? That's why I called you! You're the one and only person who can help me here."

"He doesn't have a lawyer," Callie told Brian. "The only one I know is George Blake, who handled Aunt Mel's will."

"Hank needs a criminal lawyer. Let me see what I can find."

Callie told Hank to hold on. He didn't take that well but she ignored him, refraining from reminding him of his limited alternatives. Finally Brian held up his phone's screen for her to read.

"I have the number of a local defense attorney," she said to Hank. "Can you take it down?"

"Babe, you're my one phone call."

"Okay. I can call him for you."

"Get him over here fast!" There was a pause, and then Hank spoke in a quieter tone. "I mean, please get him here fast. Sorry, babe. I'm kinda stressed."

"I get that. But try to stay calm. Hang in there." Callie wanted to add *it'll be fine* but couldn't say it. She wasn't at all sure about that.

She followed Brian into his closed café and placed the call to Clark Allard, the defense attorney. She spoke briefly to Allard's assistant, who then put her through to Allard. He asked a few questions, then promised to get right on it. Callie ended the call and relayed the conversation to Brian.

"What do you know about Allard?" she asked.

"Nothing. I fortunately never needed a criminal lawyer, nor do I know of anyone who did. I did a search and his name popped up."

"Allard. Probably listed alphabetically. So if there'd been an Aaron Aardvark, that's who Hank would have gotten?"

"Most likely."

"Well, he'll just have to hope for the best, and it has to be better than nothing." Callie thought for a moment. "What happens next?"

"I don't know all the ins and outs, but hopefully Allard will get Hank out on bail and start to work with him on this murder charge."

Brian had maintained a neutral tone throughout, but Callie was pretty sure about what must be running through his head. "There's no way Hank could have done it," she told him. "I can safely say I know him as well as anyone, and it's just not in him."

"You haven't seen him in close to a year though, right? Could he have changed in that time?"

She shook her head. "No way. Not that much. He was the same Hank I've known." Though as she said it, she had to admit they'd spent only minutes together in the last two days. The rest of the time had been watching him perform on the stage. There was nothing to learn from that.

"Well, we'll have to see what kind of evidence they have. And hope it's not a reliable eyewitness."

Callie's heart sank at the thought. She'd spent the last year wanting to fully distance herself from Hank. But not this way. Definitely not this way. She shook her head. No use thinking like this. It all had to be a terrible mistake, and Hank's lawyer would quickly see that it was cleared up.

She thanked Brian for his help. "I guess all we can do now is wait."

He gave her a squeeze. "Want some company for that? I have supplies to pick up for the café, but you could ride along."

"Thanks. That's tempting, but I have a ton of my own supplies waiting to be dealt with. That'll keep me busy and my mind occupied." Though she knew she'd have her phone within reach at all times.

As she left the café, she was glad to see that most of the group had dispersed. But Delia remained, waiting, Callie was sure, to offer help despite not knowing exactly what for. Callie went over and filled her in. She was swiftly engulfed in a hug.

"I'm so sorry," Delia said. "For Hank, of course, but also that you're being pulled into his problem. It doesn't seem fair."

"I'm probably Hank's only helpline, so I can't see not doing what I can. What isn't fair and what I didn't appreciate at all was Duane trying to shift the blame for the festival's closing early onto me. Just two days ago he apologized for bringing Hank here and told me he hadn't known about our connection."

Delia shook her head. "Typical Duane, I'm afraid, always quick to look after his own skin. But nobody will take that seriously."

"Maybe not yet. But what about when they find out about Hank's arrest? Well," Callie concluded, "first things first. Hank was really anxious to be released. A lawyer is heading over to work on that. Do you know anything about how quickly—or not—that all works?"

Delia shrugged. "'Fraid not."

"Wish I'd thought to ask that lawyer, Allard, when I had him on the line." Callie thought a minute, then nodded. She had an excellent source—not a lawyer, but probably the next best thing and luckily not far away.

Nine

Callie called Lyssa to clear it, then headed on over to her friend's new home just outside of Keepsake Cove. As she waited for a response to her knock at the front door, she glanced around. She'd been to Lyssa's place before, of course, the first time shortly after the author had bought it. But that was in the fall, and her second visit had been in the middle of winter. Lyssa only left DC for her country home when both her mood and her schedule of writing commitments coincided.

The fall and winter seasons had given very different looks to the property than it had now, and Callie could understand her friend's desire to do a little gardening work. Whether Lyssa intended to do it herself or hire someone, the yard could definitely benefit from some sprucing up, though its view of the water made up for any shortcomings on the landscaping side.

Lyssa's ideas about buying a vacation home in the area had sparked to life when she and Callie had met with a realtor in Easton while searching for answers to the two fall murders. At the time, Lyssa had only pretended to be interested in buying a place, and her list of "must-haves" was a mishmash of every house feature she could think of. But the experience seemed to have planted a seed, and within weeks she had purchased a house.

"Hi!" Lyssa cried, swinging open the door. "Sorry to make you wait. I had an email from my agent that needed a quick answer. C'mon in!"

She waved Callie into the house, which had proven to be the complete opposite of what Callie had expected her to choose. It was a very modern A-frame with a huge two-story window that faced the water. A wrought-iron staircase wound its way from the living room up to a bedroom loft that shared that same view. All lovely, but quite different from the Victorian-era B&B Lyssa had been so delighted to stay in, with its hidden door and other mysterious features. It seemed she'd had enough of that style, though, and Callie felt the same way given the experience they'd had at the B&B. The old inn was the kind of place Lyssa tended to feature in her books, but apparently this contemporary Eastern Shore home was meant to be her escape from all that.

"Coffee? Tea? Wine?" Lyssa asked as she led the way into her stainless-steel-and-butcher-block kitchen.

Callie suddenly remembered that she'd left her half-finished coffee in Brian's café. "Is it really only ten thirty? A small coffee would be great."

"I won't tell anyone if you want the wine. It sounds like maybe you could use it."

Callie had filled Lyssa in on the basics when she'd called. "More likely Hank could, though I don't think that'll be on his menu." She grimaced. "He's pretty stressed over being held. I'm hoping you can tell me about the process so I can estimate how soon he'll be able to get out."

"Well, it all depends." Lyssa set her Nespresso machine to work fixing their brews. "You got him a lawyer, right?"

"Right."

"Then from what I remember from the research I did for *Dark Grave*, after you're arrested you go through booking. That means getting fingerprinted and photographed. That shouldn't take long. Maybe he's already gone through that?"

"I don't know. But if it's all a big mistake, which it has to be, can't his lawyer stop things before it comes to that?" Callie hated the thought of Hank getting a mug shot.

Lyssa handed Callie her coffee. "You said he's been arrested, Callie. It's already come to that. It means they're sure they have enough evidence on Hank to charge him."

Callie sank onto one of the bar stools at Lyssa's counter. "But how could they? This is a murder! I know Hank, and it's just not possible."

"I'm sure you know Hank well enough to say that. But it's the police who get to make the decision." Lyssa pulled out her own stool across from Callie. "Now, his lawyer can try to get him out on bail. If all goes well, that shouldn't take too long."

"Like, how long?"

"In Maryland, he has the right to be seen by a commissioner for bail review within twenty-four hours."

Callie groaned.

"But it could happen right away. It depends how busy they are. I wouldn't think here on the Eastern Shore there'd be much of a back-up."

"So Hank should be out on bail any time now?"

"Again, it depends."

Callie didn't like those qualifiers. "On what?"

"Well, the commissioner could set the bail really high, and Hank might not be able to handle it. Or want to. Does he have much money? Or property?"

Callie rolled her eyes. "We're talking about Hank, here. All his money goes into guitars and things like snakeskin boots. He wasn't much of a saver."

"Well, don't worry too much about the bail money. You don't have to cough up the entire amount—just a percentage to a bail bondsman. All that will take some time to arrange. But with luck, maybe only a few hours."

Callie wasn't thrilled with the *you* that Lyssa had used in connection to coughing up bail money, but she'd realized it might come to that. If it meant keeping Hank out of a cell, she didn't see that she'd have much choice.

"So, several hours," she said.

"At least." Lyssa took a long sip from her mug. "I'm sorry. When I warned you there'd be a bumpy ride, I didn't know it would hit so close to home."

Callie shook her head. "Not home. But close enough to shake it up."

"Sure. And maybe too close to get involved, do you think? I mean, investigating like you were for Dorothy Ashby. Which was great, but you weren't as emotionally involved as you are with Hank." Lyssa held up her hand to forestall Callie's protest. "I know, I know. You've been broken up for a long time and have no desire to get back together—"

"None whatsoever."

"But there's still a connection from those years together. You can't deny that. And it can get in the way of clear thinking sometimes. Make that a *lot* of times."

"Lyssa, either Hank is innocent or he's guilty. I know what I believe at this point, but if I'm wrong, if totally credible witnesses say with one hundred percent certainty that they saw Hank kill Bobby, then that'll be that. I can't imagine such a thing happening, which means Hank'll be released, whatever flimsy evidence they had against him will be dismissed, and that'll be the end of it. No further action on my part needed."

Lyssa was silent for a while, her expression sympathetic but not exactly agreeing. Eventually she nodded, saying, "I hope so." She drained her mug and pushed her stool back. "More coffee?"

Back at her cottage, Callie tried to work at her stockpile of food. She pulled out celery, carrots, and multiple other ingredients from her refrigerator and started chopping to make the soup she'd planned, telling herself she couldn't just sit and wait for her phone to ring. Neither did she want to let all that food slowly turn to mush. But it was difficult. As someone who seldom cooked from scratch, the process didn't come automatically or easily. It required concentration, a state that had evaded her all day, and she found herself rereading the recipe several times after her thoughts had wandered off.

"Ow!" she cried, having cut a finger while struggling to slice through a fat parsnip. Just then there was a knock at her door. Callie grabbed a towel to press against the wound and went to answer.

"Hi," Brian said. "Just thought I'd check in, see how things are ..." He looked down at the towel with its spreading dark red blotch. "Should I call 911?"

"It'll be fine. I keep forgetting how sharp Aunt Mel kept her knives."

"Where's your first-aid kit?" Brian asked, heading for the kitchen and locating the box at Callie's direction. He helped her wash and disinfect the cut, then wrapped it neatly, brushing off her embarrassed claims to klutziness. "Happens to me all the time." He stowed the kit and looked over her piled-high counter. "What are you doing?"

"Trying to make a soup first, then a casserole and a few other things I can freeze. I bought it all last night and can't just let it go. Delia made it sound like a breeze."

"Delia's been doing it for years. It takes practice. These are your recipes?" He picked up the print-outs Callie had made from the internet. She nodded. "Go relax," he said, "and keep that bandage dry. I'll take care of this."

Before she could protest, he walked her over to the sofa and plumped up a cushion before firmly setting her down. Then he rolled up his sleeves and got busy in the kitchen, chopping, braising, simmering, and seasoning, looking like Emeril Lagasse in fast-forward to Callie's impressed eyes but without the "Bam!" or, happily, the girth. She'd never seen Brian at work in his café kitchen and had only vague visions of what he actually did back there. Now she knew. He worked magic.

Wonderful aromas soon wafted through the cottage as Callie sipped at the tea Brian had fixed in between recipes. The only help he'd allowed from her was to produce the freezer containers he needed. The mounds of fruits, vegetables, and meats gradually compacted into freezable entrees or smoothies. It was mind-boggling, and Callie's feelings of guilt were diminished only by the look of pure enjoyment she saw on Brian's face. He was in his element.

As the last casserole baked, he washed up a few pots, then poured himself an iced tea and came over to sit beside her. "How's it feeling?" he asked, sinking down and nodding at her hand.

"Fine. I could have pitched in a little more, you know."

"Room for only one in that kitchen. And you would have been a distraction." He smiled. "In a good way."

Callie smiled back. "I am totally impressed. How did you get so good at that?"

He was about to respond when Callie's phone rang. "Sorry," she said. "I'd better take it."

"Miss Reed? Clark Allard." Callie sat up straighter on hearing the name. She mouthed the word *lawyer* to Brian.

"Yes, Mr. Allard?"

"Hank asked me to call. He's authorized me to share what's going on."

Callie's stomach clenched. Hank not calling himself didn't sound good, but she wasn't ready to give up hope yet. "Yes? Did he get bail?"

She heard Allard's throat clear. "I'm afraid not. There's been a complication." Another pause. "Did you know," Allard asked, "about Hank's prior conviction?"

"What? No!"

"I thought not. It was years ago, perhaps before you knew him. That, along with the slight possibility of flight risk, and of course the evidence against him in a highly serious charge, caused bail to be denied. Hank would like to speak with you himself about the first two. But the physical evidence comes from the murder weapon."

Callie held her breath, expecting to hear about a hunting knife or a gun, which to her mind would prove Hank's innocence since he owned neither. What she heard instead shook her.

"A music box. It had a guitar pictured on the top, and it played—"

"'Achy Breaky Heart.'"

"Yes. Hank admitted it was his, and his fingerprints are the only ones on it, along with, though this has yet to be officially confirmed, Mr. Linville's blood."

"Only Hank's fingerprints? But mine should have been on it."

"Hank said he polished it before showing it around and wouldn't let anyone touch it." Allard's tone was almost apologetic.

Callie groaned. "But Hank didn't admit using it against Bobby, did he?"

"No, he denies that. Vehemently."

Thank goodness. "When can I talk to him?"

Allard gave Callie details about Hank's transfer to a detention center, which she scribbled down, all the while thinking this couldn't be real. Not Hank. How could it be? "Can I call him?"

"Hank will have to call you," the lawyer said. "It won't be until sometime tomorrow. I'm sorry for the bad news."

Callie thanked him, feeling numb. She turned to Brian and saw he'd caught the gist of the call. She filled him in on the details. "It's not what I expected," she said. "I'm stunned."

She paused, thinking, then added, "But I'm also mad. It's all terribly wrong."

Ten

The next day in the shop, Callie couldn't stop thinking about Hank's situation. Plus, the thought of her music box being used to kill someone was horrible. She remembered its weight and compactness and couldn't deny that it would be deadly in the right hands. But not Hank's. That, to her mind, was not possible.

But did she know Hank as well as she thought? Brian had asked her this, and she'd been so sure that she did. Apparently not well enough to have known about something criminal in his past. What was it? It was bad enough for Hank to hide it from her. And serious enough to deny him bail.

Tabitha's arrival only meant having to put most of those disturbing thoughts into words. Her assistant wasn't aware of anything beyond the fact of a death at the festival, having been busy working on the special orders her beaded jewelry display had garnered. Callie caught her up in a hurry, only slightly disconcerted at the end to hear a solitary ding come from Grandpa Reed's music box overhead. If it was a comment from Aunt Mel, it was as glum as Callie felt.

"Wow," Tabitha said, "that's pretty awful. I can hardly believe they're charging Hank. He seemed so ... I don't know ... harmless? up there on the stage Saturday night. But I guess nobody's going to look murderous while they're singing about a breaking heart. Not that this means he ... well, you know what I mean."

"I do, and I think you're right about him being harmless. He could drive you crazy in a lot of ways, but never due to aggression. The Hank I knew went out of his way to avoid disagreements." As she said it, Callie thought again of the argument she'd witnessed at the festival. Hank hadn't exactly been avoiding whatever that was about at the time and had to be dragged away by one of the other band members. Something had made him angry enough with Bobby to go against his usual inclinations, at least to the point of shouts and curses.

A UPS truck pulled up in front of *House of Melody* and the driver hopped out with a delivery. Tabitha accepted the boxes, and as they got busy unpacking them, Callie's phone rang. She jumped at the sound and saw that it came from the detention center. As she hurried toward the back of the shop, she responded to the female voice that yes, she would accept the call, then closed her office door.

"Babe, you there?"

"I'm here, Hank. How are you?"

She heard a long exhale. "I'm okay. I hate bein' here, but I'm okay. Allard call you?"

"Yes, last night. He told me about bail being denied. I'm sorry."

Hank gave a dry laugh. "Yeah, me too. Guess I have some explainin' to do, huh?"

"Tell me first about what happened between you and Bobby. I saw the two of you arguing Saturday night."

"What happened was I *wanted* to kill him. I was madder'n hell with the SOB. But I didn't kill him."

"What made you want to kill him?"

"His drinkin'. The drinkin' he swore was over and done with but wasn't, and which blew the record contract we shoulda got right out the window! It was our big chance, babe, and it went right up in smoke because of him!"

"Calm down, Hank." He'd begun to shout, and Callie feared he might be forced to hang up. She wanted to know how Bobby had lost the contract but put that on hold until later. She waited until she heard steadier breaths from his end. "Hank, I have to ask. Did you have anything to do with his death?"

"Babe, nothing what-so-ever! I wasn't even there when they said it happened."

"When *did* it happen?"

"Late. After everything closed down. They said between twelve and two."

"Weren't you with the other guys in the band? You always used to go out for a couple of beers after a gig to wind down."

"They went without me. I was too steamed. The others, they just didn't get what Bobby did! They think, 'Hey, we'll get another chance,' or 'Bobby can make it right.' It doesn't work that way. They're newer, younger, and they don't know. They think chances like this come all the time. I've been in this business longer. It was my last chance. I couldn't be around them."

"So where did you go?"

"First, I drove by your place."

"My place!"

"Yeah. I thought maybe you'd be up and we could talk again, you know, like we used to? But all your lights were out. So I just kept going."

"Going where?"

"Just away. That's all I wanted, just to get away for a while. I ended up in a bar somewhere. Don't ask me where. I don't know the roads around here. I just saw the sign after a while and pulled in. I had a few drinks, probably too many 'cause when I left and started drivin' I knew it wasn't good. Yeah, I know. After cursin' at Bobby for his drinking, I go and get drunk. But you know it's not somethin' I generally do. I just needed it that night.

"Anyway, I pulled over on some little dirt road and fell asleep. When I woke up it was gettin' light. I drove around in circles for a while until enough signs popped up to get me back to the motel. Then I slept off the rest of it. Until cops came banging on the door."

Callie groaned internally. "Okay. It is what it is, for now. Maybe you'll remember the bar, or somebody there will remember you."

"I don't have much more time to talk."

"When can I visit?" There was a long pause. Fearing they'd been cut off, Callie asked, "Hank? Are you there?"

"I'm here." Hank's voice had lost its strength. "You can't visit till Saturday. That's what they told me. That's four days away. I don't want to *be* here four more days."

"I know it's tough, but you can last, Hank."

"You don't know, babe. I shouldn't be here at all. I gotta get out."

A robotic voice warned that their time was up. They quickly said their goodbyes, and Callie heard the line go dead. She tucked away her phone and stared out the window of the back door, a door she could walk through any time and go anywhere she chose. Unlike Hank. What could she do to get him released from his horribly wrong confinement?

The simple answer was to find out what really had happened to Bobby while Hank was miles away. She'd taken on similar challenges before, though the memories of how they'd nearly ended still shook her. But if not her, then who? Hank could go to prison for life if the police and the prosecutor stayed on their present course. The least she could do was try.

"Yeah, I figured you'd get involved," Lyssa said when Callie told her. She'd shown up at the shop shortly after Hank's call. "That's why I went over to talk to the other band members before they took off. I called around and found where they were staying."

"They're leaving?" Tabitha asked. She picked up the UPS box she'd just emptied and dropped it behind the counter.

"They seem pretty broken up about it, but there's no way they can hang around. They have gigs lined up that they can't just back out of."

"I can understand," Callie said. "It's their livelihood."

Lyssa nodded. "They were glad to give me their contact numbers, so we can always reach them."

"What did they have to say about Saturday night?" Callie asked.

"Well, they're each other's alibis, for one thing. They stuck together like glue after the festival wound up, all except Hank."

"I know." Callie told the two what Hank said he'd done that night.

"Then all we have to do is find that bar," Tabitha said. "Right? And Hank will have his alibi."

"I wish it were that easy. He didn't have anything to go on," Callie said. "He was driving aimlessly to work off steam, and he doesn't have a location or name for this place."

"I imagine it's also a pretty slim chance anyone would remember his being there. It was a Saturday night. Bound to be busy," Lyssa said.

"But you never know. I could work on it," Tabitha said. "With a little help from a few friends. Give me a good photo of Hank I can send around. We might get lucky!"

"That's a great idea," Callie said. She started to pull out her phone but stopped. "I got rid of the photos on this, but I'm sure I can find one somewhere."

"He was still in his performance clothes, right? Look for one like that," Lyssa said.

"I will. Now, there's something that's been bothering me. The music box."

Lyssa nodded. "Why was it there, right? One of the guys in the band, Randy Brewer, said Hank brought it with him and had it backstage. He had an idea about working it into one of their songs. Maybe to impress you, or point out his connection to you to the crowd? Randy didn't know, but he talked him out of it."

"I should have asked Hank, but did Randy know if Hank left it behind?"

"He had no idea. There was plenty of commotion after they finished their set, with the guys trying to calm Hank down and keep him from catching up with Bobby."

"Catching up? Where did Bobby go?"

"That's not clear. Tried to keep out of Hank's sight, but exactly how, they couldn't say."

"He must have stayed at the festival, though," Tabitha offered. "That's where his body was found."

"Not necessarily," Lyssa said. "He had his car. He could have gone anywhere."

"But he came back," Callie said. "Why?"

"Million-dollar question," Lyssa said, blowing away a piece of formerly spiked hair that had drooped over one eye.

Eleven

"There you are!" Delia paused at the door of *House of Melody*, delighted to see Lyssa. They hugged, and after a few words about the terrible end to the festival, turned to more cheerful catch-up questions about Lyssa's latest book, travels, and new house. When Lyssa turned the questions around to Delia, she shrugged and said, "Well, it looks like I have a new housemate."

"What! You mean Jill?" Callie asked.

"Uh-huh. Just temporarily. But right now she has nowhere to go. When I invited her here for the festival, I didn't realize she'd lost both her job and her apartment. She'll have trouble getting another place without a steady salary to put on the application, so I told her to stay until she finds something."

As Delia explained to Lyssa about the costume photography Jill did at the festival, Tabitha asked, "Does Jill do regular photography?

"Oh yes, and she's good!" Delia said. "I thought a while back that she was ready to open her own portrait studio. But that fell apart for some reason. Her latest work was doing kids' photos at a department store. She wasn't thrilled with it—said it was very limiting. But at least it paid the rent. I don't know exactly why that ended." Delia winced. "But I can make an educated guess. Jill has a bit of a temper, I'm afraid."

"Ooh, not what you want in a housemate," Lyssa said.

"No, no worry there. I know her well enough to say it flares only when she feels she's been seriously wronged. But she's aware of how it's caused her problems, like losing jobs she can't afford to lose, and she's working on it."

Callie remembered the scene at the festival when Jill drove away customers with her anger over a ripped costume. Not exactly a serious wrong, and she'd admitted later that she'd overreacted. Unfortunately, the damage had been done.

"Well, good luck to you both," Lyssa said. "I hope she finds something and you get your house back to yourself."

"I'd like to talk to Jill," Callie said. "There's a chance she might have seen something at the festival that would help Hank. Would you ask her to stop in?"

"Sure." Delia's tone turned solicitous. "How is Hank doing?"

"About as well as can be expected," Callie said.

"In other words, miserably," Lyssa added.

"I can only imagine," Delia said. "I wish there was something I could do."

Callie saw Delia's genuine concern, a trait she'd truly appreciated when it had shown itself during her early days at Keepsake Cove. But she worried her friend might be too big-hearted for her own good. She hoped Delia hadn't taken on something in her willingness to help Jill that she might regret.

"Oh," Delia asked, "did you get the word about the association meeting tonight? Krystal sent out an urgent email."

"I'll check. That's a surprise—an unscheduled meeting."

"It must have to do with the hassle from the festival being cut short. Can you make it?"

Callie's first thought was that she had more than enough to deal with. But she reconsidered. Who knew what she might learn from the other shopkeepers, all conveniently gathered in one place. "I'll be there," she said.

After Tabitha left a few hours later, armed with a digital photo of Hank that Callie had found on the Badlanders' website, Callie was alone in the shop. She thought about Lyssa's last comment before she'd taken off.

I get why you want to help Hank, Lyssa had said. *But be careful it doesn't hurt what you've got with Brian.*

It had startled her. Could Brian take her desire to help Hank out of a bad situation the wrong way? She'd hate that, and decided to talk it over with him. Maybe after the association meeting, if they went together. She was about to text him and suggest it when Jill walked in.

"Delia said you wanted to talk to me?"

"Hi!" Callie put her phone away and looked out the window for any approaching customers. "Yes, thanks for coming over."

"Cute shop," Jill said, glancing around. She picked up one of Callie's novelty musical globes from the children's table and smiled at the Tinker Bell figure inside.

"Thanks. I love Delia's shop, too, with that amazing variety of salt and pepper shakers."

"Isn't it something? She wants me to pick out a set for myself, but I think I should get *her* a nice gift for what she's doing for me. As soon as I can afford it, that is." Jill's general air of tension that Callie had noticed at their first meeting was still there, and then some. Understandable, of course, from what Delia had shared about Jill's job situation. The photographer's gray-streaked dark hair was tied into the messy bun style that could look chic when done right; Jill's bun looked more "I don't really care," which Callie guessed was likely the case.

"Did Delia tell you about the band member who was arrested for the murder at the festival?" she asked.

"Yeah! She said you know him. That must have been a shock, huh?"

"Definitely, and I believe the police have it all wrong. So I'm trying to help him out. You were at the festival Saturday night pretty late, right?"

"Um, yeah, I guess."

She guessed? Delia had said Jill didn't come home before eleven thirty and likely much past that, but Callie didn't press the point.

"What I want to know," she went on, "is if you saw anything that might help my friend."

"Like what? I mean, I wasn't near the stage where the band was, and I was busy with my photography."

Except when she wasn't. Callie remembered Jill sitting morosely by herself when she and Brian had walked up. This was starting to feel like pulling teeth.

"What I'm most interested in are the activities of Bobby Linville, the man who was murdered. He was the band's manager, but he didn't stay only in the stage area. He moved around during the festival. You would have recognized him from seeing him at Dino's Diner the night you were there with Delia. He came in with Hank and went around passing out flyers about the band from table to table. I noticed that you seemed disturbed by it."

"Yeah. I remember. I thought that was really gross. I mean, bothering people like that when they're trying to eat? He was lucky he didn't come to our table." Jill's color had risen, evidence of the temper Delia had mentioned. What would she have done if Bobby had approached her?

"So, did you see him around at the festival?"

Jill frowned and fiddled with another one of Callie's smaller music boxes. "You know, I did see him one time, maybe around ten-ish? I was taking a break, getting something to drink, and as I headed back I heard some kind of argument going on. I looked over—I think they were between the Christmas ornaments booth and another one. Not too many people around that area then, with the band pulling most everyone to the stage. It surprised me, 'cause, you know, everyone else was having such a good time and all, and I stopped. They looked over at me and dropped their voices in a hurry, but they were still hissing-like. I moved on."

"They? Bobby and who else? A man?" *Please, let it not be Hank.*

"No, a woman. Short dark hair, and a kind of sparkly T-shirt on."

Krystal Cobb? "Designer jeans?"

"I guess. Nice ones, anyway."

"You didn't hear what the argument was about?"

"Nope, sorry. That's all I can tell you."

"Well, that's good. Thanks! If you remember anything else, please let me know, okay?" When Jill nodded rather gloomily, Callie said, "I'm so sorry the festival didn't work out for you. Delia told me you're looking for a new job. I guess you want to stick to something in photography, huh?"

"That's what I'm best at and what I love. If nothing comes up, though..." Jill shrugged. "I can't impose on Delia forever. I've done waitressing before. I suppose I can do it again if I have to. Funny how that goes, isn't it?" She smiled grimly. "On TV they said Bobby Linville dropped out of the music business a while back for 'personal problems.'" Her fingers made air quotes. "That's usually code, you know, for 'he ticked off a lot of people.' But there he was, back in and all was forgiven. But me? I stand up for myself once or twice and what do I get?" She shook her head.

Callie was sure Jill wouldn't want to end up how Bobby had ended up, but doubted she'd care to hear that at the moment. And she did sympathize. Everyone certainly had the right to stand up for themselves, though how they handled it made a big difference. She genuinely wished Jill the best of luck and hoped that she would find work in her beloved profession, which could go a long way to brightening her attitude. Otherwise, she hoped any future diners who might be waited on by Delia's friend would be extremely careful about voicing any complaints.

Twelve

"Thanks for coming with me." Callie smiled at Brian as they got out of his car at the library. She knew meetings were not Brian's favorite way to spend an evening, not by a long shot. But when she'd explained what she hoped to glean from it, he'd been agreeable.

"No problem." Brian smiled back and took her hand. "Might as well find out what our association's up to."

Their walk through the parking lot was pleasant, with a few thin clouds softening the otherwise bright sunset, and the temperature was mild. But Callie could feel a change in the air as they drew closer to the library's meeting room. Keepsake Cove shopkeepers heading there walked briskly, and though they greeted one another, the smiles struck her as a bit tight. In the room, people didn't actually huddle, whispering in small groups, but circulated, which Callie took as a good sign, though the chatter was quieter than usual.

Brian pitched in to set up chairs, and once that was done, Krystal tapped the microphone and asked everyone to take a seat. She'd returned to a more formal style of dress for her role as association president, with a navy cotton blazer over a striped skirt. But something was missing. After a moment, Callie realized that nothing sparkled—either on the jacket, the cami underneath, or even Krystal's jewelry, which were simple turquoise beads. Highly unusual for the woman, and Callie couldn't help wondering if it signaled anything, especially after what Jill had told her about Krystal and Bobby's apparent fight. She intended to ask Krystal about that as soon as she could manage.

She and Brian settled into two end seats in the third row, and the other chairs soon filled up. She saw Delia near the back and finger-waved to her. Jill must have decided watching TV would be more her cup of tea, and Callie couldn't blame her.

"All right, folks," Krystal said. "Let's get started. Thank you all for coming out on such short notice. A lot of you have been emailing me about the losses we took from the festival, so I thought we might as well lay it all out at once." She turned to Duane and said, "For that, I'll turn it over to our treasurer." She handed Duane the microphone and stepped aside.

"Thank you, Krystal," Duane said. He looked his usual genial self, smiling as he glanced around at the group. But Callie couldn't bring herself to smile back. His bald claim, in front of the others, that he'd only hired the Badlanders because of her still rankled. She'd remained cordial with him for months despite becoming aware of his self-serving ways, and she supposed she'd have to continue to do so. But that wouldn't start tonight.

He went through the figures, listing the expenses of the festival and the proceeds from its single day of operation, which left the association with a loss. Everything seemed to add up, and he promised that the figures would soon be uploaded to the association website for all to study. "So you see, though I'm totally sympathetic with those of you who lost the cost of your booth rental for the second day because of the festival being closed, there's no way to refund those fees. It's simply not doable."

"And keep in mind," Krystal stood up to say, "the Keepsake Cove shops that didn't set up booths on the festival grounds also lost out on the sales they'd hoped for when the crowds we expected stayed away."

"They're still staying away," a plaintive voice called out. It was Emily Frazier, whose shop carried collectible cookie jars. The petite, ponytailed woman's head could barely be seen, surrounded as she was with much larger people. "My business was terrible today."

"Mine, too!" a male voice seconded. Soon half the room had joined in with the same complaint.

Delia rose, calling out over the others, "It's natural after what happened, but it's just temporary, folks. We can get through it. What we should be thinking of is what to do next to bring the crowds back. Memorial Day isn't that far away. How about planning something for then?"

"That's three weeks away!" Howard Graham cried.

"Yes, but surely your shop can hang in there," Delia answered.

"I wouldn't have to hang in if the festival hadn't turned into such a disaster. And who's going to want to come to anything we have on Memorial Day? They'll be afraid for their lives!"

"Come, now," Duane soothed. "They will be no such thing. The murder wasn't some kind of mugging gone wrong that would make people afraid it could happen again. They've already arrested the person who did it. So it's over and done with."

No it's not! Callie squirmed in her seat but kept her mouth shut.

"It still ruined things for all of us," Howard fussed. "You never should have brought that country-western band here."

"Well, as I explained, it wasn't—"

Brian jumped up and interrupted. "I think Delia's idea of a Memorial Day celebration is great. I'll volunteer to head a committee for that. Suggestions, anyone, for something a little different that will catch people's attention?"

The group was silent for several moments. Then Lyle Moody rose slowly. "I'm new to the Cove, as you all know," he drawled, automatically reminding everyone of the type of memorabilia he sold. "But from what I understand, Memorial Day is practically a stampede to the beaches around here. No use trying to detour those folks when they smell water. Would Mother's Day be better?"

"Too soon!" someone called out. "It'll have to be in June."

"June!" Howard eyes popped, as he obviously feared bankruptcy by that time.

"Um, people?" Duane said into his microphone. "May I remind you we don't have money for another event right now."

The group went silent.

After a few moments, Brian said, "Then how about the entire Cove having a fantastic sale? The day before Mother's Day. All we'd have to do is advertise."

Heads nodded and murmurs of agreement ran around the room. Even Howard looked okay with the idea.

"Great," Brian said. "We have a consensus."

"Terrific," Duane said. "I knew we could work this all out." He babbled some more about deadlines for the ads and other details while Callie locked onto his use of we. He'd quickly taken credit for the solution Brian had thought of.

Krystal took back the microphone to bring up a couple of more mundane topics, then officially adjourned the meeting. Chairs scraped as a general chatter and gradual scatter began.

"Thanks for jumping in when you did," Callie said to Brian. "But you almost got yourself stuck with a huge committee job."

"You're welcome. I'd say it would have been worth it, but I'm actually feeling lucky that things went the other way."

Callie saw Krystal wrapping up the microphone cord at the front of the room, several feet away from anyone. "Excuse me, Brian. I'd like to talk to Krystal for a minute."

But before she could act, a voice called out from the meeting room's doorway. "Krystal! One of the library ladies wants to talk to you."

Krystal set down the microphone and hurried over.

Shoot. Callie glanced around and saw shopkeepers scuttling for the exit, none apparently in the mood to extend the evening.

"Looks like I'm not going to be able to pick any brains here tonight."

"Not unless you tackle them first. I think I hear engines revving already."

Callie smiled ruefully. "Well, it's not my only chance. I can still track them down. It'll just take longer."

She grabbed her purse and left the room with Brian—a little less rapidly than the others—then waited until they were on the road to bring up her other concern.

"You've been very supportive, and I really appreciate it. But I don't want this to be a problem between us."

"This, being…?"

"My getting actively involved with Hank's situation. I'm doing it only because I'm so sure the police are mistaken. And because he's alone here. The rest of the band has taken off."

Brian was silent, so Callie went on. "I haven't forgotten what a total jerk he can be, so I don't want you to think in the least that I might be doing this because of some old feelings being stirred. It's not

75

that at all. I might do the same if one of his band members had been wrongly charged, someone I didn't know but who needed help."

Brian smiled. "I wish it *was* one of the other band members. And that it was Hank who'd taken off. But I understand your reasons, and I'm okay with it."

"Really?"

"Really. Just be careful, okay?'

Callie promised, and she was happy with Brian's reassurance. After savoring it for a few moments, her thoughts moved ahead to her next concern. "I'll be talking to Krystal soon about an argument Jill saw her having with Bobby, but I don't know that much about her. It'd be good to have a clearer picture. Is Krystal single? I've never heard of a Mr. Cobb."

"Divorced. I think I heard she moved here from western Pennsylvania."

"Children?"

"Don't know. With our level of interaction, that topic never came up."

"She was president when I came to the Cove last year. Has she done it for long?"

Brian considered that. "This must be her third year. It's a thankless job, if you ask me, but she's good at it. And she must like it, or she wouldn't keep doing it."

"She obviously knows everybody in the Cove. But is she particularly close to anyone?"

Brian shook his head, laughing lightly. "You're asking the wrong ... wait! Now that you mention it. She's probably good friends with Rhonda Furman. Rhonda runs *Timely Treasures*."

Callie thought for a minute. "Collectible clocks?"

Brian did a thumbs-up. "I've seen them with their heads together at the end of meetings. Looked like friend-type talk instead of business."

"Okay. That's good to know. Gosh, it's amazing the shops I still don't know about in this place."

"And just when you think you know them all, more pop up. Like mushrooms."

Callie grinned at the image. Whack-a-Mole came to mind next, but then her smile faded. That sounded too close to what had happened to Bobby Linville. Somebody had certainly whacked him. But why? His popping up in Keepsake Cove must have been a big problem for someone. What that problem was, exactly, and for whom, was going to be Callie's job to find out.

Thirteen

The next day, Callie took off within minutes of Tabitha's arrival at the shop and headed to the other end of Keepsake Cove where Krystal Cobb's collectible dolls shop was located. She remembered assuming, at her very first association meeting, that the group's president must own a glass-related shop, until Delia set her straight. Callie had always thought it was a regrettable loss of a good name for a shop. *Krystal's Goblets?* But Krystal's interests lay in a different direction, as evidenced by *Forever Dolls*.

Lyssa had called that morning, and she and Callie agreed to team up, so Callie wasn't surprised to spot her standing outside the shop's window studying the display. She easily recognized the author from a distance by her spiked red hair, which the sun had turned into tiny flames. In addition, Lyssa had thrown a brightly colored scarf around her neck, adding to the glow. Callie thought it was a good thing they weren't doing anything undercover that day, since they'd never get away with it.

"I had a doll like that once," Lyssa said as Callie drew near. She pointed to a rosy-cheeked, gingham-dressed doll with a white bonnet tied under its chin. "An older relative gave it to me, but my mother never let me play with it. It was too special."

"Now's your chance," Callie said. "You could start a collection."

"Nah. Not my thing." Lyssa dismissed the thought with a head shake, but Callie thought she saw a wistful look in the author's eyes. "Ready to go in?"

"Ready."

Krystal was dealing with a single customer when they entered the shop, so Callie and Lyssa browsed. "Had a few of those," Lyssa said, gesturing at a table of Barbie dolls. Unopened packages of sequined dresses surrounded the dolls, along with sets of tiny high-heeled shoes and accessories.

"Who didn't?" Callie asked. "I used to think she was how we'd all look when we grew up."

"Good thing we didn't. We'd be struggling just to stay upright. Way too top-heavy for those little feet. Pretty hair, though."

"Thank you so much, Ms. Cobb," Krystal's customer said as she gathered up her package. "I've been looking for Caroline for years." She gently patted her box, which apparently contained a named doll.

Krystal beamed and assured the woman it was totally her pleasure, then shifted her gaze to Callie and Lyssa as her customer turned to leave.

"Hello there! How nice to see you both again. Ms. Hammond, did you come for our spring festival? If so, I'm sorry for the disappointment."

"Actually, I came to do a few things with my house. I didn't know about the festival until I got here. But it was more than a disappointment for a lot of people, wasn't it? I mean, it totally crashed!"

Krystal flinched at the blunt statement. She'd doubtless been dancing around the subject with her customers. "Well, yes. We were forced to close down after what happened."

More circumspection. Callie took her cue from Lyssa for directness. Maybe keeping Krystal a little off balance would be useful. "What happened was a murder, of course," she said. "The murder of a man that you seemed to know."

"Me! Why would you say such a thing?"

"Because you were seen talking with Bobby Linville around ten o'clock. Arguing, actually."

"Oh!" Krystal looked from Callie to Lyssa. "But that was nothing! Nothing to do with his murder, I mean."

"What was it about?" Lyssa asked.

"It … it was about money." Krystal's expression darkened. "Mr. Linville thought he could demand more from us since the band was going over so well with the crowd. I told him we intended to stick to the contract. He then threatened to cancel their performance for the next day, which I told him was despicable. I was furious!"

"I see," Callie said. "But why did he come to you and not Duane about that?"

"I told him he needed to see Duane when he first mentioned money to me. He said he couldn't find him."

"So how did it end?" Lyssa asked.

"It ended with me threatening legal action if they didn't honor the agreement. But he just laughed. He must have guessed we didn't have the finances to back that up. He told me to come up with the extra pay by morning or they would pack up and leave. Then he walked off. He knew he had me in a bind. If our headliner band wasn't there, people who showed up expecting it would never trust our events again. Of course, things pretty much turned out that way anyway." Krystal sighed. "I tried to reach Duane, but he wasn't answering his phone. I didn't talk to him until the next morning when he called me about the body. Bobby Linville's body."

"I don't suppose you brought up Bobby's squeeze tactic at that time," Lyssa said.

"Not then, no. I did tell him later."

"Did Duane say why he hadn't picked up your calls?"

Krystal looked puzzled. "Why would he? It didn't matter anymore, did it?"

Maybe not, but Callie decided to find out herself. Knowing the location of as many people as possible during that critical time period was important. "Did you stay at the festival much longer after talking with Bobby?"

"Maybe for half an hour or so. When I couldn't get Duane by phone, I looked around for him. But then I gave up and went home. I was sure he'd get the messages I left. Though what we were going to do, I had no idea." She looked from one to the other. "Now, why all these questions?" If they'd had Krystal off balance for a while, she'd apparently regained her footing and once again sounded like her call-to-order self.

"I'm trying to learn as much as possible about Bobby Linville's movements that night," Callie said. "It could help uncover what really happened and who really killed him."

"Oh! You mean, you think the man they arrested isn't ...?"

"I'm *sure* he isn't the murderer. I know Hank very well. He isn't capable of such a thing."

"I didn't realize you knew him. I'm sorry about that. I wish I could help you more." Krystal looked sincerely regretful. "But as I said, shortly after Mr. Linville and I ended our, ah, *discussion*, I went home, so I can't tell you any more about what he was up to."

Lyssa had been glancing around, and she changed to a chattier tone. "Do you live in one of those little cottages they have here? Behind your shop? I know not everyone uses them."

"No way! They're much too small. Even though it's just me, I need more space."

"I know what you mean," Callie said. "Half my clothes have to be kept in storage." Having seen Krystal in dozens of different outfits over the past year, she couldn't picture her being okay with doing that.

"Exactly!" the older woman confirmed. "I use the cottage for storing my shop inventory." Her shop phone rang, and she excused herself to answer it.

"I think we've learned all we can for now," Lyssa said quietly to Callie.

Callie nodded agreement. When Krystal had finished her call, she thanked her for her help. As they were about to leave, Lyssa said, "Oh, by the way, one of the projects I hoped to get started on at my house was fixing the landscaping. Things like replacing overgrown bushes. I could use a recommendation, if either of you has one."

Callie looked blank. Elvin Wilcox had done basic yard work for her but he wasn't a landscaper. Besides, he'd moved away a while ago.

Krystal said, "I think you'd be happy with Gavin Holder." She picked up her cell phone and began to scroll. After a moment she read off the man's contact information, which Lyssa added to her own phone.

"Perfect. Thanks!" They took off then, and once outside the shop, Lyssa said, "Well, we know a little more about the murdered guy. A slime ball. But it doesn't put us any closer to finding out who killed him."

"Not yet, but it might inch us closer. I'd like to learn a little more about Krystal."

"Why?"

"Well, she's a bit of a mystery to me. Even Brian couldn't tell me that much. If we're going to take her at her word about Bobby Linville, I'd like to understand where she's coming from. Brian thought she might be good friends with Rhonda Furman, another Keepsake Cove shopkeeper. I looked her up, and her shop's on one of the side streets, not too far from here. Want to come?"

"Sure, why not. What's her shop carry? I assume we're going to play customers. Or at least I am."

"Vintage clocks."

"Okay, that works. I wouldn't mind adding one to the house."

"As long as you're good with an eclectic look," Callie said. "Rhonda's stock will probably lean heavily toward cuckoo clocks."

"Hmm."

Callie laughed at the pained look on Lyssa's face. She remembered the Kit Kat clock she'd seen at *The Collectible Cook*, a shop that had closed last fall for serious reasons. That kitchen clock, with its moving eyes and black pendulum tail, would have provoked an even worse expression on Lyssa's face. Or maybe not. Lyssa's tastes were unpredictable. It would be interesting to see what she gravitated to at *Timely Treasures*.

Fourteen

"Good lord!" Lyssa muttered. "The entire shop is pulsating! This place should have been called *The Ticking Time Bomb*." A grandfather clock behind her suddenly bonged, and she jumped. "Just what I'd love in my house," she said, turning to look. "Something to wake me every hour on the hour."

"And probably on the quarter hour," Callie added.

"Lovely."

"You should visit Howard Graham's *Christmas Collectibles*. A life-sized Santa Claus greets everyone with 'Ho-ho-ho, Merry Christmas!' as 'Jingle Bells' plays."

Lyssa shuddered. "I'll pass on that, thanks. Thank goodness most of the other shops around here have better sense."

Callie didn't see any Kit Kat clocks, but she did spot one labeled *Klocker Spaniel* that had a red-painted dog face. Along with the kitschyness, though, there were several lovely pieces. Callie understood how shopkeepers needed to stock a little something for everyone.

Rhonda Furman had leaned out of her back office as they'd walked in, a phone held to her ear, and promised to be right with them. When she finally stepped out, Callie was surprised, realizing she'd expected someone closer in appearance to the stylishly dressed and coiffed Krystal. Rhonda looked much more grandmotherly, with a hairstyle from the Princess Di era and a shirtdress that could have hung in her closet at that time, too. Nothing wrong with either, of course; just miles away from Krystal's up-to-the-minute style.

"So, what can I do for you ladies—oh! You're Callie Reed, aren't you? I've always meant to stop in at your place and say hello. Now you've saved me the trouble!" She turned to Lyssa. "And you're that author, aren't you. How exciting!"

Lyssa admitted she was "that author" who'd done the book event in Keepsake Cove last fall, and she gave her actual name but pooh-poohed the idea of excitement. "We're actually very boring people. It's our books that are exciting. We spend hours and hours at our computers, which is why it's good to get out once in a while. I've been slowly putting my new house together and thought I might like a decorative clock of some kind over the mantel. I'm not into cuckoo clocks. Got anything a little more modern?"

"Oh heavens, yes!" Rhonda steered Lyssa toward a section at the back where a variety of choices were displayed on the wall. Callie hung back, interested in a table of small clocks, one of which reminded her of a clock Grandma Reed had owned. What had happened to it, she wondered. Aunt Mel had inherited all of Grandpa Reed's music boxes, but Callie hadn't seen any of her grandmother's things in the cottage. Perhaps the size of the place had simply made keeping them impossible.

"Oh, I love that one!" Lyssa cried, waving Callie over to see a zig-zag-shaped metallic piece that had the hands of a clock but not much else to identify it as such.

"Art Deco," Rhonda said.

"Doesn't it look exactly like something Hercule Poirot would have on his wall?" Lyssa was clearly enamored. "I've got to have it."

Rhonda smiled happily and reached to take the piece down. Callie wasn't sure if Lyssa truly loved the item—for which Callie couldn't see much to get excited about—or if she was trying to put Rhonda in a cheery and hopefully chatty mood. A glance at the price tag caused her to suck in her breath. At that price, Rhonda should spill her social security number to them along with several passwords.

As Rhonda gathered packing materials, Lyssa said, "We just came from *Forever Dolls*. Some nice things there, too."

"Yes, Krystal manages to find wonderful dolls. She has quite a knack." Rhonda lowered Lyssa's clock into a box cushioned with bubble wrap. "I've learned a lot from her over the years. We go way back."

"Do you?" Callie asked. "You're from Pennsylvania?"

Rhonda looked up, smiling. "Baldwin, just outside of Pittsburgh."

"Baldwin? Is that where the pianos come from?" Lyssa asked.

"No, those actually originated in Cincinnati," Rhonda said. "I found that out after being asked the question several times and finally looking it up. Our town was named after a congressman from the nineteenth century, Henry Baldwin."

"Ah, Henry," Lyssa said, nodding. Callie smiled, sure that her friend had never heard of the man, or the town, in her life. "So, what, you and Krystal went to school together or something?"

"No," Rhonda said, chuckling. "Not that far back. But our daughters went to school together. That's how we met. Krystal was president of the PTA."

"I'm not surprised," Callie said. "She has a talent for leadership."

"Yes, she does," Rhonda agreed. She added a layer of bubble wrap over Lyssa's clock.

"That's nice, staying friends for so long. Did your daughters do the same?" Lyssa asked.

Rhonda's face clouded, and Callie expected to hear that the daughters had had a falling out somewhere along the line. She was startled, then, when Rhonda instead said, "I'm afraid not. Krystal's daughter, Tiffany, passed away."

"Oh! I had no idea," Callie said. "An accident?"

Rhonda bit her lip and looked like she regretted saying anything. She shook her head. "A sad story, but it's Krystal's to tell."

"Of course. I'm so sorry for her."

"She's been very strong," Rhonda said. "But as sometimes happens, her marriage didn't survive."

"Grief can drive people apart," Lyssa said. "Instead of pulling them together."

"So true. But Krystal's been amazing. She's picked up the pieces and thrown herself into making a new life. When my husband's job brought us to Maryland, she encouraged me to turn my passion for clocks into this business, now that our kids are on their own."

"Good for her," Callie said. "And for you, too. It's not easy making a new beginning." She thought of her own new start in life and the struggles it involved.

"It *isn't* easy," Rhonda agreed. "But the rewards can be great." She clipped a small handle onto the string she'd wrapped around Lyssa's box.

To shift the focus to the night of Bobby Linville's murder, Callie asked, "Did you have a booth at the festival?"

"I didn't. Don and I were away the entire weekend." Rhonda's eyes lit up. "To meet our newest grandchild. Our son and daughter-in-law's little boy. Such a sweetie! We didn't get back until late Monday and have been playing catch-up ever since. Too busy even to go to the association meeting!"

Rhonda's smile stretched from ear to ear, and Callie returned a version of it. But to forestall a detour from her subject, she quickly asked, "So you probably didn't learn about what happened until you came back, huh?"

"No, and what a shock. Some stranger found dead on the festival grounds!"

"Not exactly a stranger," Lyssa said. "It was the manager of the band that was booked for the festival."

"Oh?" Rhonda apparently hadn't fully caught up since her return.

Lyssa nodded. "His name was Bobby Linville, and—" She stopped when Rhonda blanched. "Did you know him?"

"No!" Rhonda insisted, shaking her head. She swallowed and added more quietly, "I mean, I thought I did at first. The name. It's very close to someone else's I happen to know. But, no, it's not him." She laughed in an odd, gargling way. "It just caught me for a moment. Sorry."

"You're sure?" Callie asked.

Rhonda flapped a hand, looking embarrassed. "Yes, absolutely. So it was the band manager? What a shame. And terrible, of course." She picked up Lyssa's box. "Well, here you are!" she said, handing it over. "Thank you so much. I hope you'll enjoy it."

"I'm sure I will," Lyssa said automatically.

"So nice to meet you both," Rhonda said. "I'll have to stop over to see your shop, Callie." She was talking a little more rapidly. "You'll have to excuse me now. I have a few calls to return. Still catching up! Thank you, and come again!"

Dismissed, Lyssa and Callie had no choice but to leave, though Lyssa pulled Callie up once they'd walked a short distance away.

"Sound fishy to you?"

"I think she recognized Bobby Linville's name."

"But she didn't want to say so. Why not? What is she hiding?"

"I wish I knew," Callie said, looking back at *Timely Treasures*. "But she's obviously not going to tell us. We'll have to come up with some other way of finding out."

Fifteen

*L*yssa wanted to take her clock home as well as give the land-scaper, Gavin Holder, a call, so Callie headed back to *House of Melody* where she found Tabitha sweeping imaginary grains of dust from the shop's floor.

"Not much business," Tabitha explained.

Callie nodded. "It seems like that all over the Cove. Lyssa probably made one of the few buys of the day." She told Tabitha about her visit to *Timely Treasures* and *Forever Dolls*, along with Rhonda Furman's surprising reaction to hearing Bobby Linville's name.

"That's weird," Tabitha said. "I mean, how many names sound like Linville that could have made her think of someone else? She must be covering up."

"But for who? Not herself. Rhonda was miles away all weekend and obviously didn't know it was Bobby who was murdered. Krystal, on the other hand, actually had a fight with Bobby at the festival."

Callie shared what Jill had seen, as well as Krystal's explanation for the argument.

"Oooh. Something's definitely up. Rhonda said she and Krystal are old friends. Rhonda must know something."

"Which she's not about to spill. I wonder if Hank might know about a connection between them? Or one of the other band members?"

"Maybe! Oh, by the way, nobody's had any luck tracking down the bar Hank was in Saturday night. Yet."

Callie noticed Tabitha hadn't put it as "the bar Hank *said* he was in," and she appreciated that.

"Of course, it's early days," Tabitha went on, "and none of us has had piles of free time to work on it."

"I understand. I'm grateful for any bit of help."

The door opened and a customer walked in with a look about her that signaled serious shopping rather than "just looking." Tabitha, excited to have someone to wait on, hurried forward to help. Knowing she wouldn't be needed, Callie left the woman in her assistant's highly capable hands and went to the office. There she sat at her desk and gathered her thoughts.

She wouldn't be able to talk to Hank until he called her again, and the timing of that was unpredictable. She had the contact numbers of the other band members from Lyssa, but, though she knew everyone from Hank's last band well, she hadn't even met these new guys. Everything she knew about them came from watching their performance at the festival and from the episode she and Brian witnessed between sets. One of them had pulled Hank away when his fury with Bobby escalated. That had been Randy Brewer, the fiddle player Hank introduced on stage as his collaborator on the next song. Randy was who she'd call.

She glanced at the clock. The time should be good—not too early or too late. She knew all too well the habits and routines of professional musicians, who worked late and generally slept late. She pulled out her phone, found his number, and pressed call.

"Randy? This is Callie Reed. I'm—"

She was ready to explain further, but Randy quickly broke in with "Hi, Callie. How's Hank?" He knew who she was and was eager to talk.

"Well enough," she said, "all things considered. But pretty unhappy."

"Gosh, I can imagine. It tore me up having to leave, tore us all up. But we just plain couldn't afford to hang around. You know how it goes. You back out of a gig at the last minute and the chances of getting another one there are zero. And word spreads."

"Right. I'm sure Hank understands. Listen, Randy, I'm hoping you can help me with something."

"Sure. Whatever I can do."

"I believe Hank is innocent"—Callie heard an encouraging "absolutely" from the other end—"and I'm trying hard to find out what really happened. I need to know a lot more about Bobby. For starters, did he ever mention a connection to Krystal Cobb or Rhonda Furman?"

"Not to me."

"What about the town of Baldwin? It's near Pittsburgh."

"Baldwin," Randy repeated. "That rings a bell. I think Bobby used to live there. I remember Baldwin because of, you know, the piano thing."

Callie let that irrelevant error go by. "Do you know when?"

"Back when he was in school. College."

"Really." Bobby hadn't struck her as the college type.

"Uh-huh. I'm pretty sure he didn't finish. He used to laugh about all the classes he missed from oversleeping."

"Do you know which school?" When she heard a long "Ummm ...," Callie said, "Hold on. I'll pull up names of colleges near Baldwin. Maybe that'll help." She woke up her laptop and typed rapidly. A long list came up. Since it was barely outside of Pittsburgh, Baldwin was loaded with colleges and universities. But as she read the names, none struck a chord for Randy.

"Sorry. Can't help you there."

"That's all right. Is there anything else you can tell me about Bobby?"

"Oh, gosh. He could talk your arm off, sometimes, but a lot of it went right outa my head. Let me think. You know about his drinking problem, right?"

"Yes. Hank thought Bobby had it under control but apparently was wrong about that."

"Yeah, we all were. Bobby swore up and down he was off the hard stuff. He had us all fooled. But it caused him his own trouble, money problems, job problems, you name it."

"Yes, I heard he'd been in and out of the music business. Did he talk about any other work he did?" Callie heard a loud exhale and took it to mean Randy was thinking hard.

"I can't come up with anything right now," he said. "But I'll work on it, okay? And I'll ask the guys. Maybe they'll know."

"That'd be great."

Callie was considering what to ask next when Randy said, "I'm really sorry, but I gotta go now. Heading to our next job. A little place in Ohio. I promise I'll get back to you if we come up with anything, okay?"

"Thanks, Randy. I'd appreciate it."

They disconnected, and Callie stared at the computer screen before her with its list of Pittsburgh-area colleges. Randy had at least placed Bobby in Baldwin, which could be important. It didn't automatically connect him to Rhonda or Krystal, but it was too much of a coincidence not to mean something.

As she thought about that, she heard the soft ding that signaled an email had arrived and automatically reached for her mouse to click over. The email was from her mother, something that didn't come every day, and Callie opened it.

I'd like to call tonight, it said. *Let me know the best time.*

Callie's mother, Elizabeth Reed Jablonski, lived on the West Coast, so calling was often tricky with the time difference. Which was why they emailed each other much more often. Long, chatty emails. This short, text-like email was unusual. What was up?

Callie quickly typed, *Sure, Mom. Any time after 6:00 my time works for me. If it's not urgent, 7:00 gives me time to grab a bite first. OK?* She hit send, then wished she'd asked more questions, like, what the call was about. But she'd find out soon enough. She heard more voices coming from the shop and thought Tabitha might need help, so she put her laptop back to sleep and went to join her.

Callie had just carried her end-of-meal mug of tea into the living room when her phone rang. She didn't have to look at the screen to know it was her mother, and she set her mug down and got comfortable.

"Hi, Mom!"

"Hi, darling. How are you?"

A loaded question that Callie didn't want to go into, so she said, "fine" and mentioned the great spring weather they'd been having. She was more concerned about why her mother was suddenly calling. "How are *you?* Everything okay?"

"I know about the murder there, Callie," Elizabeth said.

"Oh!" Darn the 24/7 news programing, desperate for anything to fill its time, even murders of obscure people hundreds of miles away. Or social media, or whichever way her mother had stumbled on it from as far away as Oregon.

"And I know about Hank being arrested for it." Elizabeth had never been happy about Callie's relationship with Hank, and Callie was sure she'd been over the moon when it ended, though she'd never actually said so.

"He didn't do it, Mom. I'm absolutely sure of that."

"Does he have a lawyer?"

"Yes."

"Then he should be okay. I'm sorry, of course, for him, but..." Elizabeth paused. "I know you, Callie, and I know how you want to make things right for everyone. But that so often comes with great sacrifice on your part. I'd hate to see that happen again."

Callie had never told her mother about the two highly serious situations she'd gotten herself into, either of which could have cost her her life, so Elizabeth didn't know the half of it. But nothing like that—nothing life-threatening—was going to happen this time.

"Mom, Hank doesn't have anyone else close by who really knows him. I can't just abandon him."

"I'm not suggesting that you abandon him, dear. Certainly check in by phone now and then. Keep his spirits up. But..." Elizabeth paused again, this time longer. "It happens, sweetheart, that I could use your help right now."

"What? What for? Is something wrong?"

"Well, I'm going to have a little surgery. It's nothing. They're going to fix my knee, the left one that's been giving me so much trouble. You know how I've always loved hiking, but I haven't been able to do much of it at all, lately. Not the kind I'd like to do."

Callie knew that had always been her mother's favorite activity. She and Callie's dad had gone on multiple hiking trips when he was still healthy, and Elizabeth and Frank, her new husband, had met through a hiking club.

"I didn't realize your knee problem was that serious, Mom. Gosh, surgery."

Elizabeth laughed a bit nervously. "It shouldn't be a big deal, sweetie. Every other person my age seems to get it done. But you know me and surgery."

Callie did know. Her mother, a rock in every other way, turned to mush at the thought of needles and incisions. Callie's father had been the one who'd accompanied her when Callie needed a root canal as a teen. "I'd just be a wreck thinking about it in the waiting room," her mother had explained at the time.

"Frank, it turns out, is just as bad as me," Elizabeth continued. "Maybe worse. I wish you could just come to be with me for the few days up to the surgery. It would help me so much."

"Of course, Mom. If I can. When is it?"

Callie expected to hear a date a month or two away. She was startled when her mother said, "The day after Mother's Day."

"So soon!" That was twelve days away.

"Well, it got moved up. Will that be a problem for you?"

Callie thought rapidly. With luck she could get Tabitha to open the shop for at least part of a couple of the days she was away. And, if necessary, closing for a day or so wouldn't cause a financial crisis. Business had been slow lately anyway. But how could she look into Bobby's murder from three thousand miles away? It would be impossible.

"It would be ... complicated, Mom."

"I realize that, and I hate to ask it of you. I'll pay for your plane ticket, of course, once you say the word. Just think about it, will you?"

"Of course, Mom."

"Sometimes I wish Melodie hadn't left you that music box shop. I know, that's selfish of me. But it's tied you there, so far away, when I always hoped ... well, that's neither here nor there."

Callie knew her mother had always hoped she would split from Hank and return home. But it was inheriting *House of Melody* that had finally pushed Callie to do what she'd been dragging her feet on doing, because of the sudden opportunity to start a new life. In that way, Elizabeth had gotten at least half of her wish. At the time, Callie hadn't thought much about the fact that she was settling in the East instead of back in Portland. Her mother was happy in her second marriage and busy with travels to exotic places and other interests. Callie hadn't felt needed. Until now.

Now that her mother was facing what, for her, would be a difficult time and asking for emotional support, Callie couldn't simply run over for a few hours each day. Traveling across the country would definitely be disruptive and difficult, but not impossible, and at any other time she wouldn't have hesitated. But leaving Keepsake Cove now, when Hank was in such trouble and when she might be the only person who cared enough to get him out of it, was a whole different thing.

Sixteen

Callie woke the next morning feeling undecided and torn. Her strong sense not just of duty but of doing what was right called for her to be in two places at once. One minute, traveling to be with her mother won out, the next, Hank's grim situation pulled at her. Her only solution was to put the decision on hold for the time being and continue to do what she could on Hank's behalf. But how effective that would be was another worry.

As she walked from her cottage toward the shop to start her day, movement to her right caught her eye. She spotted a figure through the greenery between their yards and at first thought it must be Delia. Looking harder, she realized it was Jill.

"Good morning!" Callie called.

Jill turned, then walked over to a narrow opening in the bushes. "Hi. I guess you're heading over to open your shop now, huh? Delia's already in hers. She's going to show me the ropes a little later. Enough to help out."

"That'll be great," Callie said, stepping closer. "It'll give Delia a chance to take a break once in a while."

Jill nodded. "But she insists I spend most of my time working on finding a new job. I was just about to go back into the house and do that."

"Any nibbles?"

Jill grimaced. "So far just part-time things. I need more than that."

"Are you looking here or back home?" Callie realized she didn't know where Jill had lived.

"Definitely back in Portis."

"Portis?"

"It's in western Pennsylvania."

"Oh! Near Pittsburgh?"

"That's right. I love it there. My hope—my dream!—is to be able to save enough to set up my own photography studio in Portis. I came close to starting my own business once, a while ago. I really want to try for it again."

Knowing what she did about Jill's personality, Callie figured the photographer working for herself was probably best. Then again, she'd need to get along well with her clients. "Best of luck," she said. She wanted to ask more about Jill's hometown, but then the woman's cell phone rang.

Jill made an apologetic gesture and turned away to answer it. "Hello! Yes, hi! Sure, I can definitely send you that information." She trotted hurriedly toward Delia's cottage, still talking into her phone.

Callie hoped it was something good working out for her and continued on to *House of Melody*. As she unlocked the back door and flicked on the lights, she mulled over the coincidence of three women she'd recently spoken with all hailing from the same general area. Wasn't there a detective—was it Lyssa's hero, Hercule Poirot?—who claimed not to believe in coincidence? People did move around a lot, many of them drawn to the Baltimore-Washington area for job opportunities. But Keepsake Cove was a very small spot for all three to land in. She opened up the laptop in her office, intending to learn what she could about the Pittsburgh area.

Leaving it to wake up, Callie went into the main part of the shop, the sight of all the beautiful music boxes, as always, bringing a smile to her face. She paused below the shelf that held Grandpa Reed's music box. She'd encased it in the protective Plexiglas after learning it had historic value that went far beyond family sentiment. The box had been relatively silent lately.

Not that she minded, but after being startled by it as often as she was those first few weeks after Aunt Mel's death, it was surprising. Callie had halfway expected to hear chimes of disapproval when she'd accepted Hank's call from the detention center, but there'd been nothing. Either Aunt Mel agreed with Callie that Hank should be cleared, or her aunt had moved on, perhaps deciding that Callie no longer needed her. If that were the case—pure conjecture, Callie admitted— it brought about mixed feelings. It was good to think that her aunt might now be fully at rest. But it was a little sad, too, to completely lose her.

Sharp raps at her window shook Callie out of her reverie. An older woman who brought to mind one of her particularly strict elementary school teachers pointed to the *closed* sign on the shop's door, then several times to her wrist watch. It was five minutes after nine, she was impatiently signaling, and past time to open up! Callie hurried over to let her in.

"I came to pick up my order," the woman said, rushing inside. "Your clerk told me yesterday that it arrived. I have to wrap it up and get it over to my sister's!"

Callie got the woman's name and quickly located her music box, a particularly pretty heart-shaped piece with porcelain roses on its lid. Callie's admiring comments softened the customer's irritation, and she explained, as Callie began to pack it up, that it was to be a gift to her niece.

"Allison just got engaged. She's my goddaughter." The lines in the woman's face seemed to smooth as she gazed fondly at the music box, which clearly expressed the feelings she had for her niece. "She's always loved roses. And the music is Schubert's 'Little Rose of the Field.'"

Callie smiled, having heard similar tales from customers who found symbolism in her music boxes that meant so much more to them than their physical beauty. By the time the woman was ready to leave, she'd been chatting away, all signs of her earlier prickliness gone as she promised to return again soon.

The pleasantness of the sale lifted Callie's spirits away from the worry that had started her day, and she went back to her laptop with energy to begin the research on western Pennsylvania.

Portis, she found, was a town that appeared to have a lot of things going for it. The median income of its residents was higher than average, as well as the number of fine dining restaurants. Wedding venues seemed plentiful, too, which might help Jill find work as a photographer. In fact, the place looked to Callie like a shoo-in for someone with Jill's experience.

Why, then, had her last job been as a lower-paid, run-of-the-mill department store photographer? It seemed safe to assume that Jill had burned a few bridges. If that were the case, Callie could understand her current struggle to find something full time. But then why was she still focusing on Portis? Stubbornness?

Callie looked at the map she'd pulled up of the area. Along with Pittsburgh, there were several small towns dotted near it. The one that stood out for her was Baldwin, the town that Krystal, Rhonda, and Bobby all had a connection to. And Baldwin was a mere fifteen miles from Portis. Practically walking distance.

As she mulled this over, Callie's phone rang. It was Lyssa.

"Hi! How's it going? Anything new?" the author asked.

"Actually, yes." Callie told about Randy having placed Bobby Linville in the same small town Krystal and Rhonda had come from. "And I just found out that Delia's photographer friend, Jill, hails from another town that's very close by."

"Really! That's interesting! Can we connect any of the women to Bobby?"

"Not so far. But I'm working on it. Randy didn't know what Bobby actually did when he was in Baldwin. If I can find that out, it might tell us a lot."

"Have you tried Hank?"

"I haven't talked to him for a couple of days. I'm hoping he'll call soon."

"Okay. On another note, my new landscaper is hard at work as we speak."

"The one Krystal told you about? Gavin Holder? That was fast."

"Yeah. I think the guy's a little desperate for work. Which works for me!" Lyssa cackled. "As long as he does a decent job, of course. But he struck me as knowing his stuff. He said he's been doing this for over twenty years. Turns out he was working as the groundskeeper at the festival. I'm going to question him about what he might have seen as soon as I get the chance."

"Groundskeeper? That doesn't sound like landscaping work. It's more like maintenance work, isn't it?"

"It probably is. As I said, he was a little desperate. He seems happy to be back into planting. Anyway, I'll let you know if he's any help with the murder."

"I sure hope he knows something. Nothing really major has shown up so far."

Callie was about to mention her mother's request for a visit when Lyssa said, "I know, and I won't be around too much longer to help out."

"What do you mean?"

"My publisher called. One of their big gun authors had to cancel out of a round of talk show appearances, and they want me to take her place."

"How exciting!"

"Yeah, it is. But it means being up in New York. It's something I can't really pass up."

"No, of course not."

"It's not until the weekend, so I have a little time to keep working on this murder stuff before I go. After that, I'll have to leave it in your hands. Sorry."

"No, don't be. I've appreciated your help and support, but this is so not your problem. You need to pay attention to your writing career."

"I'd do both if I could. And maybe I can. I mean, we can still check in with each other when I'm away, right? Or maybe by some miracle this whole murder thing will be cleared up in twenty-four hours."

Callie doubted that. She felt like she'd accomplished very little and had such a long way to go. What could the two of them dig up in such a short time? And not long afterward she might have to fly off herself, which didn't leave them more than a few more days.

"Oh! Gavin's taking a break. I'm gonna go. I'll get back to you if I get anything useful out of him."

Callie hung up and stared at her computer screen for several moments, trying to organize her crowded thoughts. Then her phone rang again. It was Hank, calling from the detention center.

Once she was put through, Callie quickly said, "Hank, I'm glad to finally hear from you. I was hoping you'd call yesterday. I wanted to ask—"

Hank cut in. "I've been sick."

"What?"

"I've been sick, babe. Some kinda stomach bug. Half the people here've come down with it."

"Oh, I'm sorry, Hank. What are they doing for you?"

"Lined me up in a bed alongside everyone else who's as sick as a dog."

"Is that where you are now?"

"Naw, I'm out. Over it, they say. But I'm still draggin'."

Callie believed him. Hank, for all his faults, wasn't one to exaggerate his illnesses. "Have you talked to your lawyer lately?"

"Uh-uh. But he might come over today. Or tomorrow."

"Good. Hank, I talked to Randy Brewer yesterday."

"Randy? Where's he now?"

"He said they were about to leave for a gig somewhere in Ohio."

"Oh, yeah. I remember."

"He said they all feel terrible about having to leave you behind."

"Yeah, I know. I talked to him, that day they arrested me. I told him not to worry. I know how it goes. The only thing…"

"Yes?"

"They might need to replace me in the band. If this drags on too long, they're gonna have to. I know it."

"They could get someone short-term, you know. Don't worry about that for now. One problem at a time. And if I'm going to help you out of this, I need you to tell me everything you know about

104

Bobby. First thing—Randy placed Bobby in a town near Pittsburgh named Baldwin. It was when he attended college, so I'm guessing he either commuted to school in Pittsburgh or lived in Baldwin between semesters. Do you know anything about that?"

"Baldwin?" Hank was silent for a while, and Callie pictured him rubbing his chin with the two-day growth of beard he carefully kept, which he thought gave him a Tim McGraw look. Did he still have it? Or had they made him shave it off? Surely that wasn't required in detention centers, only in prisons. A random thought that had no use and only caused her to grimace.

"I don't remember any town called Baldwin," Hank finally said.

"Did Bobby mention his college?"

"Let me think. Yeah, I think he did. He'd brag about how he breezed through his classes after barely openin' a book. Until he got kicked out, of course. I think it was his drinkin' that did it."

"And the name of the school?"

"Huh! It's in here somewhere 'cause I know he told me. Wait! Got it! It was Daniel. Somethin' close to, like, Jack Daniels. I remember 'cause he used to joke that he liked Seagram's better." Hank grunted. "That was when he was telling us he'd sworn off his drinking. Shoulda been a clue, right? But we were too dumb to see it."

"Daniel? Okay, great. Do the names Krystal Cobb or Rhonda Furman ring any bells?"

"Uh-uh."

"How about a town named Portis?"

"Portis, Portis, Portis . . . yeah, that does! There's some kind of theater there. Not a big one, but big enough that Bobby did PR work for it. Got paid peanuts, but he said he learned a lot he could use in his later jobs so it was worth it."

"Terrific! That should help a lot, Hank."

"Will it get me out of here?"

"Not right away. But it's a step forward."

"I don't need an effin' *step*, babe. I need out!"

Callie sighed. "I know that, Hank. I can only do what I can do. I'm not a miracle worker."

"Yeah, sorry, babe. It's just … sorry."

A voice broke in, announcing the end of the call, and they said quick goodbyes. Callie hung up, telling herself to stay patient. She wasn't doing this because Hank was a perfect human being. She was doing it because he, like every other human being, deserved justice, and because she believed in his innocence. She didn't need to be thanked or appreciated, though it would be nice not to be yelled at. Then again, she wasn't the one sitting behind bars, was she?

Seventeen

*C*allie felt a strong need to talk with Brian. She hadn't brought up her mother's request for a visit with Lyssa after finding out that the author herself would be taking off; she didn't want to put a damper on Lyssa's excitement over her terrific publicity opportunity. But Callie was still trying to figure out what to do. Not that she expected Brian to decide for her, but it would help to talk. She waited until she was sure his lunch time rush was over, then left the shop to Tabitha and trotted across the street.

One couple was paying their bill at the register as she walked in, and the tables were empty, which was perfect. Brian greeted her with a light-up-the-face look as he completed the transaction, then leaned across the counter after the couple walked out as she slipped onto a stool.

"Hi!" he said, taking her hands in his. "Good timing. I was going to drop by a little later."

"Oh? What about?"

"To let you know I won't be around too much after-hours for a while. Annie's had a scare," he said, referring to his sister. "Actually, it's Ben who had the scare."

"What happened?"

"Seems that Ben woke up sometime in the night to use the bathroom. When he went back to his room, he saw a dark van and an SUV stopped in front of the house, near their driveway. There was a bright moon, so even without streetlights, Ben said he could see pretty well. He saw two men moving back and forth, carrying things, and they seemed to be arguing. As Ben watched, one of the men stopped and looked toward the house. Ben thinks he looked straight at him. Annie keeps a night light on in his room, so it's possible he could have seen Ben's face at the window. Anyway, it scared Ben—he's just turned nine, you know—and he ran over to Justin's room and climbed into his bed.

"Annie and Mike's room is at the back of the house, so she didn't hear anything, and Mike is away on a business trip. When Ben told her about it this morning, she went out and found tire tracks and lots of footprints in the soft shoulder of the road. She doesn't know what went on, but she says Ben is pretty shaken up. He seems to think the two men could be back to do who-knows-what even though she's tried to reassure him. She asked if I'd stay over until Mike gets back, to make Ben feel safer."

"Gosh, of course! If I lived in that remote spot, I'd probably feel the same way."

"While I'm there, I can fix a couple of things for them. Mike's not the handiest guy."

"You're a good brother."

Brian shrugged. "She's helped me out plenty of times. We're family, after all." Annie had stepped in once to keep the café running when

Brian had come down with the flu. She also pitched in, off and on, when Brian just needed extra help. Much as they liked to tease each other, Callie knew they were always there for each other.

"Is Justin okay?" Ben's brother was two years older and probably not as skittish.

Brian grinned. "Justin never woke up, but he took it as an opportunity to push for a dog again, which isn't going to happen with Mike's allergies. He seemed glad to know I'd be staying over."

"You're much better than a dog," Callie deadpanned.

"Glad to hear it." Brian said, grinning. "I can compete with the boys on Xbox. I'd like to see a dog do that."

"Not without thumbs," Callie said, shaking her head.

"There you go." Brian did a double thumbs-up.

"Well, I'll miss having you around after-hours, but I'm glad you're able to help Annie out." Callie paused. "I might be taking off in a few days myself."

"What, something to do with Hank?"

"No, just the opposite. It would actually pull me away from helping him." Callie told him about her mother's upcoming surgery and her desire to have her daughter with her. "It's fairly routine surgery. I mean, not like a heart transplant or anything like that. But I know my mom, and she'll be a basket case until it's over with. It sounds like my stepfather is just as bad."

"And you're the calm one?"

"At least as far as medical procedures. I guess I got that gene from my dad. Any other time, I'd happily jump on a plane, but right now ..."

"Would Skype be enough for her? Or Facetime?"

"I thought about that, but I doubt it. Would Facetime make Annie and the boys feel safer?"

"No, but then it's not the same thing. I could physically chase away an intruder. You can't keep your mom from getting the surgery she needs."

"Right, but I can hold her hand and distract her. That's what she needs. She's going to get the surgery. She wants it so she can get back to doing the things she loves. It's just thinking about it that she has such a hard time with."

"Then you'll have to go."

"But that means leaving Hank in a lurch. I've barely scratched the surface of what really happened to Bobby Linville. I've dug up a few leads, but it'll take a lot more work and time to follow them. And Lyssa's taking off soon." Callie explained about Lyssa's great publicity turn in New York.

"I'll still be here at the café during the day," Brian reminded her. "People talk a lot while they're eating, and I can't help hearing. Then there's Delia, who'd certainly be willing to do what she can."

"I know she would, but there's a problem. I've put her friend on my list of possible suspects."

"Jill?"

"Just possible, at this point. But she has a connection to a small town where Bobby worked at one time." Callie told him about Portis, where Bobby and Jill had both worked, and then about nearby Baldwin, which might connect Bobby in some way to Krystal Cobb and her good friend Rhonda Furman. "Rhonda is cleared. She was out of town during the festival. Still, she denied knowing Bobby even though the look on her face when I said his name told us otherwise."

"So she's hiding something."

"Clearly, and my guess is that it has to do with Krystal. Do you remember when we were standing in line at the ice cream stand and Krystal was in front of us? Bobby came toward us and I assumed he was coming to hassle me again about promoting the band. But then he suddenly froze and turned on his heel. I'm wondering if it was because he saw Krystal."

"But he was seen talking to Krystal later on."

"*Arguing.* Krystal gave me her explanation, which is that Bobby wanted to squeeze more money from them. What if she's lying, and instead of Bobby finding her, she confronted him?"

"About what?"

Callie shook her head. "That I don't know."

"Since we're conjecturing, here's one more thought. Might it have been Jill, not Krystal, who Bobby saw and who caused him to suddenly bolt?"

Callie frowned. "I never thought about that, but you're right. Jill's photo station was next to us. And she was upset about the torn costume right about then, wasn't she?"

"That was just after Bobby took off."

"So maybe she and Bobby recognized each other, he beat it out of there, and she got upset at seeing him and took it out on her customer."

"All possible. But still conjecture."

Callie sighed. So much more to find out. People to question. Things to do on Hank's behalf that she couldn't do from the other side of the country. She was mentally angsting over that when the café door opened.

"Hey! Thought I was in the wrong place for a minute!" Duane pointed at Callie and laughed at his own joke as he walked in. "Still open for business?" he asked Brian. "I was hoping to get a sandwich to take out. Lost track of time, and now I'm starving!"

"Sure. What can I get you?"

"Chicken salad on a sub roll, if you got it. Oh, and some fries. And a Coke. Large."

"Coming right up." Brian went off to the kitchen, leaving Callie facing a man she didn't like very much. But she had questions for him, too, so she swallowed her feelings and conjured up a polite smile.

Duane obviously picked up on the coolness, because he said, "I think I owe you an apology."

"Oh?"

"I was out of line with some of the things I said."

"Yes, you were."

"This big mouth of mine doesn't always seem to be connected to my brain." Duane rapped his head and made a goofy face.

Callie wasn't amused. "You knew I had nothing to do with your hiring of the Badlanders. We'd even talked about it."

"You're right. But that little weasel Howard Graham just kept snap, snap, snapping at me until I said whatever came into my head just to shut him up! My bad, totally. I did go to him later on and correct it."

Had he? Howard wasn't the only one in that group who'd heard it. Had Duane gone to all of them? Callie decided to let it go. "Since you're here, there's something I'd like to ask you, about the time surrounding Bobby Linville's murder."

"Uh-oh!" Duane laughed. "Sleuthing again? I thought you'd sworn off after what happened the last time."

Callie didn't recall telling Duane any such thing, though she'd told herself that privately. "When someone you know is being wrongly charged, nobody with a conscience simply stands by and does nothing."

Duane held his hands up defensively. "Understood! No problem. Ask away."

"Okay. Krystal Cobb said she couldn't reach you on Saturday night after Bobby demanded more money for the band. This was from about ten o'clock, during the festival, until the next morning. Why didn't you answer her calls? Where were you?" She put it bluntly, not in the mood for coddling.

"Where was I? Wow. You're really serious about this. Am I under suspicion, Officer Reed? Got your handcuffs ready if I don't have the right answers?"

Duane's joking was getting under Callie's skin. "Everyone is under suspicion at this point. And I'm serious about it because an innocent man could be sent to prison."

"Okay, I get it. But I do have an alibi. By ten o'clock or so, I'd had it up to here with the festival after nonstop working *on* it for weeks and *at* it since dawn that day. Everything was going well and looked to be winding down, so I took off a little before ten. There was nothing more for me to do, I thought. Of course I didn't know what Linville was going to try with Krystal."

"You went home?"

"No. I went to look at a new painting."

"A painting?"

Duane nodded. "I'd been negotiating online about it. A private seller. We agreed on the price if I could pay immediately, and I knew the opportunity would slip by if I didn't take advantage of it. Other buyers were lurking. So I arranged to dash over. It was a good hour's drive, but I got a beautiful piece at a bargain price." He looked highly pleased with himself.

Callie remembered hearing that Duane's home was filled with plenty of original artwork. She'd wondered at the time how he could afford such art, as well as several other expensive items, on the income his glass shop brought in, which couldn't be that much greater than the income of other Keepsake Cove shops. This was one of the reasons Laurie Hart had suspected he was pilfering the association's treasury, although that had proved not to be the case. As Duane eventually explained, with obvious annoyance and only after Laurie's pressuring, he had benefitted from wise investments of a family inheritance.

"I think you'd find this painting particularly interesting," Duane was saying. "It's a young woman holding what looks like a music box. Or it might be a jewelry box. Either way, it's quite lovely. You'll have to come see it."

Brian came out of his kitchen with Duane's sandwich and fries, then filled a large paper cup with soda. "Here you go."

"Great!" Duane quickly paid and grabbed his bagged-up lunch. "I'd better get going. Had to lock up the shop. I hate to miss too many customers. Are we good?" he asked Callie. When she hesitated, he added, "I can send you the number of that seller. He'll back me up. Will that do?"

"That'd be great."

"Terrific. Then I'm off. See you!"

Brian looked at Callie curiously. "What was that about?"

"Oh, Duane just took himself off my suspect list," she said, wrinkling her nose. Then she added with a wry twist of her lips, "At least for now."

Eighteen

hen Callie left the café, she glanced across at *House of Melody*. There was no sign of customers or an apparent need for her, so she turned left instead of crossing the street. She wanted to talk to Laurie Hart.

Kids at Heart was quiet as well, and Callie wondered how long it would be before Keepsake Cove would draw crowds again—if ever. Would the pre–Mother's Day sale be enough? This worry seemed to be on Bill and Laurie's minds, too, as they both looked up expectantly at her entrance into the vintage toy shop and seemed just a bit disappointed to see her.

"Sorry I'm not a customer," Callie said.

Laurie laughed. "We're always glad to see you. But your place must be just as slow if you're able to be out and about."

"It is, though some business has come in spurts. Not like it used to, though."

"Just to be clear," Bill said, "we don't blame you one bit." He pushed up one sleeve of the Mr. Rogers–style sweater he often wore. Laurie was in her usual back-room denims, her blond hair pulled into a ponytail. "Laurie told me about Duane trying to place the blame on you," Bill said.

"That's what I came to ask about. Duane just apologized to me for that, and he said he'd straightened it out later with Howard. But Howard wasn't the only one who heard it. Did Duane come by to do the same thing with you?"

Laurie made a choking noise. "Are you kidding? Duane crosses the street to avoid walking too close to our shop."

"So I'll take that as a no," Callie said, one side of her mouth curling. "I thought that might be the case, not that it matters all that much. Just a minor irritant."

"And one more indication of the man's character," Laurie added.

"We're really sorry about that band member being charged," Bill said. He moved a red and gray wooden airplane away from partially covering a collapsible spyglass, both of which had probably been polished and touched up by Laurie before being set out for sale. "We didn't realize until recently that you and he, uh ..."

"Used to be an item," Callie finished for him. "Emphasis on *used to be*. But it means I know him well enough to be sure of his innocence. I just need to find the guilty person."

"Can you make it Duane?" Laura asked.

Callie grinned. "I can only make it who it really is. Duane is probably off the hook."

"Darn."

"But I'll double check his alibi."

116

"Good. Hope it doesn't hold up. I still believe he's been siphoning from our association treasury for years. All those vacations, new cars, and other stuff."

"Honey," Bill said, "the association doesn't have enough money to pay for those things as well as its bills. It's all been explained."

Laurie huffed. "Explained by *him*! I don't buy it."

This argument had been going on between the Harts for as long as Callie had known them, and before. Somehow they managed to keep it amicable and respect each other's opinion.

Having no answer handy to settle things, Callie changed the subject. "I learned something yesterday about Krystal that was awfully sad. Perhaps you already knew about her daughter?"

"That she had died?" Laurie asked, nodding. "I can't imagine dealing with something like that."

"Do you know what the cause was, or how long ago it happened?"

"I think the girl—her name was Tiffany, by the way, which I remember because it seemed exactly the kind of name Krystal would choose for a daughter. Anyway, I think Tiffany was college-aged, but I don't know what happened. Maybe a car accident?" She shrugged. "How did you hear about her?"

"Through Rhonda Furman, when she explained how she and Krystal had become friends. She didn't want to go into details, which I could understand."

"It must be difficult for Krystal," Laurie mused, "selling beautiful dolls every day to people who probably talk about buying them for their little girls, or maybe granddaughters. She's constantly reminded of her own loss."

"No other children?"

Laurie shook her head.

Bill had wandered away during the discussion, and Laurie nodded in his direction, explaining softly, "Bill doesn't like gloomy subjects. Which is probably why he tries to think the best of everyone, including Duane."

"Then I'm sorry I brought it up in front of him. May I ask one more thing, though? Did you see anything at the festival on Saturday night that might help me find Bobby Linville's murderer?"

"Oh, gosh. I didn't even know who Bobby Linville was at the time, so probably not. But..." Laurie scrunched her face, thinking back. "There was this one odd thing."

"Yes?"

"I saw Gavin Holder. Do you know him?"

"The landscaper? Lyssa just hired him to work on her yard."

Laurie nodded. "He did a little work for us too. He's good. So I was surprised to see him doing what looked like clean-up work on the festival grounds. Anyway, I was going to go over and say hi when I realized he was kind of frozen and staring at someone standing next to the stage. It was a guy, about fifty-ish, wearing a brownish sports jacket. He had a bit of a belly."

"That sounds like Bobby Linville."

"Okay, good. So, Linville was looking down at his phone and didn't notice Gavin. I started over, but then I saw the look on Gavin's face and stopped. It was, oh, I don't know exactly how to describe it. Disgust? Anger? Whatever it was, it was pretty intense, and I decided I didn't want to get in the middle of it. I turned around and walked the other way."

"You're sure this look was aimed at Bobby?"

"Absolutely. There were other people around, sure, but the guy with the phone had a pretty good space around him. It was definitely aimed at him."

"So you just saw that look. You didn't see them actually talk?"

"Nope, that was it. Is that any help?"

"It might be." Callie mulled it over. "Can you tell me anything more about Gavin, other than that he's a landscaper?"

Laurie shook her head. "Sorry, that's all I know. Maybe Bill—?" As she craned her neck to call to her husband, a customer entered the shop. Bill immediately moved forward to greet him, and Laurie shrugged. "I'll ask him later and let you know, okay?"

"That's fine. I'd better get back to work, too. Thanks, Laurie."

Callie left, planning to call Lyssa and share this bit of information. Maybe it was nothing. Maybe Gavin Holder had simply seen Bobby toss a piece of trash on the ground instead of into the basket. But then again, maybe not.

❧

Two people were browsing through *House of Melody* when Callie got back, which after the slow-down seemed like a crowd. Tabitha took care of the younger woman, who had a gurgling baby, when she brought her choice to the counter—a lullaby-playing globe with a pink teddy bear inside. Callie lingered nearby while Tabitha was busy, in case the second browser had questions. But that woman eventually smiled and said, "Just looking today," then left.

"I did have another sale while you were out," Tabitha said, consoling Callie with a shoulder pat.

"That's fine," Callie said, laughing. "Can't win them all." She felt the phone in her pocket shiver, signaling the arrival of an email, and pulled it out to check. Duane had sent her the name and email address of the painting's seller. She'd expected a phone number, but this was at least something. She'd contact the man, but first she wanted to talk to Lyssa. A glance at the time reminded Callie that Tabitha would be

119

leaving soon. Better to do it right away. "I'll be in the back for a minute," she said before hurrying off.

"Lyssa," Callie said when her friend picked up. "Can you talk?"

"Yeah, Gavin's gone back out and is working like a beaver. This place is going to look great. I had him come inside for a break, and we had a nice chat over iced tea and cookies. Store-bought ones, of course."

"And…?

"Not that much, actually. Sorry. I was hoping Gavin would have lots to tell about things going on at the festival, what with him walking around the grounds all day. He's not much of a talker, though, and apparently focuses only on his work. I had to remind him of our murder victim's name, and his only reaction was a grunt. Nothing like our clock shop woman, Rhonda."

"That actually is interesting," Callie said. She told Lyssa what Laurie had seen.

"Whoa! So Gavin was holding back on me. Sounds like he knew Linville."

"It seems like it. Unless he's in the habit of glaring at complete strangers."

"Doubtful. He comes across as a quiet kind of guy who minds his own business. 'Course you know what they say about the quiet ones."

"That they're quietly plotting crimes?"

"Something like that." Lyssa chuckled. "I did get one tiny nugget out of him," she continued. "He's from Pennsylvania."

"Hmm. Another one to add to the growing list. It's a big state, though. What part?"

"I couldn't pin him down. Just that it was a small town nobody ever heard about. I mentioned places I've been to—or said I'd been to—to try to narrow it down, tossing in things he might comment on, like how I loved the soft pretzels in Philly or how the Steelers did last season. No bites. Not even on the pretzels."

"That's kind of suspicious in itself, wouldn't you say? It's like he was purposely hiding where he'd lived."

"Yeah, I think so too. The Pennsylvania comment only came out when he was talking about plants and where they grow best. He might have been off his guard. Hey, maybe while I'm gone, you could come by and talk with him? Pump him a bit? There are some plants that are back-ordered, meaning a lot of the work will have to wait till they come in. I also wouldn't mind having someone check on things for me. If it's convenient, I mean."

"I'll be glad to do that while I can. It's just ... well, I'm not real sure how long I'll be around next week."

"What? Where're you going?"

"I might be going to Oregon." Callie explained about her mother and her own dilemma over leaving town.

"Uh-oh. Bad timing, huh? But she's your mom. Don't you think you'd better be there?"

"Any other time and I'd be on that plane in a flash. But I worry about leaving Hank. Then there's the fact that after thinking it over, I've become just a little suspicious of the timing of this surgery. I know my mother and how she felt about Hank. She isn't past being a tiny bit manipulative."

"I've heard of fake fainting spells," Lyssa said. "But going through surgery to pull your daughter away from an ex would be carrying it a little far."

"I know. So that's why I'm wavering."

"Well, I wish I had a solution for you. Looks like the only answer is to solve this murder real fast."

"I wish," Callie said, adding, "But if wishes were fishes, we'd all … how does that go?"

"Badly. It goes badly 'cause wishful thinking will get us nowhere. So enough of that. We'll both do everything we can do while we can. And that's that."

"Yes, ma'am." Callie smiled, liking Lyssa's no-nonsense approach. She ended the call and, following her friend's direction, turned to her laptop, ready to get moving—while she could.

Nineteen

Callie typed up an email to Todd Wright, asking about the artwork Duane said he'd purchased from him on Saturday night, and the time and place. She worded it carefully, claiming only to be aiding in the investigation of the murder that had taken place at the Keepsake Cove festival—which she was. Just not at the request of anyone official. She hoped Wright wouldn't question that. She sent it off, then looked up as Tabitha appeared in the doorway.

"Time for me to go—unless you need me to hang around a little longer?"

"No, that's fine." Callie rose and followed her to the front of the shop. "Do you know anything about Gavin Holder?" she asked as her assistant slipped a light sweater over her tee.

Tabitha shook her head. "Never heard of him. Who is he?"

"He's a landscaper. He took care of the grounds during the festival."

"Huh." Tabitha pulled her purse out from under the counter and slipped the cross-body strap over her head. Watching, Callie realized something with a shock.

"You haven't been dressing up! No vintage character outfits lately."

Tabitha grinned. "You just noticed? I've been out of character all week."

"But *that's* so out of character for you! I mean, dressing, um, creatively is your thing." On Callie's first day as the owner of *House of Melody*, Tabitha had shown up for work looking exactly like a 1940s-era Joan Crawford, complete with super-wide shoulder pads, seamed stockings, and open-toed shoes. Even her hair and makeup had matched, so much so that Callie hadn't recognized the tie-dyed hippie she thought she'd hired the day before.

"Every so often I take a break. It's kind of a psychic cleansing. Clears my head. Plus, I've been crazy busy with my beading lately and haven't had the time to spend on it. It can't just be slap-dash, you know. When I do character, it has to be totally right."

Callie agreed that Tabitha never put together her "looks" halfway. Whether it was Lieutenant Uhura from *Star Trek* or simply a poufy-haired woman of the '80s, her assistant got all the details right. It was nice, though, to see the real Tabitha once in a while.

"I'm glad your beaded jewelry is picking up."

"Yeah!" Tabitha's eyes lit up. "Having that display here in the shop during the festival really helped. It brought me a bunch of new customers. Fingers crossed it keeps up!"

She hurried off to work on her burgeoning home business. Callie was truly happy for her, but also aware that she might be losing an excellent employee if things continued to go so well.

"What will I do without Tabitha?" she asked aloud, turning to Grandpa Reed's music box high on its shelf. The music box remained silent, once again stirring sad feelings within her. Though the box's unexpected playing had unnerved her at first, and she'd been reluctant to say what exactly it all meant, Callie had grown comfortable with the idea of being watched over. Had it finally ended, and had Aunt Mel moved on?

If so, she knew she should be glad. But it only added to her feeling of being deserted lately. Brian would be staying at his sister's place. Lyssa would be in New York. Callie glanced around her empty shop. Even her customers seemed to have abandoned her.

She shook herself. Enough of that. At least if her customers weren't there it gave her time to spend on Hank's problem. As Lyssa had pointed out, she needed to work faster during the time available. With that thought, she went back to her office and plopped down in front of the laptop. Time to do some serious internet searching.

First on her agenda was looking up Krystal's daughter. Callie typed in "Tiffany Cobb" and watched as the results came up. With no middle name to include, there were several Tiffany Cobbs to sift through, but knowing the girl's approximate age and location helped. Soon Callie found her obituary, archived on a funeral home's website.

A photo showed a girl clearly younger than the age at which she'd died, which was twenty-four. Tiffany looked about seventeen; perhaps it was a high school graduation photo. The obituary named Krystal and her husband at the time, Robert, as parents, along with two surviving grandparents. There were no siblings, as Laurie had mentioned, and no cause of death was given.

The obituary also listed the high school Tiffany had graduated from, along with sports and activities she'd enjoyed. Then it mentioned that she'd attended Clayton Daniel College.

Daniel! Wasn't that the same college Bobby Linville had gone to, according to Hank? Callie clicked back to her search engine and typed in "Clayton Daniel College," finding that it was located in the Pittsburgh area, which fit what she knew about Bobby. She returned to Tiffany's obituary and reread it. *Attended* Clayton Daniel. So she hadn't graduated. Neither had Bobby, according to Randy Brewer. Callie knew Bobby's age from the newspaper report of his murder: forty-six. That was a year older than Tiffany would be if she had lived. Clayton Daniel was not a large school. It seemed highly possible they would have known each other. Had they?

Tiffany's obituary didn't give any occupation at the time of her death. Thinking that was odd, Callie went back to her original search on the young woman. It didn't take long to discover a newspaper article that revealed Tiffany's manner of death: a fatal car accident, single vehicle involvement, no passengers, with driving under the influence as the cause.

Callie sat back and absorbed that, several emotions running through her along with the information, including sympathy for Krystal for losing a daughter that way. But the situation Jill had described, of Krystal and Bobby arguing at the festival—hissing at each other, as she'd put it—came to mind. Had it really been about more money for the band? Or was there an older and much deeper reason for Krystal's anger?

Callie was ready to begin a new search when she heard her shop's door open. An interruption that normally would have brought a smile to her face instead made her groan. But she hopped up, put on a welcoming face, and went out to meet her shopper.

The customer was Mrs. Frey, a regular who'd bought many music boxes from Aunt Mel and then added a couple to her collection during Callie's tenure. When Mrs. Frey first visited *House of Melody* after Callie inherited it, Tabitha had greeted the gray-haired woman by name and thrown Callie a look that signaled there'd be notes on her in Aunt

126

Mel's list, an important document Callie had copied to her phone. There she'd learned that Mrs. Frey liked bird-themed music boxes. She'd watched Tabitha guide Mrs. Frey over to those, and ever since that day she'd made sure to watch for similar unique pieces to have on hand. Her smile grew genuine, since she not only liked Mrs. Frey but could reasonably expect to make a decent sale.

"Oh, nice and quiet!" the woman commented as she glanced around the shop. "No one to pull you away from me today." She said it with a cheery laugh, and Callie politely joined in, as the likelihood of their being interrupted was slim to none.

They strolled around the shop, Callie pointing out the music boxes she'd acquired since Mrs. Frey's last visit. She was pleased to see some interest in two boxes that weren't bird-themed, since it was growing harder to find new good ones in that style. Her customer, clearly enjoying the experience, eventually chose a box that featured a lovely Japanese-style painting of cherry tree branches with a tiny bird perched in their midst. The tune, "What A Wonderful World," seemed to fit the mood, and Mrs. Frey smiled as she listened to it, saying, "I'll take it."

As Callie packed it up, Mrs. Frey brought up the spring festival and, as she put it, the "unfortunate happening" there. "I'm so glad I didn't go after all," she said, despite Callie assuring her that the hours the public attended had been perfectly fine.

"Even so, I would have had nightmares just knowing I'd been close to such a terrible thing. I've very sensitive that way. My sister, on the other hand, is quite the opposite. She went on her own when I couldn't make it."

"Did she?" Callie waited as Mrs. Frey inserted her credit card and signed.

"Donna loves festivals." Mrs. Frey looked up. "But they're not really my thing. Besides, I knew you wouldn't have a booth there, so why bother?" She chuckled merrily.

As she slipped the receipt Callie handed her into her purse, Mrs. Frey looked thoughtful. "Donna said she recognized someone there."

"Oh?"

"The woman taking pictures, with all the costumes. Donna remembered her from Portis. That's a little town up near Pittsburgh."

"Yes, I've just learned about that place." Callie had been thinking about what she'd put in the empty space left by the sale of Mrs. Frey's music box, but she quickly refocused.

"Never been there myself. But Donna has a good friend who was in a play, and Donna went up to see her. This was eighteen years ago. She can say that for sure because it was a week after her fortieth birthday and the trip was her special treat to herself. There was a photographer there who did a lot of publicity shots for the theater, including of Donna's friend. The woman stuck in Donna's mind because of the special care she took to present her friend, who frankly wasn't very attractive, at her best. They both appreciated it. Donna thought this photographer was very professional, so she was surprised to see her at the festival running a costume photography booth. It seemed like ... oh, I don't know, a come-down?"

It *was* a come-down for Jill, and Callie doubted she would want this information widely known. "She happens to have a friend in Keepsake Cove," she explained. "It was probably a fun thing for her to do, combined with a visit."

Mrs. Frey nodded. "Donna will be glad to hear that. She worries about people, even ones she barely knows."

Callie smiled and handed Mrs. Frey her music box, then walked her to the door, which she held as the woman continued to chatter away, barely noticing where she was going. After Mrs. Frey made her way out, Callie remained at the open door, gazing toward *Shake It Up!* and thinking that Jill might be there at the moment, learning her way around Delia's shop.

So Jill had done publicity photos for a theater in Portis. Bobby Linville had done PR work for a theater in Portis, according to Hank. Was it the same theater? Portis was a small town. How many live-performance theaters could it have? Callie planned to check, but it was starting to look like Brian's conjecture that Jill and Bobby had a connection of some sort just might be spot on. Which moved Jill a notch higher on the suspect list.

This was good news for possibly getting them closer to clearing Hank. But Jill was a person Delia cared about. Of course, the truth would be the truth, no matter what. But Callie knew she'd need to tread carefully in uncovering it. One mistaken assumption could be devastating to a friendship that she valued highly.

Twenty

*B*ack at her laptop, Callie found an email from Todd Wright waiting for her and immediately opened it.

Dear Ms. Reed,

Yes, Duane Fletcher was at my home on Saturday night at 11 o'clock. An unusual time to do business, but I was eager to settle on the sale of my painting before leaving on a planned trip, and Mr. Fletcher was willing to both meet my price and pay immediately in full. We had a pleasant drink together afterward, and I believe he left around midnight. I hope that covers all you needed to know.

Yours sincerely,

Todd Wright

Well. That was that. Callie mentally filed the email away under "disappointing information," at the same time shaking her head at herself for wishing someone she'd come to dislike could be legitimately sent to prison.

She returned to the search engine and typed in "Portis Theater." A string of movie theaters came up, along with a single live-performance venue: the Portis Playhouse. Callie clicked on that link and scanned the website. The home page naturally featured the playhouse's current offering, a new play by an "Up-and-coming playwright!" titled *Song of the Iguana*. After reading the brief synopsis of it, Callie wished them luck selling tickets, but then again, who knew? Tastes differed.

She clicked on the "About Us" page, hoping to find mention of either Bobby Linville or Jill in the theater's history. But the page displayed old photos of its modest beginning in a church basement, then told of a successful fundraiser and community support that led to the building of its beautiful new home about twenty years ago. Photos showed the various stages of construction, inside and out, up to the opening-night ribbon-cutting ceremony. All very interesting, but of no help to her. She clicked out of it and thought for a minute.

It was almost time to close shop. Should she do so now and run over to *Shake It Up!* to catch Jill? Callie went out front to check on nearby foot traffic. All looked quiet, as it had been most of the day, so she could safely assume no new customers were coming. She was ready to grab her keys when she spotted Delia and Jill step out of the salt and pepper shaker shop and turn down the street toward Delia's car.

Had she imagined it, or had Delia purposely avoided looking her way? Callie shook her head. That wouldn't have been like her friend at all. Delia was probably preoccupied or deep in conversation with Jill.

Callie heard her phone signal a text message and smiled when she saw it was from Brian. She'd thought he'd already left to go to Annie's.

Coming over in a sec, his text said. *Don't disappear.*

Callie texted back: *Too late. Poof!* ☺ Then she hurried to close up her register, wondering what was up. When Brian arrived, he had an unexpected invitation.

"Annie would love to have you come for dinner."

"Tonight?"

"Last minute, I know, and she apologizes, but still hopes you'll come."

"Well, I don't know. Can she top any of the frozen meals you stocked my freezer with, one of which I was planning to heat up tonight?"

"Doubtful. But she'll come close. I've taught her a few things over the years."

Callie grinned. "I'd love to come." She felt a twinge of guilt about setting aside her investigative work but told herself she had to eat, after all. "You'll be staying over, right? So I'll drive myself."

"I'm heading there pretty soon to start work on one of the repair projects. You could come with me and I'll bring you back later."

"No, that's too much bother. And I'd love a few minutes of down time. I'll meet you there," Callie said. Annie's home was about a fifteen-minute drive from Keepsake Cove, and Brian agreed that her arriving around 6:45 would be fine. He took off, and Callie finished closing up the shop and went back to her cottage.

Jagger was waiting eagerly, as usual, and she fed him, then kicked off her shoes and gave him some lap time to make up for having to leave again for the evening. She felt his purrs gradually loosen every taut muscle in her body, which was wonderful, but she had to put an end to it before too long to avoid turning into total mush. A bit of freshening up and a change of clothes, and she was soon out the door.

The drive to Annie's through the countryside was always lovely, no matter what the season. But in early May, with the fresh green leaves, emerging blooms, and temperature mild enough to lower her car's windows, an evening drive was particularly great. Life on the Eastern Shore could be pretty darned good. Except, of course, when things like murders happened. But Callie refused to let any guilt about enjoying herself while Hank was stuck behind bars ruin her mood. She would pick up her work on his behalf later, and likely with renewed energy for having a few hours off.

Annie's eleven-year-old, Justin, opened the door at Callie's knock, and she was struck once again with how much he resembled his father, Mike, with his dark hair and square jaw. "You're just in time," he said. "Uncle Brian's cutting up the chicken."

"Smells great!" Callie said, glad to hear that the menu fit the white wine she'd thought to grab at the last minute. It was the only bottle she had on hand and might have originally been a gift to her, though she couldn't remember for sure. Hopefully it hadn't come from Annie and Mike.

"C'mon in!" a woman's voice called, and Callie followed Justin through the house to the kitchen, where Annie stood filling salad plates from a large bowl, her son Ben lined up forks and knives on the table, and Brian worked at carving a perfectly roasted, golden-brown, crispy-skinned hen. He lifted his knife in greeting.

"Wow, everything looks wonderful," Callie said after giving Annie a hug, one that was somewhat awkward between her wine bottle and Annie's salad tongs. "I haven't had roast chicken in ages."

"You have to have the time to cook it," Annie agreed. "Justin, get out three wine glasses from the cabinet, will you?"

"Only three?" He said it with a sly grin that made him look even more like his dad.

"Yes, three, smartie! Thanks, Callie. That'll turn this into a real company meal." To Callie's relief, Annie didn't show any signs of recognizing the bottle.

After asking what she could do to help, she put the potatoes, gravy, and broccoli on the table, then joined them all in settling down around it. Much passing of dishes was soon followed by their concentration on Annie's good food, punctuated only by short comments and small talk. The salad lettuce, it turned out, had come from Annie's garden and was tender and delicious.

"I picked the bugs out of it," Ben said, which made Justin cry "gross" while Annie declared it very helpful. Callie couldn't help looking a little more closely at her own salad and happily saw nothing at all that shouldn't have been there.

It wasn't until after the main dishes were cleared and Callie, Brian, and Annie were sipping coffee while the boys went to do homework that Annie brought up the more serious topic.

"You heard about our little scare last night, right?" she asked.

"Yes, Brian told me. How is Ben doing?" Callie hadn't noticed anything obvious, but then, she wasn't Ben's mother.

"He's still a little jittery. We had a good talk, both when he first told me about it and again this afternoon. Turns out our neighbor across the road happened to see a tow truck show up around two this morning, which Ben *didn't* see. So that pretty much explains it."

"Which of the two vehicles got towed?" Brian asked.

"Huh? Oh, our neighbor said he only saw one besides the truck. A van."

"But Ben also saw an SUV?" Callie asked.

"Yes, and he was very sure about that."

"So, why did the SUV not hang around?"

Annie shrugged. "I guess you'd have to ask them. Him. Ben said there were only two men, so probably one for the van and one for the SUV."

"And they were arguing?" Brian asked. He reached for the coffee pot Annie had placed on the table and refilled his mug.

"Seemed to be, according to Ben. He couldn't hear them, but he thought they looked mad. Their gestures, I suppose. Body language. He remembered that one of them, the shorter one, had a sweatshirt with a number five on it that reflected the light, and he seemed the most upset of the two. What scared him, though—and still does—is that he's convinced they were burglars because of the stuff they were transferring from the van to the SUV. He's written this scenario in his head that the two were making off with their loot when they spotted him in the window. He thinks they'll want to come back and take care of him."

"Poor guy," Callie said. "I don't suppose there were any burglaries reported?"

"None that I've heard of."

"Here's a thought," Brian said. "How about we track down the tow truck driver?"

"That's a great idea," Callie said. "If the driver could confirm it was something very ordinary, it would put Ben's mind at ease. There aren't too many tow trucks outfits around, are there?"

"Probably two, maybe three," Brian said. "Remember when you needed one last fall? I only had to make one call."

Callie nodded. She'd called Brian one night after being run off the road and damaging her car. Brian had sent the tow truck and shown up himself, something she hadn't asked for but deeply appreciated after that nerve-wracking incident.

135

"I'll start with them," Brian said. "We should be able to get it all straightened out for Ben."

"That would be so great," Annie said. "Thanks."

There was no joking follow-up comment, which was unusual for Brian's sister. It told Callie how concerned Annie was for her young son, though she'd shown few signs of it until then. An example of how worries and pain could be deeply hidden from view. Krystal Cobb, with her daughter's death, came to mind as another example, along with other people Callie had known.

Hank, on the other hand, was never one to keep his anxieties to himself. She sighed. Her fondest hope, beyond proving his innocence, was to wave a final goodbye as he drove off to rejoin his band. The first action—proving his innocence—had to happen before the second one could, and was possibly her strongest impetus to keep working and get it done soon.

Twenty-One

*L*yssa called the next morning as Callie was unpacking a recent delivery—a special order for a customer who collected music boxes with Broadway songs. This one played a tune from *Les Misérables*.

"I'll be taking off for New York pretty soon. Just wanted to check in before I go. Anything new come up?"

"A couple of things." Callie got up from the floor and settled more comfortably into her desk chair. "I've placed Jill at the same Portis theater that Bobby did PR work for."

"Wow. At the same time?"

"It seems very possible. I looked up the theater's website—it's the Portis Playhouse—but I couldn't find any mention of either of them. Not that likely that I would, I suppose, though there was a page covering the theater's history. I'll have to talk to Jill and see what she has to say."

"That'll be tricky," Lyssa said, "if it's information she wants to keep hidden."

"I know. I'll need to come up with a plan. Oh, and I discovered a few things about Krystal's daughter." Callie told Lyssa about Tiffany Cobb's DUI-related death and the college she attended. "Hank thinks Bobby may have gone to that same college. From their ages as well as the size of the school, they might very well have been in a class or two together, or at least run into each other."

"Well, well, well. Perhaps our clock lady, Rhonda, would know that. She said their daughters went to school together. Think that included college?"

"It's possible."

"More questions for you to dig up answers to. I'm sorry. I wish I could pitch in."

"No, don't feel that way. Just concentrate on your interviews for now. What's the schedule? I'll want to catch them."

Lyssa rattled off the list of talk shows she'd be guesting on and Callie scribbled them down. "I'll record them all to watch. That's so exciting!"

"I guarantee it won't be after you watch the first two or so. I'll be repeating myself and probably babbling by then. Ever try to come up with ten different ways to say how you come up with your ideas? As if I knew in the first place. Hah! Oh, shoot," she went on. "I just remembered I'll need to pick up a blouse to go with my green jacket while I'm up there. The one I usually wear looks yucky on camera. And I'd better pack the stilettos, much as I despise them. Some of the shows like to stick you up on those tall stools, which means shoes matter. Hate those stools. I got my heels caught on the rungs once and nearly landed on my face. Not a pretty sight."

Callie wished her luck, wondering as she spoke if "break a leg" was really the proper thing to say. Lyssa didn't correct her, just continued to mutter as they discussed other things she needed to remember. Apparently even seasoned pros like her could get nervous, though Callie doubted any of it would show once she got started talking about books.

A few minutes later Brian called. "I found the garage that sent out the tow truck," he said. "The driver is out on another call, so I'll try to catch him when he gets back."

"Great! I hope what he has to say will settle things for Ben."

"We had a little talk after you left last night. Annie thinks he's doing better. But it can't hurt to totally clear it up."

"Absolutely. Let me know what you find out."

"I will. Hey, is there any chance you could pop in at Ben's baseball game tomorrow? It'll be at the park, starting at one. I'm going to close up around one thirty to run over."

"I wish I could. But tomorrow's visiting day at the detention center. Tabitha's shifting her schedule to come in so I can go."

"Ah, the detention center."

"It's the only day I can see Hank."

"Right."

"We need to talk more than we get to on the phone. Plus, he's been sounding pretty down. Seeing a friendly face will be good for him."

"No, I get it. You should go, absolutely." Brian exhaled. "Sorry, I'd go with you—if you wanted me to, that is. I mean, because it's probably not the greatest place to have to visit. But I promised Ben ..."

"I wouldn't have expected that, honest. And it's best I talk to Hank alone. At least this time." As she said it, Callie realized how much both she and Hank didn't want there to be a next time. What if this dragged on because she couldn't find anything that would get him out? A terrible thought that she shooed away.

"Gotta go," Brian said. "Customers."

They disconnected, with Callie struggling over what more she could do to forward Hank's cause. She'd come up with a plan of sorts by the time Tabitha arrived, calling out her hello.

"Still no luck finding the bar Hank went to last Saturday night," Tabitha said as Callie came out of the office. "And the more time goes by, the less likely it's going to be. I mean, for people to actually remember him and all."

"It's a long shot. But I appreciate you and your friends giving it a try."

Tabitha grinned. "Checking out area bars? We were more than happy to do it." She dropped the grin. "Sorry. Didn't mean to make a joke out of it."

Callie flapped a hand. "No problem. By the way, did you happen to see who was covering *Shake It Up!* when you walked by?"

"I saw Delia heading over to the café, so I'm guessing her friend is watching the shop."

Callie smiled. "Then I'm going to run over. Call if you need me."

Pausing outside of *House of Melody*, Callie looked across the street at the Keepsake Café. It appeared crowded, so Delia might be held up for a while. If she planned to eat her lunch there, Callie would have even more time, though she wouldn't count on it. A few minutes alone with Jill might be all she'd need. She hustled next door.

Jill looked up as she walked in. "Hi! Delia's out for a few minutes if you wanted to see her."

"No, that's fine. So you've learned the ropes, huh?"

"More or less. Ringing up sales is no problem. But tracking down specific kinds of salt and pepper shakers for people—ugh! There's so many! But Delia's a text message away if I need her."

Callie glanced through the window. No sign of her friend. "I have a question for you." Jill's eyebrows rose expectantly, as she probably anticipated something innocuous and shop-related. "Why didn't you mention that you knew Bobby Linville?"

"What?" Jill's voice squeaked and she stepped back. The surprise had thrown her off balance, just as Callie intended, hoping it might break down some of her barriers. "Why would you think that?"

"It's true, isn't it? You both worked at the Portis Playhouse." Callie hadn't been sure if the timing coincided, but Jill's stunned reaction told her she'd hit the mark.

"I … I didn't think it was important." Jill reached behind herself and slumped onto a nearby stool. "No, that's not true. I just didn't want to talk about it. Period. It was a bad time for me."

"Bad because of Bobby?"

Jill nodded. "The way it ended. Things were great at first. I was in love, and we had plans, or at least I did. I didn't know his plans were going in a very different direction." She rubbed her temples. "I was young—twenty-four, but very naïve—and he was good at convincing people he meant exactly what he said."

"In other words, he lied."

"Yup." Jill straightened. "And it cost me. Cost me a lot, in more than one way. But that's neither here nor there." Her eyes flashed. "It was just something personal from my past. I didn't see the need to make it public."

"Normally, no," Callie said. "But we're talking about the man's murder."

"And you think I did it?" Jill's voice had risen, loudly enough that neither of them heard the shop door open.

"What's going on?" Delia stood in the doorway, her bag of take-out from the café in her hands. Callie's and Jill's heads swiveled toward her.

"Your friend thinks I'm capable of murder!"

"I never said that," Callie corrected her mildly.

"You might as well have. Just because I didn't inform you I knew Bobby, you think that means I killed him."

"You knew Bobby?" Delia stepped in, dropping her food on a nearby table.

"Yes, I knew Bobby! Is that so terrible? We had a fling. It ended. I didn't want to talk about it. So there!" What she'd said earlier sounded like much more than a "fling" to Callie.

"Oh, Jill," Delia said, rushing forward. "You could have told me. It would have been okay. And you can tell Callie. She's just trying to find out all she can so she can clear her friend. Isn't that right Callie?"

"Definitely. I have to piece together as much as I can about Bobby's past life, and soon, to find out who would have wanted to kill him. I know it wasn't Hank."

"And it wasn't me," Jill said more calmly. She smiled grimly. "Maybe I could have killed him back then. But I got over it."

"I'm so sorry," Delia said. "He broke your heart?"

Jill's mouth twisted. "Demolished it." She laughed, but Callie saw the lingering bitterness in her eyes.

"So now you know Bobby Linville was a cad," Delia said to Callie. "That must have shown up in other ways."

"I'm sure I'll find more examples." Callie turned back to Jill. "At the festival early Saturday night, Bobby was heading in my direction while I was in line at the ice cream stand. That was close to your booth. It looked to me as though he suddenly saw something or someone he didn't want to face. Would that have been you?"

Jill's face flushed but she shook her head. "I wouldn't doubt it, but like I told you, I only saw him the one time. It was later in the evening and he was arguing with that woman."

"Yes, Krystal Cobb, around ten o'clock. You must have been shocked to recognize him. Did you speak to him?"

"No! No way! I told you the truth. I got away from there fast and went back to my booth."

"How much longer did you stay at the festival? Business must have been winding down around then. And you must have wanted to avoid running into Bobby again."

"Yeah, but I had to pack up all my stuff, you know? That took a while. I really don't know. Eleven-ish? Yeah, that was probably it."

Callie saw Delia's eyelids flicker at Jill's *eleven-ish*, though she said nothing. Delia had told Callie about waiting up for Jill as late as eleven thirty. Had Jill just lied, or did she actually not know what time she left?

Callie decided she'd done as much as she could for the moment. She thanked Jill and left, wanting to give Delia a chance to discuss things further on her own with her friend. It seemed highly likely that there was much more to Jill's story than they'd both heard so far.

Twenty-Two

*B*rian called again later that afternoon. "I got in touch with the tow truck driver."

"Good. What did he say?"

"He was called out to pick up a van in front of Annie's house around one a.m. Thursday. He said there was only the van, and no SUV. That fits with what Annie's neighbor said. He also said this van has been in their shop for repairs before. The owner always gets only the minimum done, even though he's been told this could lead to other problems before too long."

"Did you get a name?"

"Earl Smith. No address given. But he must be local. Once the van was fixed by late Thursday, he picked it up pretty quick. Not likely to be a pillar of society—'kind of scruffy' is the description I got—but not a known criminal either, at least not to the people at the garage. Just someone with enough money to keep his rickety van running until it happened to break down in front of Annie's. That should be enough to settle Ben. At least I hope so."

"Me too. Thanks for letting me know." Callie updated Brian about Jill, and he agreed there was probably more to come out.

"Whether you'll hear it or not is the question," he said. "Delia can be very protective of her friends."

"I hope only to a point. Surely she wouldn't cover up a murder if it came to that."

"No, but... well, there's other... I don't know. I'm probably way off base about that. Forget I said anything. I'll talk to you later."

Callie hung up, wondering exactly what Brian had started to say. Forget what he said? That only made it more likely to stick with her.

A customer came in and Callie waited on her, though she was not as fully engaged as she should have been by then. Luckily it was a simple sale—someone who'd already been to the shop and knew exactly what she wanted—so handling it on auto-pilot wasn't a problem.

Not long after that, she got a call from Lyssa.

"Hey," Lyssa said rather loudly, with much background noise coming through. "I'm in New York, waiting for my bag, and I wanted to tell you something before I have to run."

"What's up?"

"While I was on the plane, I went to that website you told me about. For the Portis Playhouse?"

"Okay..."

"You were right. There's nothing there about Bobby Linville or that photographer, Jill. But I saw someone else on it."

"Who?"

"Oh, wait! Here comes my bag. Hold on a minute."

Callie heard scraping noises and voices, including Lyssa's firm "excuse me" that sounded more like "move!" Callie's impatience was growing the longer it went on. Finally Lyssa was back.

"Got it! Sorry. The crowd here is rough! Anyway, what was I saying?"

"You saw someone on the playhouse website."

"Oh, yeah! You'll never guess."

"Don't do this to me, Lyssa!"

"Okay. Plain and simple. It was my landscaper guy, Gavin Holder! He was in the photos of the grand opening ceremony."

"Gavin! What was he doing there?"

"I'll give you a hint: he was holding a shovel. He did their landscaping, you ninny." Lyssa cackled. "And he was there helping to plant a memorial tree that honored some donor. I might not have recognized him—it was twenty years ago, you know—but the caption gave his name. It said he'd made their outdoor areas beautiful, and that he'd continue to keep it that way, which means he was on their payroll. So he really must have known Bobby Linville. He wasn't glaring in his direction at the festival because of an upset stomach."

"Wow, good catch, Lyssa. That ceremony happened around the time Jill was working there, too."

"You're sure?"

"A customer of mine put her there in that time frame. Plus, we know Jill's age when she was in a relationship with Bobby—she said she was twenty-four. It all fits."

"Aha. The plot thickens. Can you go over to my place sometime and see what Gavin has to say about this? He should be around. Wish I could do it myself, but ..."

Callie wished Lyssa could do it too, especially since she'd said that Gavin wasn't particularly gabby. She'd struggled to get anything out of him, and she was highly skilled at that. But Callie would have to try.

Lyssa, who'd been walking through the terminal during their conversation, apparently made it outside, since Callie heard changes in the background noises. "Oh" she suddenly cried, "I got a taxi. Better go. I'll check in with you later!"

Callie heard the abrupt disconnect and put her own phone away. As she thought about all they'd been talking about, along with what else she'd recently learned, she realized there was a lot she needed to keep straight. She pulled out a pad of paper, sat down behind her counter, and began to write.

At the top of the page, she wrote:

Time of Murder: Between 12 and 2 a.m. Sunday morning

Below that she wrote:

Opportunity and/or motive:

1. Krystal Cobb

Krystal admits to arguing with Bobby at ten p.m. She claims it was over Bobby's demand for more money for the band, but there's no one (alive) to back that up. She also says she left the festival soon after, but again, there's only her word for that.

Krystal's daughter, Tiffany, might have known Bobby at college, and she died from a DUI. Bobby had a drinking problem. Is there a connection? Might Krystal blame Bobby for her daughter's death?

2. Jill Burns

Jill admits to a years-ago relationship with Bobby that turned bad, and there's obvious lingering bitterness. But Jill seems angry at a lot of things. Could this be blamed on Bobby and whatever happened between them? Jill named eleven o'clock as the time she left the festival, but according to what Delia said Sunday morning, it couldn't have been that early.

Callie paused, then added another name.

3. Gavin Holder

All we know about Gavin so far is that he probably knew Bobby from when they both worked at the Portis Playhouse twenty years ago. The only suspicious thing is that he wasn't forthcoming about having lived and worked in Portis. Of course, Lyssa was his employer, not a police detective requiring full and complete answers. But it's worth looking into further.

Then Callie reluctantly, but for complete honesty, added a final name:

4. Hank

Hank's anger with Bobby over his mismanagement of the band, particularly the loss of a good recording opportunity, is well known. Bobby was killed with the music box Hank recently bought. His alibi for the time of the murder—getting drunk at a bar, then sleeping it off in his car— can't be confirmed.

Callie sighed. Once it was all put down in writing, she had to admit it looked very bad for Hank. She could understand why the police stopped looking beyond him. But had they, actually? Hank's lawyer, Clark Allard, might know. She picked up her phone and called his office, only to hear he was out. She left a message with his assistant, asking the attorney to get back to her.

After hanging up, she looked back at her list of suspects and stopped at Gavin Holder. If Laurie had read Gavin's expression right at the festival, Bobby was not only known to Gavin but had left a pretty bad impression on him. And Gavin had the best reason of all to stay late at the festival: it was his job. How long had he been there?

Another question Callie had was why Bobby had stayed late—or returned—to the grounds after the rest of the band had gone. Nobody seemed to have an answer to that, but she knew it might make all the difference in identifying the murderer.

She was pondering it all when her shop door opened. She looked up to see Rhonda Furman smiling cheerily, the blue shirtdress she'd worn the other day at her clock shop replaced with a gingham blouse tucked into a denim skirt. She held up a ring of keys and rattled them.

"I've been dying to come see your place, so with business as slow as it is, I asked myself, 'Why not now?' and locked up to run over here." She took in Callie's array of music boxes in a sweeping gaze. "Wow! Can I try a few?"

"Go right ahead," Callie encouraged her as she came out from behind her counter.

Rhonda wound the key on a small child's music box nearby, smiled at its tinkly tune, and then moved on, eventually lifting the lids or winding nearly a dozen to play simultaneously. She clasped her hands with delight at the sound. "I love it! Much better than all the tick-tocking at my place." Remembering Lyssa's horrified reaction to that, Callie smiled. As though reading her mind, Rhonda asked how Lyssa was enjoying her new clock.

"I know she loves it. But she's left it behind for a few days to do some book promotion in New York."

"Ooh, how fun! I'm going to look for one of her books. I'd love to have her sign it."

"I'm sure she'd be happy to."

Rhonda went around to carefully close the music boxes, then turned to Callie. "You know, I think I should explain a little something."

"Oh?"

"When you two were in my shop and you told me about the murder at the festival, I wasn't perfectly honest. I actually did recognize Bobby Linville's name."

Callie wasn't exactly stunned to hear that, though she was surprised to hear Rhonda say it. She waited, expecting to hear something to do with Krystal. Instead, Rhonda said, "It's a little embarrassing, which is why I fumbled around about it. But it happens that I once bought a car from that man."

"A car?"

"Yes, some years ago. It was totally on impulse. I saw it advertised in our PennySaver, and it was so reasonably priced. My husband was out of town, so I met with Mr. Linville, drove the thing around a little, and bought it on the spot."

"I have a feeling that didn't turn out very well."

Rhonda grimaced. "It didn't. The car had lots of problems. When we tried to contact Mr. Linville, it was like he'd vanished. He did tell me he was moving away, which was why he needed to sell the car in a hurry, but still. As I said, embarrassing. I tried to put it behind me long ago, but when you said his name, it came flooding back." She winced. "Which was probably what that car went through: a flood."

"You didn't know Bobby before that?"

"Oh, no."

"Because I learned that he went to Clayton Daniel College. I believe Krystal's daughter went there for a while. Did yours?"

"CDC? Yes, our Jamie graduated from there. Bobby Linville did too? Wow!"

"Not graduated but attended, and possibly around the same time."

"Well, the college is fairly close to where we lived back then, so I guess it's not such a coincidence."

"And your daughter didn't know him?"

"No, I'm sure she didn't, or she would have said something." Rhonda checked her watch. "I'd better be going. My husband will be picking me up soon. I just wanted to clear that up."

"Thank you for telling me this," Callie said, walking with her to the door. "It's one more piece in the puzzle of Bobby Linville."

"Yes, I'd heard you were working to clear your friend of the murder."

Callie knew she hadn't mentioned that to either Krystal or Rhonda and asked, "How did you hear?"

"Duane Fletcher." Rhonda cast another glance at her watch. "Well, I wish you luck. I do love your shop, by the way. So many pretty music boxes!"

She hurried off, Callie looking after her, glad to have the question answered about what Rhonda had obviously been hiding. She admired the woman's willingness to share her uncomfortable tale.

Then Callie wondered how and why Duane had happened to bring up her investigation, and finally put it down to his typical gregariousness. How many others had he talked to about it? She supposed she'd eventually find out. What she didn't know yet was if that would be a help or a hindrance.

Twenty-Three

Callie had just closed her shop when her phone rang. It was Hank's lawyer.

"Thank you for returning my call, Mr. Allard," Callie said, noting the rushed, halfway-out-the-door tone to his voice. "I wanted to know if the police have been looking at anyone else besides Hank."

"Others? It doesn't appear so. I get the strong impression they feel they've done their job and are just waiting for a trial date."

"Tunnel vision, then? Saves them a lot of work, doesn't it?" Callie said, hearing her anger and frustration coming through.

"You can't blame them. Things look pretty solid from their point of view."

"Then we'll have to point out alternatives to them."

"Do you have any information I can use to do that?"

"Nothing solid," she admitted. "But I'm exploring a few possibilities." She ran through what she'd learned so far, hearing Allard react with "Uh-huh, uh-huh" as hopefully he wrote it down.

152

"Is that it?"

Callie said it was and let the lawyer go, wishing he'd been able to tell her that things weren't nearly as bad as they looked. Unfortunately, it seemed they probably were.

She went out the back of the shop to her cottage, feeling down and looking forward to the lift she knew would come from Jagger's happy greeting. He didn't fail her, and she cuddled her purring pet for several moments before carrying him to the kitchen and feeding him. She then pulled out one of Brian's frozen dinners to heat for herself.

She'd finished eating, washed the dishes, and just put her feet up when her phone rang. Hoping it might be Brian calling to say hello from Annie's, she grabbed for it, but saw it was her mother instead.

"Are you busy? I can call back later if you are."

"No, Mom, this is good. How are you?"

"Fine, except for this stupid knee, of course."

"Is it very painful?"

"Bearable, but bad enough that I'm willing to put myself through the surgery," Elizabeth said. "Which tells you something. I just wish they could knock me out now and wake me when it's over. It's this waiting ten more days and thinking about it that's the hardest part. I'm starting to climb the walls."

"I'm sorry."

"Have you decided one way or the other about coming? It'd be wonderful to have you here for Mother's Day, of course, but also a huge help in taking my mind off what's scheduled for the next day. Frank, you know, is as bad as I am about hospitals and surgeries. He's trying his best, but he's really making me more anxious. I'm actually thinking of sending him off somewhere until it's over." Elizabeth gave a short, humorless laugh.

How could Callie say no? Yes, she'd be leaving Hank behind. But not right away. There was always the possibility that between now and next weekend, she'd discover something that would get him released. She knew that the way things were going, the likelihood of that was slim, but she'd have to go with it.

"Sure, Mom, I'll come. Just let me work things out with Tabitha about her schedule and what she can do."

"Wonderful!" The relief in her mother's voice filled Callie with a flood of guilt for having hesitated. "I know you feel some sort of responsibility for Hank. But after all, what can you possibly do?"

Not much, it seemed. "I'll at least be seeing him tomorrow," Callie said. "It might cheer him up a little." For an hour.

"That's very kind of you, Callie. And of course, you can always talk to him from here, can't you?"

"Yes, that's true." *And hear how miserable he is and be helpless to do anything about it.* But wasn't that exactly how things would be going in the Cove, anyway?

"I met that man who was killed, you know," her mother said. "Did I tell you that?"

"Bobby! You met him? How? And when?" Callie would have added where and why, but she was eager to hear her mother's tale.

"Oh, it was some weeks ago. I forget exactly when. Hank and this man—name's Linville?—showed up out of the blue on our doorstep. Their band was in the area, and Hank seemed to think I'd be perfectly delighted to see him."

Callie groaned. How typical of Hank to be so tone-deaf to how her mother—who'd always been perfectly polite though never, ever warm—truly felt about him.

"I invited them in, of course, and offered something to drink. Frank, unfortunately, wasn't home, so I had to deal with it by myself.

154

Anyway, while I was pouring out the iced tea in the kitchen, this Linville person went wandering around as though he was buying the place. Very annoying."

"I only met him once, but I agree. That's exactly how he was."

"And he kept it up even after I'd brought in the drinks and Hank and I sat down. He picked things up and turned them over as if looking for a price tag. When he finally joined us, he pointed to a picture on the wall—the one hanging near the window. Do you remember it? The blue flowers? Frank gave it to me for my birthday?"

Callie vaguely remembered a picture of flowers in a vase. "Uh-huh."

"He said he could get us *real stuff*, as he put it, at a good price because he knew someone. I could barely contain myself. Frank's painting is as real as they come. Perhaps not by a famous artist, but I love it. I didn't appreciate hearing my gift put down like that."

"If it's any comfort, Mom, Bobby Linville treated everyone like that. And I highly doubt he knew what he was talking about, so his opinion meant nothing. How did Hank react?"

"Well, to his credit he looked embarrassed, and he changed the subject. They didn't stay much longer after that, to my relief. Callie, Hank had his good points, I'll grant you, but his choice of friends left a lot to be desired. I was so glad when you moved away from that scene."

"Bobby wasn't a friend, Mom. He was the band's manager, a business associate. Hank figured out what kind of person he really was— or wasn't. It just took a while. And it was that realization and his anger over it that got him into the mess he's in right now."

"Well, I'm sorry for him. But bad luck, I'm afraid, just seems to follow some people around. I'm sure it'll work out all right." Elizabeth's voice brightened. "By the way, we're thinking of making the Greek islands our next trip. A cruise, so it wouldn't mean too much walking for me. As soon as I get the go-ahead on my new knee, of course."

Elizabeth went on about all the things she and Frank would get to see. Callie was glad to hear that her mother wasn't ready to give up on the travel she loved just yet, though her thoughts occasionally strayed to her upcoming visit with Hank. They ended the call with Callie's promise to nail down the time for her visit and a happy promise from her mother to then immediately buy her ticket.

After she set down her phone, Callie reached over to Jagger, who'd curled up on the sofa cushion beside her. "Lucky you," she said as she scratched his ears. "An uncomplicated life with few demands beyond being adorable."

The gray cat snuffled, whether in agreement or derision she couldn't guess, and tucked his nose back under his paw.

Twenty-Four

"Oh, gosh," Tabitha said when Callie asked if she'd be able to keep *House of Melody* open when she was in Oregon. "Doing full-time hours would be really hard right now. My beading orders are getting backed up, and I can't afford to lose my new customers."

"I understand." Callie truly did, but it was going to make things more difficult.

"Wait! What if I brought my stuff here? There's always slow periods in the shop. Lately, more than usual. I could work on my orders in the back during those times. Would that be okay?"

"That'd be perfect," Callie said, greatly relieved. "I hated to ask this of you, but I really appreciate it. My mom will too. If I get there by Friday night, I think it will help her cope much better."

"Sure, absolutely."

"And really, if it gets to be too much, just close up," Callie said. "It wouldn't be a disaster." At least, not *total*.

"Well, I might take you up on that if I have to. I'll see how it goes."

With that settled, Callie emailed her mother and got ready to see Hank. But she planned a stop at Lyssa's house on the way to the detention center. She hoped to find Gavin Holder working on Lyssa's yard.

On the drive over, Callie thought about Tabitha's burgeoning business. She'd known from the start that creating beaded jewelry was her assistant's passion and long-term career goal, and that Tabitha had been working at *House of Melody*—first for Aunt Mel, then for her—because she wasn't able to support herself on beading alone. Was that on the verge of changing? Would she be losing her wonderful employee before too long? It had always seemed light years away, but that reality was suddenly approaching. What would she do without Tabitha?

The turn-off for Lyssa's house came up and Callie took it, soon pulling up in front of the A-frame. She was elated to see that a van was parked in the driveway with potted shrubs, bags, and various tools spread out next to it. As she climbed out of her car, the memory of Ben looking out into the night at a van in front of his house flashed through her mind. But there were plenty of vans around, and Ben's had already been linked to another owner.

Callie glanced around for the landscaper, then followed a buzzing noise to the far side of the house. She found Gavin attacking a tall, weedy-looking shrub with energy, sawing off branches and yanking them out of the way. She waited until he set down his saw.

"Mr. Holder?"

He jerked and turned in her direction.

"Sorry to startle you. I'm a friend of Lyssa's. Callie Reed. Do you have a minute?"

Holder pulled a handkerchief out of his pocket and wiped his tanned, slightly lined face. "Sure. Lyssa change her mind about something?" He gestured toward a wooden picnic table, set close to the water, and led the way over to it. He pulled a chilled water bottle out of a cooler and offered it to her. When Callie declined with a head shake, he closed the lid and pulled out a bench to sit.

Callie slid onto the bench across from him and waited as he opened the bottle and took several swallows. He looked fit and trim, as his line of work likely would keep him. The receding hairline and gray hairs that showed as he took off his hat suggested a man in his late forties. He set the bottle down and looked across the table at her.

"So, what's the bad news?" he asked. "I hope it's not something about the bush I just hacked apart."

"No, I'm not here on Lyssa's behalf, although she did ask that I stop by to see how things were going. It's looking much better already."

"There's a ways to go." He waited, and Callie got to her point.

"I've been looking into the murder of Bobby Linville. I'm here to learn more about him."

Holder blinked. "You're with the police?"

"No, I'm a friend of the man who's been arrested for the murder. I know he didn't do it, and I need to find out who did because the police seem to have stopped looking any further."

Holder's pleasant expression turned dark, and Laurie Hart's description of him glaring at Bobby at the festival came to mind.

"You knew Bobby Linville in Portis, Pennsylvania," Callie continued. "I would appreciate your telling me what you can about him."

"Portis." Holder took another swallow of water. "How did you know about that?"

"It doesn't matter."

Holder stared at her hard. "He was someone I'd hoped never to run into again."

And yet he had. "Why?"

Holder held her gaze for several moments while Callie remained silent. "I don't like talking about it. Why should I? Let the police deal with his murder. If they want to talk to me, let them come."

"They might want to talk to Jill Burns, unless you give me a reason not to send them to her."

"Jill! Why would you do that to her?"

It had been a long shot, but Callie had thrown out Jill's name in hopes of getting Holder talking. It seemed to have worked.

"It's clear she has plenty of bitterness concerning him. She told me he led her on and then dumped her. But I think there's more to it. If I can't find out what it was, the police probably can."

"Don't do that to her. It could destroy her."

"What do you mean?"

Holder exhaled and leaned his face into his hands, rubbing hard. "You probably think she's tough," he said, looking up. "She comes across that way. But it's all an act. She's fragile and protecting herself. She let her guard down with Linville. And it almost did her in."

Callie waited.

"He played her. I saw it all and couldn't do a thing about it. She didn't see through his smooth talking. I tried to warn her, once, after I heard him giving her all kinds of excuses for why he couldn't come up with his part of the deal. It was all baloney, but she swallowed it."

"Deal? What kind of deal?"

"I think the plan was to set up her own studio. Some kind of fancy photography. Like that woman—what was her name? Who did all those celebrity photos?"

Callie thought for a bit and came up with a name. "Annie Leibovitz?"

"Yeah, that's it. Not that Jill expected to draw celebrities, but she wanted to tell stories with her photos. At least, that's how she put it one time when we had a coffee together. She wanted to be creative."

And ended up taking kids' photos at a department store.

"So Bobby was going into this with her? As what, a business partner?"

"Business partner, marriage, the whole thing. Jill was walking on air."

"And then it all fell apart?"

Holder nodded, his jaw working hard.

"How?"

"He just up and disappeared. She'd taken out loans, signed papers, put down deposits with every penny she could scrape together, thinking he was getting his part of the investment in line, too. When he skipped town, she lost it all. It hit her hard."

"Yes, I imagine it would."

"I mean, really hard. She fell apart. As I said, she isn't as tough as she pretends. I was the one took her to the hospital when she tried to kill herself."

"Oh!"

"She claimed later it was an accident, that she'd taken too many pills when she was half asleep, but it wasn't." He slapped his hands onto the picnic table and pushed himself up. "And that's all I'm going to say about it. Except that's why you can't put her through anything more. Yes, she has good reason for wanting to do away with Linville. But she'd sooner do away with herself. Don't push her to it."

Holder walked back to the house and picked up his chain saw, yanking it hard to start it. The resulting roar effectively told Callie to leave. She did, the sound buzzing in the background as she drove away.

She'd succeeded in getting Gavin Holder to talk, and in sharing Jill's sad story he must have felt he'd convinced her of the woman's innocence. But he might also have given Callie his own reason to want Bobby Linville dead. Bobby had badly hurt the woman Holder loved, and he'd clearly never forgiven him.

161

Twenty-Five

From Lyssa's house, Callie headed north, traveling mostly on major roads so that the drive went swiftly. She found the detention center easily. It surprised her. She'd been picturing a large prison, yet the facility was more like a small town high school, which made her feel better about Hank's situation, although only slightly. Small building or not, he was still incarcerated.

She shuffled through the security check lines with a mix of other visitors, glancing around and finding the facility modern and coldly clean to the point of sterile. She stole glances at the other visitors. Some, like her, looked nervous, rubbing bare arms in agitation rather than due to the air conditioning. Others appeared bored, as though they'd been through this routine many times before. A sad thought, and worrisome. She hoped never to reach that stage.

The visitors room was crowded. A guard led her to one of the few remaining seats at a small table and told her to wait. Within minutes, another guard walked Hank in and Callie's heart lurched to see him dressed in a prisoner's jumpsuit. She tried her best to look upbeat.

Hank took the seat across from her. "Thanks for comin'."

"How are you?" she asked, really wanting to know.

"See this bruise?" He pointed to a bluish mark near his eye.

"What happened?"

"Got caught in the middle of a fight between two crazies. There's a couple more under this getup. Babe, I got to get out of here." He'd said that before to her, but this time Hank sounded worn down, as though he'd become resigned.

"I'm working on it, Hank. I've been finding out things from a lot of people and I might be getting somewhere. But right now I need an answer from you. Explain to me why you didn't get bail."

Hank leaned back and exhaled loudly. After a long pause, he said, "Okay. I should have told you about this a long time ago, but ... I didn't." He ran his hands through his hair, his eyes darting around like he wished he could get up and pace. Callie figured that wouldn't be a good idea.

"All right. It's like this." Hank leaned forward, gripping his hands together tightly on the table. "This was before us, you know. There was this other girl. Stacy. She turned out to be a big mistake. Anyway, I'd been scraping along in some rinky-dink bands, barely making ends meet, until I had this windfall."

"With the band?"

"No, gambling. We were in Vegas. I got lucky—really lucky—at roulette. And I didn't report it." Seeing Callie's look, Hank scrambled. "Babe, it was the first time I had any money like that at all! Yes, I should have paid the taxes, but I was stupid and didn't."

"And that's why you were denied bail?"

"Not exactly." A second, long pause. "Stacy? Well, when we broke up, she was really mad. I didn't do anything wrong, I swear, but she was the kind who thinks they're the one who calls things off, never the one who *gets* dumped. So she went and turned me in to the IRS."

Callie winced and waited, suspecting that wasn't the end to Hank's story.

"When I found out what she did I got mad, and we had a real shoutin' match. Just words, I swear. But it was loud, and a lot of people overheard."

"And?"

"And she got hurt, but it wasn't because of me. It was her own fault, wearing those skinny heels and not lookin' where she was going. So she fell down these steps and got hurt, bad enough to go to the hospital. That's when she pointed the finger at me."

Callie groaned.

"Yup. I got charged with assault on top of tax evasion and did some time. Not much, but it's twice as hard when it's for something you didn't do—I mean, the assault thing. And I hated it so much that I never wanted to talk about it, so I never told you about it."

Callie nodded automatically, but she was processing Hank's story, understanding better why he was stuck where he was. A previous record that included violence. A current charge of murder. And maybe considered a flight risk since he didn't have roots in the area. She wouldn't have been surprised to learn that Hank mouthed off at his hearing on top of all that. He would call it standing up for himself, but it wasn't the time, and a judge wouldn't have appreciated it. Whatever had happened, Hank was where he was.

They moved on to talk about what Callie had dug up about Bobby Linville. Hank was surprised to hear about certain incidents, but not about Bobby's behavior.

"Yeah, I can believe that," he said when Callie told him about Bobby's treatment of Jill. "Especially now, after seeing how he bungled the band's record deal. He probably got himself in too deep with all his phony promises, then got scared and went on a binge or just took off."

Callie shared Rhonda Furman's tale about the car sale, and he shook his head. "Wish I'd known what a con man he was. He sure conned me."

"How did he get into band management?" Callie asked. "Surely the Badlanders wasn't his first."

"No, he managed others, but I don't know exactly who. Maybe Randy can tell you."

"I'm wondering about this because he seems to have jumped from one thing to another. My mother told me about you and Bobby dropping in on her a few weeks ago."

"Oh, yeah. That was Bobby's idea. We were in Portland, and I mentioned you and your folks having lived there. Going to see your mom seemed like a good idea at the time." Hank grimaced.

"Bobby gave Mom the impression he had connections in the art world."

"Yeah. Who knows? He didn't explain that to me." Hank shrugged. "Probably just more of his talk."

"Five minutes!" a guard called out, warning that visiting hours were coming to an end.

"Listen," Hank said, leaning forward. "I really appreciate your coming and all you're doing for me. I mean, I wouldn't have blamed you if you'd just walked away. I've been a jerk sometimes, I know. And I'm really sorry. Having the time to think a little, here, I've seen that, and I wish it'd been different. When this is all over, you're going to see a changed man."

"Hank, I'm glad to hear that, but..." Callie's immediate thoughts were that she hoped not to see much of him at all after it was all over, and that he shouldn't be thinking otherwise. She was trying to think of the best way to put it when a loud buzzer sounded, ending the session. Detainees stood and left with guards, Hank looking over his shoulder one last time, and Callie tried her best to look encouraging.

On the drive back, she thought about Hank's past run-in with the law. Though she'd tried not to show it, it had shaken her to hear news like that come from a person she thought she'd known so well. Brian had mildly questioned her faith in Hank's innocence, suggesting he might have changed since she'd seen him, and Callie had remained steadfast in her belief.

But now she knew that Hank had kept a significant part of his past hidden from her for years! Was that all he'd kept from her? Had he been totally honest about the night Bobby was murdered? The thought was distressing enough to make Callie want to push it away. But she knew she'd have to keep it with her from that point on as she continued to search for the truth.

The truth, she realized, just might turn out to be something she didn't want to find.

Twenty-Six

Callie relieved Tabitha at the shop and was looking over an order written up for a specialty music box when Lyle Moody walked in.

"Mr. Moody!" she said. "What a nice surprise."

"Lyle will do," he said in his deep-pitched but quiet voice. "If that's all right with you, ma'am."

"Of course. And I'm Callie."

The proprietor of the John Wayne memorabilia shop nodded and touched two finger tips to his forehead, causing Callie to picture a cowboy hat perched there, which would blend well with his denims and checkered shirt. White sneakers, however, completed his outfit instead of boots.

"What can I do for you?" she asked. She couldn't imagine Lyle shopping for a music box, but stranger things had happened.

"Well, I happened to have a little something to tell Mr. Greer, but I see his café is closed. I wondered if you'd pass it along for me?"

"Brian? Sure, I'd be glad to." Although Lyle Moody was a new-comer to Keepsake Cove, he'd apparently already been informed or picked up on the relationship between Callie and Brian, casual though it was.

"I happened to be at a garage that he contacted about a certain van. My ornery pickup has been having engine troubles lately. As I was waitin' on it, I couldn't help overhearing Joe, who handles most of the tow truck jobs, talking about the call."

"Oh?"

"I don't know what Mr. Greer needed to know about the van, but I know a little about the owner. If he's wanting to hire him, I wouldn't recommend it."

"You know Earl Smith?"

"Just enough to know he's not reliable. I was having a beer with Gavin Holder, the landscaper, the other night, and Smith was running off at the mouth after a few too many."

Callie perked up at mention of Holder's name but stuck with Smith for the moment. "The reason Brian was asking about the van," she said, "was that it apparently broke down in front of his sister's house in the middle of the night, worrying her young son. There was some transferring of items from the van to another vehicle. He wanted to be clear about what was going on."

"I don't know about that, but I'm not surprised at the breakdown. According to the guys at the garage, the thing's just this side of falling apart. Not too bright of Smith, since he uses it for hauling jobs when he can get them. That's what I wanted to warn Greer about."

"That was good of you, Lyle." So the argument going on in front of Annie's house must have been between Smith and whoever had foolishly hired him and ended up finishing the haul themselves. "Do you happen to know how to reach Mr. Smith? Not to hire, but Brian might have more questions about the incident the other night."

Moody shook his head. "Somebody at Dave's Pub might know. I got the feeling Smith is a regular."

"Thanks. You mentioned Gavin Holder. He's doing landscaping for a friend of mine. It's taking shape very nicely."

Moody nodded. "He's a pro. Knows what he's doing."

"My friend said he seemed anxious for the work. That's surprising to me, since good landscapers are usually pretty busy this time of year."

"Gavin's new to the area, like me."

"Did you know him before moving here?"

"Nope, just ran into each other at the pub once or twice and started talkin'." Moody smiled, adding, "More about John Wayne than about flowers. But he sounds pretty experienced in his line of work. Your friend's most likely in good hands. Well, I'll be on my way. Just wanted to pass on that little nugget about Smith." He started to turn, then stopped. "Oh, and I'm sorry about your other friend. Hope things work out for him."

"Hank? Thank you."

"He stopped in at my shop that first day he was here. Didn't buy anything, but that's okay. He sure didn't seem like anyone who'd do what they say he did."

Callie hadn't thought so either, and she'd been so sure about that. Yet Hank's admission of what he'd hidden from her had shaken that conviction. She didn't say so to Lyle, and simply thanked him.

Later that night, Callie turned on her recording of the first talk show Lyssa had appeared on earlier that day. She'd fixed a mug of tea and curled up on the sofa with Jagger by her side. Though it looked like Lyssa would appear later in the program, she watched from the beginning, enjoying the chatter and the luxury of a small break from thoughts of murder.

When the chatter got to be a bit much, Callie fast-forwarded, stopping when one of the hosts held up Lyssa's latest book. She listened to the glowing introduction, after which Lyssa walked into view. Callie sat upright, excited to see her friend on TV exchanging hugs with the show's hosts and looking wonderful in her green jacket with a new blouse and a dark pencil skirt. The total image said *successful author*, at least to Callie, but Lyssa's easy, joking manner made her relatable and perfect for daytime viewers.

She enjoyed the interview, and the fact that, if Lyssa was as nervous as she'd sounded on the phone, it never showed. When the segment ended, she pulled up a recording of a show that had taken place later in the day. When Lyssa appeared in that one, she'd changed into a dress. New clothes, new hosts, but the questions and discussion were much the same. Though Lyssa tried to vary her answers, there was only so much she could do. Her prediction that Callie would quickly become bored was turning out to be on point, though it was still fun to see a friend on the screen.

When the second show ended, Callie turned off the TV. Lyssa's next appearance would be on a late late show, which was much too late late for Callie. She would catch it another time. She put her mug in the sink and went upstairs, Jagger following closely behind.

⚭

A loud boom woke her in the middle of the night. Callie sat straight up. What was that? She waited, listening, but heard nothing more.

Then she swung her legs down and climbed out of bed. When she stepped into the hallway, a flash of light from below caught her eye.

She hurried to the top of the stairs and saw the flash again, realizing it came through her front window. After running back to her room to grab her cell phone, Callie dashed down the stairs and to the window. More flashing light. But she also smelled smoke.

She yanked open her front door and saw flames to her right, licking the corner of her house. She immediately pulled up the Emergency SOS on her phone and called for help, then rushed back inside, intent on finding the fire extinguisher Aunt Mel had stored in the kitchen. After scrambling through the clutter on the floor of the narrow pantry closet, Callie laid her hands on it. She ripped off the safety pin as she ran outdoors, praying that the device was still operable.

The flames were concentrated on the side of her cottage, underneath the electric meter. Callie aimed her extinguisher's nozzle and pressed down. A whoosh of white gas flew out, and the flames quickly died down.

As her extinguisher fizzled out, so did the breath she'd been holding in. Her fire was out. Her head swiveled as she heard sirens in the distance. Possibly unneeded but still wonderful to hear. Then she remembered Jagger. Callie dashed back into her cottage and up the stairs, hoping against hope that the large cat wasn't hiding. To her relief, she found him still on her bed, and she scooped him up. Hearing the roar of the fire truck pulling up, she carried Jagger down the stairs and out of her cottage to meet the truck at the street.

"It's back there," she yelled, struggling to hold tight to her now-panicked cat. "I think I put it out." She got out of the firefighters' way as they took over in a rush of activity. As she watched, dazed, Delia miraculously appeared in her robe and slippers and pulled Callie into *Shake It Up!* With the brightness of the fire truck's flashing lights illuminating the shop, Delia led Callie directly to the back office and closed the door behind them, allowing her to put a frazzled Jagger down and draw a deep breath.

"Here," Delia said, pulling a stand-by raincoat off its hook and wrapping it around her friend, who'd begun to shiver in her thin pajamas, and not only from the cold. Callie slid her arms through the sleeves and went to the office window, from which she could see several firemen at the back of her cottage. They weren't rushing anymore, which she took as a good sign.

"I think the worst is over."

"Thank God. What happened? What caused the fire?"

"I don't know! It was just suddenly there. There was a loud boom that woke me up. Otherwise I might not have discovered it."

"That woke me, too. I think it came from the breaker on the pole out front."

"The flames were under my electric meter. Would that have affected the pole breaker?"

"They're connected. When a tree branch landed on the lines once, during a storm, the breaker out there boomed just like that. And all our power went out." Delia clicked a wall switch on and off to no effect. "See? We're out."

"Wow," Callie said, still stunned. "But where did that fire come from?" She saw two of the firefighters conferring at the corner of her yard. "I'm going out. Maybe they'll have some answers."

She left Jagger with Delia and crossed her friend's small yard to her own, where she identified herself as the cottage's owner.

"Looks like you had an arsonist at work here," a firefighter told her after confirming the fire was out. "Somebody built a nice pile of wood and paper right under your electric meter. Looks like minimal

172

damage to your house, mostly to the siding, but the meter's a loss. You'll have some internal damage to the wires and your breaker."

An arsonist! "Why would somebody do that?"

"It's weird," he agreed. "We've reported it. We also notified the power company about the outages, but it might be a while before they can get here. They're dealing with a major problem farther east of here. Freak wind storm and lots of lines down. They're stretched pretty thin right now."

Callie sighed. "Is it safe for me to go back in?"

The man nodded. "Soon. We're still checking to make sure the fire didn't extend internally, but so far it looks fine. I should be able to give you the final okay in a few minutes."

Callie thanked him, and then spotted Karl Eggers standing at the fence opening between their yards. She went over to tell him what she'd learned.

"So," he growled, "some idiot thought it would be fun to light fires and close down people's shops for the next day. Like the murder wasn't bad enough for business."

Callie understood the feeling. Her business was just starting to pick up again, and now her shop and several others would be dark until the power company showed up. Who was the arsonist and why would he—or she—do such a thing?

It was clear to Callie that she'd been the target, the surrounding shops and homes simply collateral damage. Had her questions about Bobby Linville's murder triggered this response? If so, it meant she'd asked them of the right person. If she only knew who that was.

Twenty-Seven

Once the fire truck left, Callie retrieved Jagger from Delia's office and took him home. She tried to get some sleep, but found it next to impossible as adrenaline and a multitude of unanswered questions continued to swirl. Exhaustion won out eventually. She dozed off just as dawn was breaking, managing to catch a couple of hours. She woke to bright sunshine coming through her unshaded window and into her eyes. She checked her phone for the time: 9:05. Still groggy, she nonetheless dragged herself out of bed. Her rest time was over. A quick shower revived her somewhat, and she dressed and pinned her limp hair out of the way. With the power out, there'd be no hair dryer use that day. Or coffee maker.

Once downstairs, she stepped outside to get a look at the damage in daylight. She was groaning over it when her cell phone rang. It was Delia.

"I picked up coffee and breakfast sandwiches in Mapleton. Come on over!"

"Delia, you're a saint!"

Callie slipped through the break in the greenery between the two cottages and saw her friend standing at her door. "I waited to see some signs of life," Delia said. "Didn't want to wake you. The coffee's staying nice and hot in my big thermos."

Callie expected to see Jill, too, as she walked inside, but Delia's living room and kitchen were both empty. She realized she hadn't seen Jill the previous night, during all the commotion from the fire, and asked Delia about it.

"Jill has been having trouble sleeping, so she picked up an over-the-counter sleep aid. Sometimes those things can really knock you out. But I'm glad she's finally getting some rest." Delia waved Callie to the kitchen and told her to pick out a sandwich while she poured out a coffee.

As she unwrapped her sausage and egg-filled muffin, Callie thought about Delia's housemate. Was Jill really still in bed because of a sleeping tablet, or could she possibly have tired herself out during the middle of the night, gathering wood and setting a fire? Delia had told Callie once that she herself was a sound sleeper. She might not have heard Jill if she'd slipped out of the house.

Shortly after Delia joined Callie at the small table, they heard sounds of movement upstairs, followed soon by dragging footsteps on the steps as Jill called out, "I smell coffee!" When she appeared, wrapped in a robe and looking bleary-eyed, she stopped at the edge of the kitchen, surprised to see Callie. "Oh! Hi!"

"We're having a fast food breakfast today," Delia said, getting up. "But the coffee's good. Come on in. You can take my seat. I already ate."

"Fast food? How come?" Jill asked, staying where she was. "Not that I mind. All I really want is coffee."

"You must have been out like a light! There was quite a bit of excitement last night." Delia told her what had happened and that cooking on her electric stove wasn't going to happen for a while. Callie watched Jill's face but saw only normal shock and surprise, muted somewhat by sleepiness.

"Wow! And I slept through all that? Amazing." Jill pushed a straggly bunch of hair back from her face.

"You might want to cut your dose of that pill in half next time," Delia said. She put Jill's coffee on the table and waved her toward it. "Sit."

Jill seemed reluctant, saying she could take her coffee into the living room, but when Delia insisted, she took the seat across from Callie and began to sip her coffee. Callie told her more about the damage to her electric meter and the cottage's siding, along with the firefighter's statement that it had been arson. Jill shook her head but didn't appear all that alarmed. Simply groggy from the sleep aid? Difficult to say.

Callie munched on her sandwich a while, then told both women about her visit to the detention center to see Hank. Delia glanced sympathetically over her shoulder from the sink as she listened, but Jill continued to focus on her mug. Callie didn't bring up Hank's explanation for his bail denial, but she told about things he'd gone through since being locked up.

"He picked up some kind of bug that made him sick enough to be in the infirmary for a while. And he got caught in the middle of a fight between other inmates. He's also very worried about losing his spot with the band. They have to keep performing, and they could decide to fill his place, maybe with someone they'll like better. This could be really tough for him, the longer it goes on."

"I'm so sorry," Delia said, full of sympathy.

Jill nodded and mumbled agreement before lifting her mug for another sip.

Wanting to get at least some kind of response out of Jill, Callie tried a new subject. "I stopped at Lyssa's on the way to the detention center yesterday, to see how her landscape project was going."

Delia brightened. "I didn't know about that. What is she getting done?"

"A lot of tidying up, with old, overgrown shrubs removed. That's what's happening now, and it's already made a big difference. Then there'll be new plants put in—perennials and low-maintenance things." Callie turned to Jill. "The landscaper, by the way, is from Portis. Gavin Holder. Perhaps you knew him?"

Jill's still-droopy eyes shot open, but she instantly looked down again. "Holder? I don't know. Sounds familiar."

"He also worked at the Portis Playhouse, doing grounds management at the time the new facility opened up."

"Then I must have run into him. He's here, now?"

"Fairly new to the area and just getting started. Turns out he was the groundskeeper for the festival."

"Oh! That's a change." Jill's face showed the first signs of genuine concern. "But it sounds like he's got a good project with your friend. I'm sorry I didn't see him."

"We could run over there if you like," Delia said, "and say hello. I wouldn't mind seeing Lyssa's yard take shape. Is she there?"

"She's in New York right now," Callie said. "But I'm sure she'd be glad to have more people checking on it for her."

"No." Jill shook her head impatiently. "I have too much to do. Calls to make. I can't waste the time." She got up and plopped her mug in the sink. "I'm getting dressed."

As they heard her rush up the stairs, Callie looked at Delia, who seemed just as surprised by Jill's outburst but said nothing. After a moment she took the seat Jill had vacated. "More coffee?" she asked weakly.

Callie shook her head. "Delia," she began carefully, "do you have any concerns about Jill?"

Delia sighed. "She's had problems. Things haven't been easy for her."

"I know you've been trying to help her, and that's wonderful of you. But you didn't know about her past relationship with Bobby Linville. Does it worry you that she didn't tell you?"

"She had good reason not to. It was a time in her life she didn't want to revisit. I have to respect that, Callie. I don't need to know everything about everyone." Delia fiddled with the salt and pepper shakers at the edge of the table, realigning them, then brushed a few crumbs together.

Callie broke the silence. "I agree about a person's right to privacy. But there's a point when honesty is needed. Required."

Delia looked up. "Yes, I know. We're getting there, I think. It's just something I prefer to take gently."

Callie nodded. She'd leave it there for now. "I'd better get started lining up repairs for my damage," she said, getting up. "I'll make the calls from Aunt Mel's landline, to save my cell until I can charge it again." She thanked Delia for the unexpected but highly appreciated coffee and breakfast.

As she left, she glanced back at Delia gradually closing the door. She couldn't say at this point if her friend was right to give Jill such leeway. But since she had no concrete evidence to argue otherwise, she had to trust—and hope—that things would work out for her.

Twenty-Eight

When Callie saw Brian heading toward the café's front door later, she waved and hurried over.

"I guess you haven't heard about last night," she said.

"I just got here from Annie's," he said, his keys in hand. "What happened?"

"For one thing, the café probably has no power." Callie told about her fire and its far-reaching effect. "We don't know how long it will be until it's restored. I hope your food will be okay."

Brian smiled and shook his head. "I should be fine. With the possibility of a hurricane always looming, I couldn't afford not to have a generator. What about you? How about we bring those frozen meals from your freezer over here."

"My dinners! I forgot about them! Do you have the space?"

"Plenty. Mondays are when I stock up. Let me get the generator going, then I'll come over and help carry your stuff."

Callie went back to her cottage and pulled out her laundry basket. When she heard the generator chugging and saw the café's lights go on she got to work, filling the basket with Brian's frozen casseroles. He showed up within minutes with a cardboard box, but Callie showed him the damage from the fire first. That brought a low whistle.

"You were lucky it didn't spread farther than that."

"Believe me, I realize that. Whoever did it might not have expected the loud boom it caused on the street pole. That's what woke me up."

"Or they knew exactly what they were doing and planned this limited damage."

"As a warning to me? I thought of that too. It's a pain and a major hassle, and it'll slow me down. But it's not going to stop me. It only makes me more determined."

Brian nodded. "Which is what I expected. Your arsonist obviously doesn't know you as well as I do."

Callie smiled, glad he wasn't urging her to drop her investigation to be safe. "Well, that puts you in the clear then, I guess!"

Brian grinned. "That, plus the fact that I'm terrible at building fires. Really struggled over that badge in Boy Scouts. Let's take care of your food before it thaws."

They went inside and transferred an unopened carton of milk and several perishables from the refrigerator to the cardboard box. "Come over to the café for any meals until things get fixed," he said, spurring a grateful smile from Callie.

She told him about Delia's early morning breakfast run as they carried their loads across the street, then shared her thoughts about Jill while they emptied it all into the café freezer and refrigerator.

"Oh, and Lyle Moody wanted me to tell you something. He came into the shop yesterday after you'd already gone." Callie related what Lyle said about Earl Smith.

"Hmm. That makes me just a little curious. I think I'd like to know a little more about Smith. Feel like a little pub food tonight?"

"You mean at Dave's Pub? Sure."

"I'll pick you up at seven. With luck we'll run into Smith. If not, Dave might have more to tell us about this man or how to get in touch with him."

Callie left Brian to his work of getting things ready for Sunday lunch. The shops at their end of Keepsake Cove would be dark and therefore draw fewer people that direction, but Brian didn't seem too worried about losing customers. "People will still be hungry. They know where I am."

Callie had already decided to open her shop for the afternoon and at least try to accommodate any customers that wandered her way. She'd scrounged around and found a small battery-powered lamp of Aunt Mel's to put in the window as a sign that she was open for business, plus the lamp could be carried to darker corners as needed. She'd have to handle credit card sales manually but it was doable, as were cash sales, of course, and orders. Her next plan was to make a sign to put out on the sidewalk, perhaps a sandwich board if she could manage it.

With those many thoughts running through her mind, Callie was ready to cross the street when she glanced to her left. Howard Graham stood outside his *Christmas Collectibles* shop, two doors down, talking with Pearl Poepelman. He appeared agitated, and Callie guessed he'd just learned of the power outage. She was reasonably sure that Pearl had been told what had happened by Delia and had subsequently related it to Howard; Callie felt no need to add to the explanation, especially knowing how badly Howard tended to take any bump in the road that affected his business.

She saw him turn in her direction. She waved quickly and then trotted over to *House of Melody* before he could call out, hoping he wouldn't follow. She wasn't to blame for the fire that led to the outages, but she also wasn't in the mood for even the slightest hint that she could have done something to prevent it and thus save Howard his latest tribulation. Once she was inside, she peered out her window and saw Pearl edging Howard into his shop.

"Thank you, Pearl," she murmured. "If you could manage to lock him in, all the better."

As expected, Callie had few customers during the early part of the afternoon. When she grew hungry, she had little hesitation about locking up temporarily to run over to the café for a take-out lunch. She checked the power company's website on her phone while she waited at Brian's counter.

"Looks like they still have plenty of work to do on the windstorm outages," she said as Brian brought over her bagged sandwich and drink. "Nobody's likely to show up here for a while."

"If I have to keep the generator going overnight, I've got enough gas," Brian said. "It'll be noisy though."

"A small price to pay for access to food and electricity. My phone's power is running low," she said, pulling out her charger. "May I leave it here?"

"Of course. At no—ha!—extra charge." Brian glanced out his window. "Looks like you might have a customer."

"Wouldn't you know. Just when I take a little break." Callie grabbed her bag and hurried out, hailing the woman who was peering into the shop and welcomed her in after unlocking the door. She ended up making a sale—small, but at least a sale. And her customer promised to let others know that Callie's shop and several others were open at the darkened end of Keepsake Cove.

"I just came from *Forever Dolls*," her customer continued, referring to Krystal Cobb's shop. "The woman in there didn't say anything about power being out over here, and I almost turned around when I saw how closed up all the stores looked. Maybe she didn't know or hasn't heard? She seemed a little out of it, frankly. Half asleep."

"Really? The owner?"

"I guess that's who it was." The woman described Krystal to a T. "Must have had a late night."

"Possibly," Callie agreed. But doing what? Could Krystal have been her arsonist? Callie couldn't picture the perpetually well-dressed and polished association president slinking about in the middle of the night to set fires, but she made a mental note of the information and stored it away.

❦

Brian picked her up at seven for their pub date, the top down on his classic red convertible.

"Is that okay?" he asked as Callie climbed in. "The weather's great, but Dave's is a few miles out of town. It might get a little windy as we pick up speed."

Callie laughed. "I haven't been able to do a thing with my hair besides tie it back ever since the power went out. Wind won't make it any worse."

"It looks fine," he assured her, though she remembered with a smile that Brian had never noticed the few times she'd thought her hair looked particularly good after a trip to the salon. But she appreciated the effort.

"How was Ben's baseball game?" she asked. With all their discussion of the arson, she'd forgotten to ask before.

"His team lost, eighteen to ten." Brian laughed ruefully. "Eight- and nine-year-olds aren't that great at fielding. Ben seemed a little off. I did explain to him why the van was in front of his house in the middle of the night, and he seemed to get it, but I think the scare is hanging on. Annie hoped the game would take his mind off of it, but it looked like it was the other way around. He didn't seem able to focus."

"That's a shame."

"How did things go at the detention center?" Brian asked.

"Fairly depressing. I wish Hank could remember where he went and got drunk that night after chewing Bobby out. Confirmation of his alibi could solve his problem in a jiffy."

"And yours," Brian added.

Callie sighed. "Yes, and mine." She turned to him. "And to some degree yours, too, for having to listen to all this. I know it must be a pain, but I am grateful for your support."

Brian turned to smile at her and reached over to give her hand a squeeze. Callie appreciated it, but knew that Brian would be just as happy as she would be to wave a final goodbye to Hank. As he left to rejoin his band, that is, not left in a police van on his way to prison.

Twenty-Nine

Callie didn't know exactly what to expect as they drove to Dave's Pub. The plain, no-nonsense name indicated a male-oriented, no-frills kind of place that would appeal to guys like Lyle Moody and Gavin Holder, who both ran their own businesses but were down-to-earth types (Gavin literally so). But it also had drawn Earl Smith, who Lyle had described as unreliable and barely scraping by but who somehow managed to scrounge up enough money to pay for pub beers. What could Dave's Pub offer to such a range of patrons?

She discovered as they walked in. A horseshoe-shaped bar dominated the area, with a few booths placed against pine-paneled walls. Mounted animal heads decorated those walls, along with several framed, outdoorsy photos. A pool table and a jukebox filled the remaining space in the back. The aroma of beer saturated the air, but also the scent of fried onions and burgers. Vegetarians would need to search elsewhere, Callie suspected.

"How 'do, folks," the burly man behind the bar greeted them, the rolled sleeves of his white, button-down shirt exposing the edges of dark tattoos. "Food, drinks, or both?"

"Both," Brian said, glancing at Callie, who nodded.

They chose to sit at the bar as the best location for conversation, both exchanged and overheard. The bartender, whom they quickly learned from other patrons' banter to be Dave, slid two laminated menus over to them, then crossed to the other side to take care of a customer who'd signaled for a refill with his raised glass.

The menu was surprisingly varied and leaned heavily toward deep fat fried. Callie chose a shrimp platter while Brian went for the Chesapeake burger that promised a crab meat topping on its grilled ground beef. Both added a tap beer to their orders, which their bartender pulled immediately. He lingered after setting down the glasses. "Folks new to the area?"

"Keepsake Cove," Callie said. "But I've been there a year."

"Oh yeah? Where'd you move from?"

Callie said West Virginia, skipping the many other parts of the country she'd lived in after leaving Oregon.

"My brother lives in West Virginia!" Dave went on to name the town, Berkley Springs, which Callie said she'd been to and liked. That brought on a lively listing of the pros and cons of the area, and by the time a stone-faced waitress delivered their food, Callie felt that she and Brian had become Dave's new best friends. At least for the day.

As they dug into their dinners, Dave tended to a few other customers. When he wandered back, Brian brought up Earl Smith's name. "Is he here, by any chance? I'd like to talk to him."

"Earl?" Dave glanced around, shaking his head. "He might show up later. You looking to hire him for something? He does a little bit of everything, you know."

"That so?" Brian asked.

"Yup. Works crew as a waterman, off and on. Does plenty of odd jobs."

"Do you know how I can reach him?" Brian asked.

Dave rubbed his bristly chin, then turned to a man sitting across the way. "Joe! Got a number for Earl? This fellow wants to talk to him."

"A number? Uh-uh." The leathery-faced man lifted his ball cap briefly to scratch his head. "He hangs around the Kentmorr Marina a lot. You might find him there."

Dave turned back to Brian. "Know where that is?" When Brian nodded, he added, "He's probably looking to pick up jobs there. It must work, 'cause he's in here most every night for a beer or two. Just your luck tonight isn't one of them. At least so far."

Callie was disappointed for Brian, though she was enjoying her dinner as well as the casually friendly atmosphere. She understood its appeal to Lyle and Gavin and all the others. Despite its décor and the ratio of its current patrons, it wasn't strictly a male gathering place. She spotted a few women chatting in the booths.

She was nibbling one end of a French fry when Gavin Holder walked in and sat several seats away at the bar. When he spotted her, he didn't look all that happy about it. He nodded but then turned away, making it clear he wanted to be left alone.

Callie wasn't surprised to see Gavin, but she blinked when, a little while later, Duane stepped through the door. She wasn't sure why, except that the pub—even with its wide-ranging appeal—didn't seem like Duane's kind of place. She leaned back to be less noticeable, hoping Brian blocked any view of her as he held his burger to his face. She watched curiously. Duane glanced around and stopped at the sight of Gavin.

"Holder," he said, acknowledging him pleasantly. Gavin tilted his glass at Duane in response. Neither showed any interest in further conversation, and Duane continued on to an empty booth.

"That's surprising," Callie murmured to Brian.

"Hmm? What?"

"Duane Fletcher just came in. He went to sit by himself in the booth over there." She gestured subtly toward it.

"Why is that surprising?" Brain asked, looking toward the booth, where all that was visible of Duane was a sliver of his left side.

"Well, first because this place doesn't seem quite his style. Then he goes and sits by himself in a booth instead of at the bar. He's a talker. Gavin Holder would be the one I'd expect to want privacy. But Gavin's sitting up front."

"Maybe Duane's just here for the food. It's pretty good. And he might want some time off. Even garrulous types get tired."

Dave came by and asked if they wanted another beer. Both declined, and Brian asked for the check. They were waiting for it when a new patron came through the door, on the thin side and wearing denims that had seen better days along with a faded ball cap. He grinned at one man who turned and greeted him with a straight-faced "hey!" and then exchanged a couple of halfhearted high fives before slipping onto a stool.

Dave had his back turned, so the new arrival called out, "Hey, Dave, how about some service here!" He rapped on the bar jokingly.

"Keep your shirt on," Dave answered, handing Brian his bill before turning. "Hey, Earl! Wondered when you'd come by. Guy here's been looking for you." He jerked his thumb toward Brian.

"Yeah?" Earl's face lit up. He scrambled off his stool and came over to Brian and Callie. "What can I do for ya?" As he drew closer, Callie caught a strong fish odor. She also noticed at least one tooth missing in his eager smile.

"Earl Smith?" Brian asked. "How about we take a booth. Can I get you a beer?"

"Sure, sure, thanks!"

Dave heard and started reaching for one of the cheaper brands, apparently the man's usual. Earl asked instead for a draft Coors. He carried it to the empty booth Brian and Callie had moved to, two away from Duane, who was now giving his order to the waitress.

Earl slipped in, his fishy aroma intensifying in the closer quarters. "So what can I do for you?" he asked again, before taking a swallow of his beer and wiping his mouth.

"It's not a job," Brian clarified, to Earl's obvious disappointment. "I wanted to ask you about the night this week you called for a tow truck. Wednesday, or actually very early Thursday morning, around two a.m."

"That tow's paid up," Earl quickly said. "I have the receipt."

He started reaching into his pocket for proof, but Brian stopped him. "That's not why I'm here. What I need to know is if there was a particular reason your van ended up where it did. It was in front of my sister's house."

"Huh? Oh, heck, no. It just happened. Engine belt broke, that's all. Sorry if I woke her up."

"Belt broke?" Brian grimaced. "Bummer."

"Yup. Here I am, out in the middle of nowhere, and my dash lights start dimming, then the power steering goes."

"That's what happens with a belt problem." Brian nodded. "Temperature gauge probably shot up, too, right?"

"You'd better believe it." Earl's head bobbed up and down as Callie watched the bonding take place.

"So it was just by chance that you stopped where you did?" Brian asked.

"That's it. Just rolled to a stop. Couldn't do a thing about it."

"Lucky you had a friend come by. I mean, before the tow truck showed up."

"A friend?"

"Right. The guy who helped unload your van?"

Earl looked confused. Or was it nervousness? Whichever it was, instead of commenting, he dove into his beer for a long swallow. The stone-faced waitress appeared at their booth at that moment to ask if she could get them anything. Brian shook his head, waiting for Earl to respond. When he finally set down his glass and wiped the foam off his lips, he pulled up a gap-toothed grin.

"I don't know," he said. "Maybe you folks are thinking of someone else. Nobody was unloading my van. Nothing to unload." He grinned and bobbed his head. "Wish there was. I could use the job. Sure you don't have anything you want hauled?"

"Not at the moment. But something might come up. Is there a way to reach you if it does?" Brian pulled out his phone and entered the number Earl gave him. "Any limits on what you'll carry? Or distance?"

"Nah, I'll take anything you want, go anywhere, too. You pay, I'll play." He snorted and bobbed some more.

"Well, great," Brian said. "And if you need to reach me for any reason, I run the Keepsake Café."

"Oh, yeah, over in the Cove, right? I know someone from there."

"Lyle Moody?" Callie asked.

"Moody?" Earl looked puzzled again, but then he nodded. "Yeah. He comes in here."

A dark figure suddenly loomed. Gavin Holder nodded briskly as the three of them looked up, then said, "Smith. I need help cutting down a tree tomorrow. You up for it?"

"Yeah! Sure." Earl scrambled out of the booth, taking his beer with him, and moved off without further comment, presumably to get Gavin's details.

Brian glanced at Callie wryly and shrugged. "Well, I guess that's it."

Callie grimaced. "At least we enjoyed a good dinner."

They went back to the bar, where Brian settled his bill and added Earl's beer to the tab. Callie caught Dave before he turned away.

"Do you recognize this man? He might have been in here a week ago Saturday." She held up the cell phone photo of Hank that she'd given Tabitha. "It would have been late in the evening, and he might have had too much to drink."

Dave took the phone and studied the photo but eventually shook his head. "Sorry, no. Friend of yours?" When Callie nodded, he said, "Then I hope you find him."

Callie thanked him, and she and Brian took off. It had been a long shot, since Hank had described driving farther away than this pub. But she'd had to try.

Thirty

So excited about your visit! Callie read the email from her mom with mixed feelings. It included the details of her flight reservation for Friday evening.

Friday evening! It was coming up too soon. Leaving in four days meant leaving Hank behind bars and might effectively end her efforts to get him released.

Still, she had four days left to work on getting Hank out. She had to look at it that way. And if her electricity wasn't restored, there was less reason to open her shop, which gave her more free hours. Callie laughed ruefully at herself. That was positive thinking carried to the extreme and a denial of the problems the loss of business would cause for her, such as trouble paying her bills.

But since it was Monday and all shops in Keepsake Cove were closed anyway, even those that hadn't lost power, she could brush that concern aside and make the best of her free time. Doing exactly what, Callie hadn't yet figured out. So she began by crossing over to Brian's café for breakfast, which his chugging generator promised to make available.

Several other shopkeepers were already seated in the café, their own cottages affected by the outage just like hers. They greeted her as she walked in. Callie glanced around for Howard Graham and was relieved not to see him, then remembered he lived outside of the Cove. She received smiles and a few friendly words from several shop owners, with no one blaming her for their inconveniences, which, logically, they shouldn't. Howard, of course, didn't always slow down for logic.

Brian was bustling with the larger-than-usual crowd but still managed to whip up a plate of bacon and eggs for her within minutes. She was impressed but didn't dare speak to him beyond the minimum, not wanting to throw off his rhythm. It was as she nibbled at her last piece of toast that Lyssa surprised her by walking in.

"Wow! Full house," Lyssa said, slipping onto the stool next to Callie at the counter. "I thought it'd be quieter on a Monday."

"You're back!" Callie gave her friend a hug. She complimented her on the two TV appearances she'd watched, then explained the reason for the crowd at the café—the power outage—and told her about the fire that caused the outage.

Lyssa's jaw dropped. "Somebody tried to burn your house down?"

"Well, maybe, maybe not." The people who'd been sitting on either side of them at the counter had left, and the noise level in the café was high enough to cover her words, so Callie felt comfortable saying more. "It was definitely arson, but the fire was set under my electric meter. The boom from the transformer woke me up, along with half the neighborhood, in time for me to put the fire out. The intention might have been to cause enough trouble to keep me from asking questions."

"But what if that fire had really taken off?"

Callie shook her head. "It didn't. I'll need a new meter and breaker, which is a pain, plus repairs on the siding. Nothing worse."

Lyssa looked at Callie as though amazed at her calm attitude. Callie might have been amazed herself, except she had too many other things to think about.

After Brian stopped long enough to take Lyssa's order, they chatted a while about the author's experiences in New York racing from one TV interview to the next. "Of course, I use 'racing' metaphorically. Those midtown taxis move slower than turtles in mud. By the last interview, I'd gone into auto-mode. If you look carefully, you'll see the glazed look in my eyes. I couldn't relax my perma-grin until I was halfway home. But my editor says they've seen an uptick in book sales, so I guess I wasn't too bad."

Callie assured her she'd been terrific. She told Lyssa about stopping by her house and the talk she'd had with Gavin. "When I pressed him about Jill, he told me about her apparent suicide attempt after Bobby crushed her hopes and plans so drastically. But Gavin only revealed this to stop what he considered to be my badgering of Jill. He's very protective of her. He tried to conceal it, but there was love in his eyes and in his voice when he spoke of her."

"Aha. And what does she think of that?"

"She barely acknowledged knowing him when I mentioned him over breakfast yesterday morning, and she got angry when Delia suggested dropping by your place to see his work." Callie then explained about Jill's claim of having slept through the entire fire event.

"From an over-the-counter sleeping pill? I suppose she could have been highly susceptible to it, but..." Lyssa shook her head skeptically.

Brian brought Lyssa's order of French toast and coffee and refilled a few coffee cups at the counter and tables before disappearing again into the kitchen. Callie let her friend enjoy her breakfast a while and sipped at her own coffee. Then she mentioned the stop at Dave's Pub the previous night and Brian's less-than-productive talk with Earl Smith.

"What was he looking for?" Lyssa reached for her steaming mug.

"He wanted to get a better understanding of the situation. His nephew's overactive imagination has been giving him a hard time since that night. Smith didn't strike us as particularly scary, but he seemed evasive. And we're pretty sure he lied about no second person showing up. Brian doesn't think Ben was dreaming about that."

"It was the middle of the night," Lyssa pointed out.

"Yes, but Ben didn't dream up Earl Smith and his van. A neighbor confirmed that part, as did Earl. Brian trusts that Ben saw everything he claimed to, including the man with the SUV. Unfortunately we didn't get the chance to press Smith on it. Gavin came over to hire him to help cut down one of your trees."

"What! I don't want that!" Lyssa realized she was screeching when several heads turned their way. "Sorry, folks. I just learned my landscaper wants to cut one of my trees. I love my trees." She scrambled through her purse for her cell phone. "I'd better get hold of him before it's too late."

"It's okay," a voice piped up from a corner table. Rhonda Furman stood up to get Lyssa's attention. "It's one of Krystal's trees that Gavin's cutting down. The top cracked and was kind of hanging. She was afraid it would fall on her fence. He should be done by noontime."

"Oh, thank heavens. Thanks, Rhonda." Lyssa put her phone away. "Crisis averted," she said to Callie, smiling.

With more people looking their way and unabashedly listening by that point, they ended their discussion of Smith and any others. Lyssa finished the rest of her breakfast, then asked to see the fire damage.

After a quick goodbye to Brian and waves to his remaining patrons, they walked over to Callie's cottage.

"Hoo-eee!" Lyssa cried, looking at the curled and melted siding. "That's scary. I don't know that I would have handled it as well as you did."

"You'd be surprised at how fast your adrenaline kicks in when you need it."

"You're back!" Delia's voice startled them, coming from the rear door of *Shake It Up!* They turned to see her heading into Callie's yard, Jill lagged behind. "It was so exciting to see you on TV, Lyssa! You looked so poised and calm. I would have been a basket case!"

"All pretense," Lyssa claimed. "Inside I was a mess." She tipped her head toward Callie. "She's the one with nerves of steel, handling the fire as she did."

"I agree. That was pretty amazing. Is there any structural damage?" Delia asked.

Callie shook her head. "The firefighters said no, just to the siding. I need to get that fixed before I can get the meter and my breaker replaced. I'll probably be without power a lot longer than everyone else." She grimaced.

"You're very welcome to come to my place for whatever you need," Delia said.

"Mine, too," Lyssa said.

Callie was grateful for the offers, which would help mightily with her personal needs. But neither of her friends could help her run her music box store without electricity.

Lyssa looked toward Jill, who hung several steps back. "How's the job search coming?" she asked.

"Still looking," Jill said, crossing her arms. Callie noted the dark shadows under her eyes and the fact that she seemed to be looking everywhere except at the damaged area of her cottage. An uncomfortable silence followed.

Delia clapped her hands together briskly. "Well! We just came back to get a few items for the laundromat that we forgot. Better get going before somebody unloads our washers for us!"

The two women left, Jill wordlessly and Delia calling out good wishes for Callie's repairs over her shoulder.

"That woman looks guilty as hell," Lyssa muttered as soon as they were out of earshot.

"Maybe. But definitely miserable. Poor Delia."

"I hope she's sleeping with one eye open."

Callie looked at Lyssa, startled. "Surely Delia isn't in danger. She's been nothing but wonderful to Jill. If—and I think it's still a big if—if Jill is guilty of murdering Bobby Linville, it would be because of his bad treatment of her. She'd have no reason to turn on Delia."

"She would if she thought Delia had figured it out and planned to turn her in."

Before Callie had two moments to think about that, Lyssa pulled out her phone and calmly tapped at it. "Any idea where Krystal lives? I think we should head over there, don't you?"

Thirty-One

*L*yssa found Krystal's address on the internet, clucking at the same time that nothing was private anymore. She and Callie were heading toward her red Corvette, which she'd parked a short distance from the café, when Callie noticed Duane walking in their direction. He spotted her at the same time and hailed her as he picked up speed. She had no choice but to wait.

"Hey!" he said brightly as he approached, then said to Lyssa, "Heard you were on TV. I sure wish I'd caught it."

Lyssa smiled politely and pooh-poohed the idea that he'd missed anything important. "You heading to the café?" she asked. "Half the town seems to be gathering there because of their power being out."

"No outage at my place, thank goodness. Except of food!" He chortled, then said to Callie, "I saw you and Brian at Dave's Pub last night. Just as you were leaving, though, so it was too late to catch you. My bad luck."

"Oh, were you there?" Callie blinked innocently. "I guess we missed you. The place was pretty crowded. Do you go there much? I'd never been."

"Oh, off and on, for a change of pace. The food there is pretty decent. But their clientele can get a little rowdy, so I generally take a booth at the back."

"It seemed fine last night. Gavin Holder was at the bar. He's a fairly quiet guy."

"Oh, yeah. Gavin. Saw him."

"And we'll be seeing Gavin very soon, I hope," Lyssa said, pulling open her car door as a broad hint. "He's my landscaper. I need to make sure we're on the same page."

"He's working at your place now?"

"Not at the moment." Lyssa slipped behind her wheel and Callie opened the passenger door. "But we'll track him down." She turned on her ignition as Callie climbed in and buckled up, then waved and drove off, her sports car motor purring. Duane stood where he was on the sidewalk, watching them go.

"Lordy," Lyssa said, looking in her rear-view mirror. "He looks as though we abandoned him. What did he expect? That we'd spend the rest of the morning chatting with him?"

"Maybe he wanted to pump you about how to get booked on TV. He's a schmoozer. Except for last night at the pub, but maybe because it was the end of the day. As Brian said, even talkers can run down. Mornings, he's probably raring to go."

Callie was curious to see Krystal's house. Like all Keepsake Cove shop owners, Krystal had a cottage built behind her store, but some felt that the houses were too small for their needs. What requirements did Krystal, who lived alone, have that had made her decide to pass on the convenience of the cottage for the added expense of living in a different house?

When Lyssa pulled up to Krystal's address after a fifteen-minute drive, Callie saw a pretty Cape Cod set behind an expansive green lawn. The driveway curved gracefully toward a bricked walkway, which in turn led to a cozy front porch. That alone explained the woman's decision to Callie, who would have loved a front porch like that to sit on. She recognized Gavin Holder's van parked in front of the garage.

"They're probably all in the back," Lyssa said, cutting off her engine. "Might as well head right over."

When they rounded the corner of the house, a bright blue pool sparkled into view.

"Wow!" Lyssa said, taking it in. "Nice."

The broken tree in question had already been cut down, and Gavin and Earl Smith were busy slicing it into manageable pieces. The endangered fence that Rhonda Furman had mentioned was apparently what enclosed the pool and its patio. An umbrella-topped table and four chairs sat at its edge.

As they stood watching the two men work, Krystal's voice called out a surprised good morning, pulling their attention to the shadows of a screen porch. The association president pushed open a squeaky-hinged door and stepped out. She was dressed impeccably, even on a day off, in cream-colored slacks and a white linen shirt. Callie and Lyssa went over to meet her.

"Sorry for barging in," Lyssa said. "I heard Gavin was here, and I wanted to talk with him. Thanks for the recommendation, by the way. He's been doing a good job over at my place."

"I thought he would. And you're not barging at all," Krystal said. "I'm delighted to see you both. Do join me for a cool drink. I have plenty on hand ready for the men as soon as they take a break." She ignored their polite protests and led the way back into her screened porch, to a table with a full view of the yard.

"I'm truly delighted with the company," Krystal claimed as she poured glasses of lemonade from a large pitcher. "Watching the tree come down was exciting. But the rest of it has become rather boring."

"Your pool is beautiful." Callie took the glass held out to her.

Krystal smiled. "The water hasn't warmed up enough to use. But once it is, I look forward all day to swimming laps. It's relaxing, but at the same time it wears me out enough to get a decent sleep."

"Working all day in your shop isn't enough?" Lyssa asked. "That would wear me out."

Krystal shook her head. "When you reach my age, your brain doesn't want to turn off. Mine seems to search for unfinished business the minute I turn in."

"I hate to think about what mine will find, what with all those crazy scenes I've written into my books." Lyssa cackled. "Oh, the guys are taking a break. How about I take their drinks out? That'll give me a chance to talk to Gavin."

Krystal didn't argue, and Lyssa was soon out the door carrying two frosty glasses of lemonade to the men. Callie suspected Earl would prefer a cold beer, but if so, he was out of luck.

After watching for a minute, Krystal invited Callie inside. "I want to show you my new kitchen. Oh, but you've never seen the old one, have you? Terrible of me! I should have had you over ages ago."

Callie followed her into a bright kitchen, where Krystal talked about the many decisions she'd made on countertops, floor, and wall colors, something Callie had never gotten into herself. Her past living quarters had all been rented and temporary, and her current one had come so beautifully done by her aunt that she hadn't wanted to change a thing.

Krystal's living room faced the front yard, its large windows letting in plenty of light. It was also beautifully decorated but looked seldom used, one of those rooms that the owner only passed through. The same with the dining room. Callie wondered where Krystal spent most of her time. She'd mentioned swimming laps, and of course the screen porch was cozy, but both required warm weather. Where did she unwind when it was colder? Or darker?

Krystal's phone rang and she excused herself to answer it, stepping away from Callie, who, after a few moments, decided to wander. A short hallway brought her to a cozy den. The door was open, so she could see a well-worn chair and hassock, which she thought answered her question. There was also a glass-fronted cabinet. Inside were several dolls, which at first wasn't surprising, since Krystal owned a collectible dolls shop. But a closer look showed that these weren't the type she would carry in her shop. Callie recognized ones similar to those she'd had years ago, popular and ordinary. They looked well played with. Had they belonged to Krystal's daughter, Tiffany?

She heard Krystal's voice a bit nearer, apparently wrapping up her conversation. Callie went back to the kitchen.

"Sorry about that." Krystal pocketed her phone. "Something always comes up to do with the association."

"A problem?"

"No, just another shopkeeper who doesn't come to meetings and therefore is never up-to-date on things. Wanted to know when we were going to reimburse booth-holders for the festival day we lost." She sighed.

"Why would they call you and not Duane?"

"Duane's apparently not answering his phone." Krystal pursed her mouth in annoyance. "Just as he wasn't when I tried to call him at the festival about Bobby Linville's demand for more money."

"Lyssa and I met him on his way to the café, so he must turn his phone off when he doesn't want to be disturbed. Actually, he told me that when you were trying to reach him that Saturday night at the festival, he was on his way to buy a painting. He apparently decided he was off duty as the association treasurer."

Krystal snorted softly, still looking annoyed. "Another painting. He must have a storage facility somewhere full of them!"

"Why do you say that?"

"Because I don't think I've ever seen the same picture twice at his house. He obviously can't resist buying them, but then runs out of room. Why he doesn't just buy a bigger house is beyond me." Then she laughed. "Maybe he can't afford it after buying all those paintings! Well, to each his own. We're all a town of collectors, after all."

"Yes, we are. I haven't actually started collecting music boxes for myself, but I'll always keep my grandfather's music box because of the special memories attached to it. I imagine you do that, too."

Krystal's eyes softened for a moment, and Callie wondered if she was thinking of the dolls she kept in her den and of the daughter who'd probably owned them. But then the woman's mouth tightened and a flash of hot anger ran over her face. As quickly as it had appeared, it vanished. Krystal smiled tightly. "We should probably get back outside. Gavin Holder might be waiting to be paid. Oh, and that bumbling helper of his. The next time Holder does a job for me, he's going to have to bring someone who doesn't just yammer on and on when he should be working."

She clicked briskly across the tiled floor of her kitchen and pushed open her back door, not looking back to see if Callie was following.

Thirty-Two

On the way back to Keepsake Cove, Callie told Lyssa about the dolls she'd seen, and about Krystal's surprising flash of rage.

"Rage?"

"That's what I have to call it, though it only lasted an instant. We were talking about collections and memories. At first she seemed to have pulled up fond ones, then that changed quickly."

"She lost a daughter, as we know. The memory of that would be full of sadness. So the anger associated with it—"

"—would be aimed at whoever she might blame for the daughter's death."

"Which we'd like to think is Bobby Linville. Remind me. Do we have a connection between Bobby and the daughter?" Lyssa slowed for a sharp curve.

"They attended the same college at the same time. A small one."

"So they could have known each other."

"Seems possible. Then Tiffany died a few years later while driving under the influence."

"And Bobby also had a drinking problem," Lyssa said.

"Yes."

"I think we have a connection. He could have drawn her into an alcohol problem with him, which later caused her death."

"Just speculative," Callie pointed out.

"But"—Lyssa paused to negotiate a sharp curve—"there's too much there to be simply coincidental. If a relationship with him didn't actually lead to her death, couldn't Krystal at least have blamed him for it? He disappears, then shows up after all these years at the Keepsake Cove festival. He and Krystal meet face to face, and within hours he's dead. Coincidence? I don't believe it."

"But remember that Rhonda Furman, who's known Krystal for years, didn't connect Bobby to Tiffany. Only to selling herself a lemon of a car."

"If she's Krystal's good friend, she might be protecting her."

"True. But it's still speculative. There's nothing we can take to the police yet."

Lyssa had to reluctantly agree with that and was silent as she drove into Keepsake Cove and down its quiet main street. At least half of the area would be open and lively on Tuesday, or maybe the whole street if the power company was able to restore electricity to the rest of the properties. That is, except for Callie's house, which needed much more repair work. She groaned silently, then quickly shook it off. It was a problem, but there was a worse problem on hand to solve—the murder of Bobby Linville.

"Mind if I drop you off across the street?" Lyssa asked, pulling up in front of the café. "I'm going to head straight on to pick up a few groceries."

"That's fine." Callie unbuckled and climbed out, promising to call if more things came up. She was standing at the curb, waiting as Lyssa drove off, when she heard the café door open behind her.

"Nice car, isn't it?"

Callie turned to see Duane. "It is."

"Did she find Holder okay?"

"Yes," Callie answered, taking a step off the curb.

"Where was he?"

Callie sighed and stepped back. "At Krystal Cobb's. She needed a tree cut down."

"A tree! Wow. That's a big job. Hope it's going okay."

"He was nearly done when we got there. By the way, while we were there, Krystal had to field a call for you from an association member. Have you turned your phone back on?"

Duane patted his shirt pocket confidently. "Back in action. I hate being bothered during a meal."

"Or whenever you take yourself off duty, like when you left the festival that night."

"Then, too," he agreed cheerfully. "You know, I was thinking about what you said about Krystal not being able to reach me then. I realized later that I actually didn't have any missed calls from her that night. So I don't know what that was all about."

"Really? No missed calls?"

"I guess she could have misdialed," Duane said. "Sometimes I do that. Click on the wrong contact by mistake. It happens. Oh, by the way, I meant to tell you this earlier. Last night at the pub, sometime after you left, I happened to hear this guy—one of the regulars—talking about Delia's friend. The photographer?"

"Jill? What about her?"

"Well, he was a little drunk, so I don't know how much credence to give to it, but I got the impression he was at the festival and had his eye on her. Thought she was, in his words, pretty hot."

"He had his eye on her? Who was this?" Callie thought immediately of Gavin Holder, but it didn't sound like him.

"Just someone who tends to ramble on a lot after a couple of beers. A scruffy kind of guy. I've seen him there a lot. Name's Earl something."

"Earl Smith?"

"That's probably it. Anyway, if you see her, you might give her a heads-up. I don't know if he's any real trouble, like a stalker or anything, but she might want to keep an eye out."

"I'll let her know. Did he say he actually knew her?"

Duane shook his head. "Not that I heard."

Callie pictured Gavin Holder sitting at the bar and couldn't imagine he would put up with hearing that kind of talk about Jill. She asked Duane if Holder was there when this happened.

Duane shook his head. "I don't really remember. Hey, maybe it's a big nothing. But I thought I'd pass it on. Forewarned is forearmed and all that, right? Well, gotta go. Things to do."

Duane walked off, and Callie stepped back into the street to finally cross, but with more things on her mind than she'd had at the start.

Instead of returning to her own cottage, she went to Delia's. She found her in the yard, where she'd brought her parakeet out in his Victorian cage for a little sun. Delia was dead-heading her daffodils and looked up as Callie approached. Callie asked if Jill was around.

"She's probably in the shower. Want to come in and wait?"

"No, thanks. Would you tell her something?" Callie shared Duane's tale about Earl Smith. "I don't know if it's anything to be concerned about, though Duane thought it might be. Would you let me know if Jill knows this guy or not?"

"Sure. He sounds creepy."

"Maybe. He's shown up on the radar lately in some odd circumstances." She told Delia about the van breaking down in front of Brian's sister's house. "I'm still not sure what to make of him."

Delia looked concerned. Then her face suddenly lit up. "Oh! I think the electric company truck is here!"

Callie turned and saw flashing yellow lights coming from the street. "Great!" she said. "Looks like you'll have your power back soon. I'm going to check on when my siding people will be here. Then maybe I'll get back in business before too long too."

"Oh, I hope so. But don't forget you're always welcome to whatever you need at my place. Oh, to be able to cook again!" Delia said, clapping her hands together in joyful anticipation.

Oh, to be able to blow-dry and curl my hair, watch something on TV, and most importantly, run House of Melody properly again. Callie left Delia to her own joys and returned to her unlit cottage, which was likely to remain so for a discouragingly long time.

Thirty-Three

Callie fixed herself a peanut butter sandwich in her dim kitchen by the light of the cottage's small windows. She could have gone to the café for something more substantial, but she wanted a little down-time to think things over, time she wouldn't get if the café was bustling.

What did it mean if Earl Smith had been watching Jill at the festival? Anything or nothing? Had she been right to let Jill know about it?

Callie began to wonder about this. Earl didn't strike her as a dangerous man, more as someone living on the edge while scrounging up low-paying, temporary jobs. But she couldn't claim to know the man well. One thing she did know was that if he was hanging around the festival that day, she wanted to learn what else he might have seen. Brian had Earl's contact number. She'd get it from him and go from there.

Then there was the surprising statement of Duane's that he'd found no missed calls from Krystal on his phone the night of the murder. What did that mean? Was one of them lying, and if so, which one? Or was there a simple explanation related to the pitfalls of using a cell phone?

As she mulled that over, Callie became aware of a change. The ongoing chugging of Brian's generator had stopped. She knew what that must mean and stepped outside to confirm it. A small cheer came from the direction of the café, and Callie saw light shining through both Karl Eggers's and Delia's cottage windows. Nothing, of course, from her own. But her phone signaled a text that informed her that the siding people were on their way to check out her damage.

She gave a small cheer of her own at that news. Progress! With the siding fixed, she'd be able to get her meter replaced. At least on that front, things were looking up.

❧

The man in the gray uniform looked down dourly at the corner of Callie's cottage. *Hawkins Siding* was emblazoned in yellow across his back and on his truck, which had arrived three hours after his text. Since *Hawkins Siding* was an Eastern Shore company, Callie wondered about their GPS system and where it had routed him, or if "on our way" was code for "we're thinking about it."

"Gonna have to special order this," he said.

"Special order? Why?"

"That color red. It's not your everyday red." He opened up the thick catalogue he'd brought with him and flipped through it, stopping at Callie's particular type of siding. Red, for that siding, apparently came in three standard shades. The one Aunt Mel had chosen was not one of them.

Callie remembered her first sight of the cottage as her aunt led her out the back of *House of Melody*. The little house, with its beautiful red siding set off by a sage green door and a white, rose-covered trellis, had looked like something out of a fairy tale. Aunt Mel had picked everything for her home with an eye to what she most loved, and it had worked. Except for now, when Callie needed to match part of it.

She sighed. "How long will it take?"

"Depends."

Callie hated that word.

He gave her a long explanation, which she tried her best to follow and which ultimately came down to he'd have to get back to her. He left, and Callie considered trying another siding company but opted to wait on his call first. It was, after all, the company Aunt Mel had dealt with, and therefore seemed most likely to come up with what Callie needed. She only hoped she wouldn't be waiting three hours or more for the promised information.

Realizing she was rapidly running out of clean clothes, Callie thought she should make a run to the laundromat, as Delia and Jill had done earlier. Both Lyssa and Delia had offered their facilities for her use while her electricity was off, but she'd take them up on that when things got a little more dire—which she hoped would be never. With everyone else in Keepsake Cove back to normal, the laundromat would likely be available, so she gathered up her clothes and drove there.

Inside, Callie loaded two washers—one for light-colored, one for dark—and sat down to wait. She pulled out her phone to call Brian.

"Hi! Are you enjoying your lights?" she asked as he picked up.

"I am. I assume you're not?"

"No. I'm sitting at the laundromat watching my clothes churn."

"You could have brought them here."

"Thanks. Maybe next time. I called to get Earl Smith's number."

"Hmm. Should I be jealous?"

Callie grinned. "Only if you want to be." She told him about Earl's apparent interest in Jill at the festival. "I want to ask him about that."

"Good idea." He paused to find the number, then read it off to her.

"Thanks. I don't suppose you'd want to take a trip to Dave's Pub tonight if it comes to that?"

"I can't, sorry. After I put away the generator, I have to make a supply run. Everything to do with the café got off schedule with that outage."

"I know. Maybe I can handle it all over the phone. We'll see."

Callie let him get back to work and tucked away her phone. As she stared at the chugging washers, a woman who'd been quietly doing the same from a few blue-plastic seats down said, "You're Callie Reed, aren't you?"

Callie turned in surprise toward the woman, who was wearing jeans and an orange tee that set off her mocha-colored complexion. "I am. I'm so sorry. Have we met?"

The slim woman, who looked to be in her late thirties, laughed. "No, but we should have, a long time ago. My fault. You were pointed out to me at an association meeting but I never made it over to say hello." She slid closer and held out her hand. "Kendra Hollins. I have a collectible doll houses and furniture shop."

Callie shook her hand. "Hi, Kendra. I've been in the Cove a year and thought I'd caught up with everyone but apparently not. Your shop sounds really cute. Where are you located?"

Kendra described an area near both Duane's *Glorious Glass* and Krystal's *Forever Dolls*. "Mine is *Marvelous Miniatures*."

Callie smiled. "Then too bad you weren't named Mavis, or, um, Minnie."

"I know! If my folks had only had the foresight." Kendra grinned, then turned serious. "Your aunt lucked out with her name, Melodie, having a music box shop. I've only been at the Cove a few months, so I didn't know her. But I've heard she was a lovely woman."

"She was. I'm trying my best to carry on her tradition." Callie swallowed the lump that still rose in her throat at the mention of Aunt Mel. "Your part of the Cove didn't lose power. What are you doing at a laundromat?"

Kendra grimaced. "Broken washer."

"Oooh. Bummer."

"I know. Maybe it can be fixed. We'll see. Getting a new one wasn't exactly in my budget. But what can you do, you know?"

Callie nodded.

"I couldn't help overhearing your conversation a minute ago." Kendra gestured to how small the seating area was. "You mentioned Earl Smith. Skinny guy, kinda down at the heels?"

"That's him. Do you know him?"

"No, but I remember him hanging around the festival. I had a booth across from the photographer, Jill."

"Did he strike you as particularly interested in her?"

Kendra shook her head. "I wouldn't say so, but then I was busy a lot of the time. He just seemed to be trying to drum up work by going around to all the vendors. He asked me if I needed help moving my merchandise back to the shop after the festival, but I told him I was okay. He left his name and number with me in case I changed my mind." Kendra took a quick look at her washers, which had shifted into the spin cycle. "The grounds person didn't like Earl hanging around. He hustled him away from our area more than once."

"The grounds person? Gavin Holder?"

213

"I guess. I don't know his name." Kendra described Gavin perfectly. "Maybe he'd been asked to handle some kind of security as well? I got that impression."

Asked to do security, or took it upon himself to do it? "How did Earl react?"

"He didn't like it, but he moved on. Though he showed up again later. I thought it was a bit uncalled for, myself, chasing him off like that. But maybe I missed something."

Gavin had enlisted Earl's help in cutting down Krystal's tree, so apparently there was no lasting problem between them. Of course, Jill wouldn't have been at Krystal's at that time, if Earl's interest in Jill was what had bothered the landscaper at the festival.

"Ah, time to switch." Kendra got up to move her things from the washers to a dryer. When she finished, she turned back to Callie. "Hey, it's been great talking with you, but I've got to run to the drug store. Maybe I'll catch you when I get back."

She took off, leaving Callie with thoughts that churned about as much as her two loads of sudsy clothes.

Thirty-Four

The next morning Callie knocked at Delia's door, fresh clothes and a towel in hand. She'd tried to reach Earl the night before without success. She vowed to try again later.

"Hi!" Delia cried when she opened the door. "Water tank finally out of warm water?"

"Yup. I don't care for showers quite that refreshing. Is it okay if I run my hair dryer too?" Callie asked as she came in, noticing that Jill wasn't up yet.

"Sure. That shouldn't disturb Jill."

"Still taking the sleep aid?"

"I think so, though she said she's cut the pills in half." Delia shrugged. "Want your eggs scrambled or fried after you're done?"

"Thanks, but neither." Callie wasn't about to impose more than she already was. "I'm going to run over to the café for breakfast. There's a couple of things I need to check with Brian."

"But at least have some orange juice. You should have something in your stomach."

To take a shower? Callie smiled, knowing Delia needed to fuss, and accepted the glass, sipping at it on her way upstairs. It was delicious and probably freshly squeezed. Jill was very fortunate to be looked after by a friend like Delia. And the thanks she appeared to give was minimal. Callie made a mental note to find a special gift for Delia as her own thank you. Maybe in Oregon, which she had to fly to in three days. The reminder that she was leaving soon was worrisome, and she banished it soon with a stream of luxuriously hot water. First things first.

She was sitting at Brian's counter, scraping up the last of his fluffy pancakes, and had just reached for her mug of coffee when Lyle Moody walked in.

"You folks hear the news?" he asked the room at large.

Callie, Brian, and the four customers seated at various tables all turned, the grim look on Moody's face warning them it was not going to be good.

"A drowning," he said. "Over at the Kentmorr Marina." He paused. "It was Earl Smith."

Callie's jaw dropped as gasps sounded from the others. She didn't know if they all knew the man, but a sudden death, relatively close by, was always alarming.

"How did it happen?" Brian asked.

Lyle shook his head. "They're investigating. Nobody saw it happen. A marina worker discovered his body early this morning. Might have been accidental, but we won't know for sure for a while." Lyle shook his head. "Damned shame. He was just talking about landing a good-paying job. For all I know he might have celebrated a little too much and lost his balance near the water."

"What was the job?" Callie asked. "Something to do at the marina?"

"He never said, exactly. But I got the impression it involved his van 'cause he said he'd be getting it fixed up right and proper first off so there'd be no more breakdowns. I don't know. Maybe he just meant he'd finally have the money to do that."

"Poor guy," a lone, heavyset man at one of the tables said. "Finally getting a break, then this happens."

Lyle nodded. "Well, I'll be on my way. Just wanted to let you know."

Callie rubbed at her arms, shaken. She turned to Brian. "We just spoke to him Saturday night."

Brian leaned closer. "Right," he said quietly, "and I thought at the time that he was holding back on us."

"About there not being any other car there before the tow truck arrived."

"Uh-huh. Ben is still sure of what he saw. I'd love to know who was wearing a sweatshirt that night with the number five reflected on it."

Had she ever seen a shirt like that? Callie searched her memory for times she'd been with Gavin, Jill, and Krystal, then moved on to anyone at all in Keepsake Cove, even her new acquaintance Kendra Hollins. Had a number five shirt possibly been spinning in one of the washers?

Finding this effort ridiculous, she gave up. As more people arrived at the café and the news was shared and discussed, there was little chance to talk privately anymore with Brian. She took off to open up *House of Melody* with its single, battery-powered lamp, and to mull over the latest death and what it might mean.

When Tabitha arrived for her shift, her puzzlement over the dim shop reminded Callie that her assistant had been out of the loop since last working there on Saturday afternoon. Callie updated her on everything, but particularly the fire. Tabitha's shocked reaction matched Lyssa's of two days ago.

"I had no idea," she said.

Callie pictured her busily working on her beaded jewelry most of the weekend. "I should have called to let you know."

"No way! You had enough to deal with. Mind if I run out back to take a look?"

"Go right ahead."

Callie watched Tabitha hurry out, aware that as distressed as Tabitha was over the problem, there was a certain amount of excitement there too, just as rubberneckers react to a highway accident with an adrenaline rush along with genuine sympathy. For that reason, Callie was glad her damage was in back and out of public view. Though, as she considered it, something to see at the front of her shop might have drawn more customers than she'd had so far.

Tabitha commented on just that when she returned. "We need to have a better way to let people know you're open. That cardboard sign you have out front? I'm sorry, but it's pitiful."

"What?" Callie cried in mock-indignation before ruefully agreeing. "I know. It was the best I could do on short notice."

"I think I can perk things up. Okay if I make a run to the craft shop?"

"Please do." Callie pulled out her credit card and handed it over. "Just please don't break my bank," she added with a smile, though she'd seen Tabitha put together her amazingly creative outfits for pennies and wasn't worried.

Left alone and tired of wandering about her dim shop, Callie soon stepped outside, thinking a visible presence might be some improvement to her sad homemade sign. Since she'd never managed to install the small bench in front of her window that she'd long had in mind, she strolled, occasionally extending her path in front of Delia's shop. That caught her neighbor's eye, and Delia soon came out to join her.

"Lovely day," Delia said, lifting her face to the sun.

"It is." Callie decided not to bring up Earl Smith's drowning right then. Instead, after small talk of a more pleasant kind, she simply asked if Delia had ever seen anyone wear a sweatshirt with a prominent number five on it. "Like a football jersey," she said. "The five would have been reflective."

Delia frowned in concentration. "I don't think so. Does it have something to do with Bobby Linville's death?"

Did it? Callie shook her head. "For now it's just an unanswered question. Would you let me know if something comes to you?"

"Of course."

Their attention was drawn to two women who began crossing the street, heading directly for *Shake It Up!* As they reached the sidewalk, Delia welcomed them, adding that Callie's *House of Melody* was open as well despite having temporary lighting problems.

"Oh, I thought it was closed!" one of the customers said. She quickly veered toward Callie's shop, telling her friend she'd rejoin her in a few minutes.

As Callie followed the woman into her shop, she thanked Delia with a smile. By the time Tabitha returned from the craft store with an armful of supplies, Callie had sold a very nice music box to the pleased customer.

She gave Tabitha free rein in the back office to work on her project, which turned out to be a vast improvement over her own with its large, brightly colored lettering and much more visible sandwich board arrangement.

"Perfect!" Callie cried. They set it up outside and stood admiring it for some time, after which Callie said she'd leave the shop with Tabitha for a bit. She explained about the sweatshirt with the number five that she hoped to track down. "You don't happen to have seen one like that around, lately, have you?"

"It's not that noticeable," Tabitha pointed out. "Unless the person wearing it was doing something really unusual—like, oh, holding up a convenience store?—I don't think it would stick in my head."

"I know. It stuck in Ben's head, though, and Earl Smith denied the existence of the person Ben saw wearing that shirt. Now Earl is dead. Why, I don't know. Did it have anything to do with his van breaking down in front of Annie's house? Another thing I don't know. But if I can somehow identify the person wearing that shirt, it might help us find out."

"Good luck." Tabitha went back into the music box shop as Callie struck out on her possibly hopeless quest.

One shopkeeper after another shook their head at her question about the sweatshirt. All commiserated with her on her ongoing lack of electricity, but none could say with any conviction that they'd ever seen that particular kind of shirt. Kendra Hollins was delighted to see Callie again after their laundromat meeting, but she couldn't help out either.

"But I'll be glad to ask around for you," she said.

"That'd be great," Callie said, checking the time. "I didn't talk to everyone at this end of the Cove, and it's getting late, so I better go back to relieve my shop assistant. Love your shop, by the way!"

Kendra beamed, obviously proud of her unique collection of doll houses and their furnishings, and with good reason. If Callie had had more time, she would have enjoyed looking through many of them—Victorian, modern, Barbie doll houses, and even one that resembled her own cottage, minus the damaged siding, of course.

She took off, hurrying past shops busy with customers, returning to her own, empty except for Tabitha.

"I did have one sale," Tabitha said, striving to be upbeat. "And one guy said he'd be back ... sometime." She grabbed her purse. "Don't worry. It'll get better."

Callie appreciated the thought, only wishing there could be a time-line attached.

The rest of the afternoon saw one more small sale, and she laughed ruefully over the fact that at least she hadn't wasted any electricity by staying open. She locked up, then trotted over to the café where Brian promised to have one of her frozen casseroles warmed up and ready to eat.

"I'm sorry to just hand it over like this," he said. "But I have to leave for the airport soon to pick up Mike."

"This is fine," Callie assured him, taking the hot, towel-wrapped dish from him. "So Mike's coming home, huh?"

"Annie and the boys are excited. It was touch and go for a while if he'd make it back in time. There's some sort of school project that has Justin going in with Mike to his office tomorrow, and they were both looking forward to it."

Callie was sure that Brian was looking forward to sleeping in his own bed once again, though he had been more than happy to help his sister out.

"Say hi to Mike for me." She carried her dinner to the cottage, set up the battery-powered light, fed her eager cat, and sat down to feed herself.

It was after she'd cleaned up the best she could with her limited resources and sat down to relax that the cottage's landline rang.

"Callie Reed?" a hushed-sounding voice on the other end asked.

"Yes. Who is this?"

"Doesn't matter. But I can tell you what Earl was up to."

Thirty-Five

Callie sat up straight at the words that came through the phone. "Who is this?" she demanded again.

"Earl was my pal. He didn't deserve what happened to him. Someone's gotta know."

The voice was male, Callie was pretty sure. But with the raspy sound of it that was all she could say.

"Okay," she said. "Tell me."

"No, I have stuff that'll prove it. I'll give it to you."

"Stuff? What do you mean *stuff*, and why not give it to the police?"

"Uh-uh. No cops. I figure you can do that."

"Why me? And how did you get this number?"

"Look, I know you two've been askin' around. Earl had your boyfriend's number. But he's not answerin'. So it's gotta be you. You're not so hard to find."

She wasn't. But she wasn't about to meet up with anyone who said he couldn't talk to police, and she said so.

"Yeah, okay, I get it. But we can meet at Dave's. They know me there. They can tell you me and Earl go way back. I'm doing this for him. Sticking my neck out! But I can't hold on to this stuff. Just let me give it to you. His and that other guy's murder, that's bad stuff!"

"Other guy's? Do you mean Bobby Linville?"

"Yeah! Earl got sucked into the same crap. Look, I gotta go. I'll be at Dave's in half an hour. Ask for Earl's pal Jimmy. You gotta do this!"

The line went dead. Callie thought hard. Should she go? This person claimed that Earl Smith had been murdered and promised some sort of evidence that might also help Hank. Could she believe him? Then again, did it matter? She could meet him in a safe place, so why not?

Her first wish was to go with Brian, but he'd left for the airport and wouldn't be back in time. What about Lyssa? Callie picked up her phone. The call to Lyssa's cell phone went to voicemail. She left a message about her hurry-up trip to the pub, then tried Lyssa's landline. That call wasn't picked up either.

What should she do? She was losing time just thinking about it. "Jimmy" might not be willing to wait around. Callie chewed at her lip for several moments, then grabbed her keys. This could be the break that she—and Hank—needed. She couldn't let it slip by.

As she drove out of Keepsake Cove, Callie tried to keep her hopes realistic. She'd met Earl and could see he wasn't the brightest bulb, to put it mildly. She shouldn't expect his pal Jimmy to be either. Whatever he had to tell or give her might be a waste of her time. But there was always the chance he might have something to at least point her in a good direction. She held on to that idea.

She'd set her GPS to guide her to Dave's Pub, since she hadn't paid close attention when Brian drove them there. She was glad she did, since part of Dave's neon sign wasn't working and she nearly passed _ave_s _ ub despite the robotic voice claiming she'd reached her destination.

The parking lot was crowded. A sign in the window proclaiming Tuesday night to be *Ladies Night, 1/2 Price Beer!* was likely the reason. After searching, she squeezed into a spot at the side of the building, butting up against thick shrubs. She locked her car and headed to the front entrance, following two couples already on their way in.

The pub was as crowded as she'd expected by this time of night, with standing room only around the bar. How to connect with "Jimmy" might be a problem. Callie slowly worked her way to the bar to order a small ginger ale from Dave, then leaned in closely to be heard above the din. "Is Earl's friend Jimmy here?" she asked.

"Jimmy? Which one?" Dave asked. "Miller? Saunders? Green?"

Callie's heart sank. "I don't know. He said he and Earl went way back."

Dave glanced around but clearly didn't have more than two seconds to spare. He shook his head. "Sorry." He went off to serve another customer.

Callie picked up her soft drink and started to wander. Hopefully, Jimmy could identify her. She'd made it to the pub within half an hour. The rest was now up to him.

Wandering through a busy pub and checking male faces, she quickly found, was not the best course of action for a woman on her own.

"Hey there, pretty lady, buy you a drink?" was something she began to hear often. Her best course of action was to repeat, "Meeting someone" and keep moving, not the easiest thing to do in the crowded space. Where was Jimmy?

Fifteen minutes went by. She'd just turned away one of the more persistent men when she bumped into someone. Turning to apologize, she was surprised to see Duane Fletcher. He looked equally taken aback.

"Hey! Nice to see you again." He glanced around. "Brian here too?"

"No, he couldn't make it." Callie wasn't thrilled to run into Duane, but since he seemed to be at least a semi-regular at the pub, she hoped he might be able to help her. "I'm trying to find a man named Jimmy. He was a friend of Earl Smith. Would you happen to know who that is and if he's here?"

"Jimmy?" Duane rubbed his chin. "Yeah, I think I know who you mean." He craned his neck to search through the crowd. After several seconds he cried, "Aha! There he is. Near the back." He pointed.

Callie looked. "Which one?"

Duane stepped to the side to give her a better view. "The one in the black T-shirt, with longish hair. See him?"

Someone stepped in front of her, briefly blocking her view. When he moved, Callie stretched her neck, searching for the person Duane had described. "The one with the goatee?"

"Right! Want me to go with you?"

Callie got his point. Jimmy didn't exactly look like someone you'd want to run into in a dark alley. But this was a crowded pub. And they needed to talk privately.

"No thanks. I'll be fine." Someone bumped her elbow, which splashed a bit of her ginger ale over her hand.

"Want me to hold that for you until you come back?"

Callie shook her head. She had no desire to return. Instead she took a long drink, to avoid more spills, and began working her way through the crowd, keeping her eye on Jimmy as well as she could.

Why hadn't he been trying to find her? As she drew closer, she was frustrated to see him moving farther away. She followed, then stopped when she realized he'd gone into the men's room. There was nothing she could do except wait nearby—and fend off more "buy you a drink?" offers.

Jimmy took a long time, and Callie sipped her ginger ale as she waited, growing more and more annoyed. When he finally reappeared, she hurried over.

"Jimmy?"

The black-shirted man kept on walking.

"Jimmy!" Callie repeated more loudly.

He looked over. "Talkin' to me?"

"Aren't you Jimmy?"

He shook his head. Then a smirk appeared. "But I could be, if you want me to."

He stepped closer, but Callie quickly turned away. "Never mind, sorry." She kept on moving. *Thanks, Duane,* she silently cursed. *Thanks a bunch!*

What to do? Had Jimmy not turned up after all? Or was he having as much trouble finding her as she was with him? She checked the time. Over half an hour had passed. The noise and the crowd was getting to her. The room was much too hot. She felt tired. Exhausted, actually. She should go. This had been a total waste of time.

She struggled to wind her way again through the crowd. It seemed a lot harder than before. Too many people bumped into her. Or was she bumping into them?

"Hey, there!" somebody cried as she stumbled, nearly dropping her glass. She apologized, confused.

"Here, let me take that from you."

Callie turned to her right. It was Duane. He took the glass and set it on the bar.

"Are you okay?" he asked.

"I'm ..." She couldn't seem to find the word.

"Come on," he said, taking her arm. "You need to get some fresh air."

She let him walk her out the door. The cool air felt good. "My car..." She pointed vaguely to the side of the building.

"I'll drive," Duane said, turning her firmly in another direction.

She climbed into his SUV, needing help. When she fumbled with the seat belt, he leaned over to do it.

Then everything went black.

Thirty-Six

Callie woke up in the dark. But where? She was lying on her side on something. Cardboard? Her hands were bound behind her! And her feet! What was going on?

She tried to pull herself up. Bending her knees gave her some leverage, but when she lifted her head, the rush of dizziness stopped her. How did she get here?

She remembered being at the pub and walking outside with Duane, and ... That's where her memory stopped. Had Duane done this to her?

As if in answer, a wide door began sliding upward, letting light into her enclosure, which seemed to be some kind of a shed. The light came from a car's headlights, angled slightly but with a glare that made her blink. After a moment, she was able to perceive a figure outlined in the doorframe, a figure whose rounded shape she instantly recognized. Duane Fletcher stepped forward.

"Good. You're awake." He held a roll of duct tape and a box cutter. Callie eyed the box cutter nervously. "I couldn't gag you right away," he explained as he ripped loose several inches of the tape. "You might have died on your own vomit. Died too soon, that is. I need to keep you alive a little longer." He sliced off a section of tape.

"Why, Duane?"

"Why do you have to die? Because, my dear, you were getting much too close. If you'd just minded your own business you wouldn't be in this predicament." He paused and tsked to himself. "Partly my fault, of course, for hiring that band. That name, Linville, didn't click soon enough. And then your old boyfriend gets blamed for his murder, which would have been just fine with me except it got you all worked up and snooping around. That's your fault, and now you're paying for it. Sorry, sweetie."

He leaned down and, despite Callie's efforts to turn away, quickly slapped the strip of duct tape over her mouth. "Can't have you calling for help, can we? Somebody might actually hear, though the chances of that are pretty slim." Duane straightened up. "Uncomfortable, I know. But it won't be for too long. Try to think of it that way." He chuckled.

Callie struggled to lift her head in order to see Duane's face. Could he really be doing this? How had she missed seeing the monster that he was?

"Don't bother," he advised. "Waste of energy." He paused, appearing to think. "It'll be a few more hours, but I'll be back. Got to get that kid, Ben."

At Callie's horrified squeal, he added, as though it were obvious, "He saw me! Oh, I already destroyed the sweatshirt, the one with the big number five on it you were running around asking everyone about. But the kid saw me from the window. I can't take a chance he'll point me out. It's all Earl's fault, you know. That stupid van of his. But I was in a pinch and had to use him. The stolen—or as I prefer to call it, *relocated*—artwork, you know." He waved one hand around the shed. "You're surrounded by some of it, by the way. Too bad you can't appreciate it. Nice stuff! Anyway, it was my mistake hiring him, I admit that. And then when he showed he couldn't be counted on to keep his mouth shut … well, that settled it."

He started to turn, then stopped. "In case you want to know—hey, it'll give you something to think about while I'm gone—Linville worked with me at one time on this, very briefly and a long time ago. His memory, unfortunately, was better than mine, and when he showed up with the band, he saw an opportunity to get money out of me. I played along and said I'd meet him back at the festival after everyone was gone. I brought my gun instead of the cash he wanted, but then I spotted that music box sitting there. Just the right size and weight and much quieter." Duane chuckled. "Maybe that could be a good selling point for those things. Pretty, plays music, and convenient for killing someone!"

He clapped his hands together briskly. "Well, gotta go. Busy day coming up." He stepped back and pulled the door down, shutting out any light. Callie heard a lock turn, then a car door slammed shut. Within seconds the car started and drove away.

Ben! He was going to grab Ben and then kill them both! The thought was too horrible to believe. But Duane had already killed—first Bobby Linville, then Earl Smith. Who knew if there were others? He was cold-blooded about it too, removing people as they got in his way. Callie and Ben had both posed a threat to him, so now it was their turn. All to protect a scheme that made him money. Lots of it, apparently.

In the brief time the shed door was open, Callie had glimpsed some of the objects surrounding her. She'd seen brown, paper-covered rectangular shapes scattered about that were probably paintings, and large and small boxes that must hold other pieces of art. Duane's tale of Bobby Linville's involvement in his "relocation" scheme reminded her of her mother's description of Bobby's drop-in visit with Hank. His annoying appraisals of her decorative pieces sounded like he'd spent time with Duane. That inflated opinion of his own abilities must also have convinced Bobby that he could handle blackmail, and that mistake had led to his death. It had been Hank's bad luck to get caught in the middle.

If she didn't get out of there, Hank would be tried for Bobby's murder. That was bad enough, but now Duane was threatening nine-year-old Ben's life! She had to do something to stop that. But how, when she was bound hand and foot and locked inside a shed that was who-knows-where! Getting herself loose seemed impossible, and with no chance of anyone knowing where she was, rescue wasn't going to happen. There was nothing she could do to save herself and Ben!

Callie had already been plunged into darkness when Duane closed the shed door. Now a deeper darkness enveloped her, brought on by the comprehension of her helplessness. Tears flooded her eyes, and it was only the duct tape covering her mouth that kept her from sobbing.

As she struggled, in this state, she heard a faint sound coming from nearby. Inside the shed but some feet away. Callie held her breath and concentrated, gradually recognizing a unique ringtone. Her cell phone was there! Duane must have tossed her purse in with her, figuring she'd never be able to reach it. Maybe he was planning some sort of accidental-appearing death and wanted it found with her. If she could get loose, she could call for help! She had to do it.

Callie's despair lifted as she began to think hard. What had she seen while the door was open that could help her? There were the paintings and the different-sized wooden crates. Crates sometimes had sharp edges. Could she use that?

Energized, she struggled to get herself more upright. After many leg swings and body rolls, some painful, she managed to leverage herself onto her knees. A wave of dizziness passed over but quickly cleared. Whatever Duane had slipped into her ginger ale was apparently wearing off. That helped. What next?

She was near a large wooden crate. With her ankles bound together it was difficult, but by inching her knees, she managed to align herself next to one of its edges. The next struggle was to press her wrists, bound together behind her, against the wooden edge. It required much contortion, but she eventually did it and began to scrape the duct tape on her wrists against the crate.

If her hands had been in front of her, there would have been little problem. As it was, the awkwardness of moving them up and down behind herself, with enough pressure against the wooden edge, all while maintaining her balance, brought grunts of frustration. But she kept working at it as pain shot through her shoulders and knees. What pushed her on was the thought of Ben being snatched by Duane.

How did the shop owner hope to accomplish that? Break into Annie's house in the middle of the night? Brian must have already brought Mike home from the airport, and she couldn't see Duane risking a break-in.

It would have to be when Ben was out of the house. Perhaps on his way to school? But surely Justin would be with him at their bus stop, which would make it too difficult. Then she remembered with horror that Justin was going to Mike's office the next day instead of school. That meant Ben would be at the bus stop by himself and vulnerable!

How much time did she have before Duane could act? Callie had no idea how long she'd been locked in the shed, though there were no slivers of daylight showing around the edges of the door. But did that mean it was still nighttime, or simply that the door fit tightly? Either way, time was running out, which meant she had to keep working to get loose.

She felt the tape tear. Not totally through, but a beginning. The edges of her hands above and below the tape had grown raw and might have been bleeding. But she couldn't stop. Her shoulders and knees ached but she kept on. She'd made some progress, and she could make more. Callie dragged her wrists over the wood edge over and over, feeling the tape tear, bit by bit. Finally it broke apart.

Thirty-Seven

Callie jubilantly pulled her newly freed hands in front of her, then reached for the duct tape over her mouth and peeled it away. She threw her head back and gulped in air, fully expanding her lungs for the first time in hours, then bent down to search for an edge on the tape that bound her ankles. When she found it, it didn't take long to free her feet. If she'd been up to it, she would have danced a jig. As it was, she simply flexed her stiff ankles and rubbed at them, basking in relief and joy.

The shed was still pitch dark, so when she stood, she edged forward carefully, hoping she was heading in the direction of the door. When her feet bumped up against a box, she felt her way around it until she could continue moving. Eventually, she came to a wall.

Callie ran her hands over the surface, inching first left, then right until she discovered what must be the thermostat. Excited, she slid her fingers further and came to what felt like a light switch. She clicked it, flooding the shed and her eyes with light, which required several seconds of rapid blinking to adjust to. When her vision cleared, she checked out her prison.

It was large, approximately fifteen by twenty feet, with a concrete floor and cinder-block walls. Wooden boxes and variously sized wrapped paintings covered about half the area. Callie guessed that items didn't stay there for long but were stored temporarily until buyers were ready for them. Where it all came from, she couldn't imagine. But the operation was definitely lucrative enough for Duane to commit murder to protect it.

She thought of his claim that he'd been off buying a painting at the time of Bobby's murder and felt gullible for having believed it. She'd gone along with the emailed confirmation from the supposed buyer, not thinking about how easy it was to fake an email! How she wished she'd pushed harder and demanded an address and phone number to speak to the person. But she hadn't been suspicious enough at the time, plus Duane had already prevented her from making that move with his fictitious seller's claim to be leaving soon on a trip.

Callie's gaze landed on her purse, lying on the floor where Duane had tossed it, containing the phone she'd heard ring during her darkest hour. She lurched forward, snatched it up, and pulled out her phone, praying it was still charged. It was! But when she checked for bars, there were none. She ran back to the door to hold the phone against it, hoping to bring up a bar that would allow her to make a 911 call. None appeared.

How could that be? She knew she'd heard the phone ring earlier. What had changed? Some mysterious shift in the atmosphere? Whatever the reason, her phone was useless. Frustrated, she grabbed the door's handle and yanked up with all her strength. It wouldn't budge. She'd expected that, but it still made her scream. Then she pounded and kicked until her fists were sore.

What good had it done to work herself free of her bindings only to remain trapped in this concrete cell, waiting helplessly for Duane to return with Ben and kill them both! Callie pounded and shouted for help until her throat grew sore and her fists were raw. She slid to the floor, leaning against the door, certain that she hadn't been heard and that she was only exhausting herself.

Duane's advice had been, "Save your energy." Though he'd meant it as "Don't bother," she realized it was what she needed to do. That, and to come up with Plan B. She'd made it this far. She could do more.

Callie began searching through the shed. She was excited to find that several of the wooden boxes weren't nailed shut, possibly to allow for quick removal or rearrangement of the contents. One by one, she opened what she could, looking for what she needed, pulling out and testing several items until she was satisfied. Then she sat down and waited.

❧

Light had begun to leak around the edges of the door. What time did the sun rise? Six? When would Ben be at his bus stop? Callie wasn't sure. Seven thirty? Later? If that was when Duane planned to grab him, she still didn't know how long it would take for them to get to the shed. It could be another half hour. That might mean two hours more to wait. But she needed to be alert. For all she knew, Duane might have other plans and could show up at any time. She only prayed that he wouldn't hurt Ben before they arrived.

She got up to stretch her muscles, then paced as much as the area allowed. Fatigue hovered from the remnants of whatever drug she'd been slipped, followed by her struggles to break free over sleepless hours, but the adrenaline that coursed through her did its best to counteract this. What worried Callie most was how quickly she'd be able to act when the time came. But she had a major element on her side: surprise. At least, she hoped she did.

Her pacing took her regularly back to the shed's door, where she always pressed her ear to listen. Over and over, she heard nothing beyond the faint chirping of birds as it grew lighter. She switched off the shed's light, now that the slivers of daylight coming in plus her memory of the shed's layout made movement through it possible. Finally, she heard what she'd been waiting for: the sound of a car's motor and tires crunching on gravel.

She flattened herself against the wall at the side of the rolling door. The car came closer, then stopped. She waited. It seemed forever until finally she heard a car door open and close, then footsteps approach. Another excruciatingly long pause. Was he searching for keys? Checking something outside? Callie had a moment of panic. Surely there wasn't another entrance, was there? Wouldn't she have seen it? Just when she was ready to move and hide behind a large box, the door began to rise. She braced herself.

She couldn't wait too long. Duane would expect to see her lying where he'd left her. How high was too high? She saw his shoes, then his shins. When she saw at least two inches above his knees, she swung the heavy metal sculpture of a woman, holding it by the head and shoulders so that the solid base connected with a knee.

As Duane screeched and stumbled back, Callie rolled under the door and struck again, this time at the other knee. This took him down as she scrambled to her feet.

"Bitch!" he cried, rolling to one side and clutching a leg.

She struck a third time, something so totally against her nature that she could barely believe she was able to do it. But Ben's life was at stake. She hit Duane's shoulder, then his head, twice. He went limp.

Callie paused, breathing hard. Had she knocked him out? Worse? All she'd needed to do was to incapacitate him. But at this point, she didn't care if she'd done more. He didn't move.

Callie spotted his keys on the ground and snatched them up. Not car keys. He must have left them in the ignition. Duane still hadn't moved, so she turned, realizing as she did so that the car wasn't his SUV but her own Chevy Malibu. Dropping the sculpture, she jerked the driver's side door open and saw Ben lying across the back seat, gagged and tied, but his eyes—thank God!—were open. He made a muffled squeal when he saw her.

"Hang on, Ben," she cried. "We're getting out of here." She had one foot inside the car when her head was jerked back.

"Not so fast," Duane snarled, one fist holding her hair as the other arm wrapped around her neck.

Callie kicked back hard and the two of them fell to the ground. Duane lost his grip on her but grabbed at her shirt as she tried to scramble up. She fell back but spun around to punch hard at his face. He rolled them both over, trying to get the upper hand, but they were on an incline and momentum continued their roll, ending with Callie pressed against a tree. She couldn't move as his weight held her down.

"Now you've done it," he cried, panting. "I was going to make it easier, but—"

The wail of a siren stopped him. As they listened, it grew louder.

"You called the cops? Bitch! I should have got rid of you last night!"

Duane clambered to his feet, but Callie grabbed an ankle and held on. He lost his balance and fell to his already painful knee, crying out. He kicked back at her. But the siren was deafening by then, as a flashing red light wound up the gravel driveway. Duane kicked again, this time connecting hard enough that her grip loosened, and scrambled away. But by the time he reached Callie's car it was too late. The squad car had screeched to a stop behind it. Two officers jumped out, guns drawn, shouting, "Face down on the ground! Now!"

Callie exhaled. It was over.

Thirty-Eight

Callie sat at the edge of the emergency room bed. She'd been examined, had her scrapes attended to, and was pronounced good to go. Lyssa stood beside her.

"You'll come to my house, of course."

"Of course?"

"Well, yeah." Lyssa rolled her eyes. "Like, I have electricity, for one thing. And a hot shower. And food. Besides all that, no way should you be alone. Not for a while, anyway."

Callie smiled tiredly. Everything on Lyssa's list sounded pretty good. "What about the shop?"

"Tabitha's got it covered."

"Okay then. Just for the night. But first you have to tell me how you got the police to Duane's shed."

Lyssa sank into the chair. It was going to be a long story, Callie guessed. But before it began, there was a knock at the door. A very familiar voice asked, "Callie?"

"Brian!" Callie responded. "Come on in."

Brian made it to her in two giant steps. He wrapped his arms around her, then stepped back worriedly. "You okay?"

"I'm okay." She pulled him back for a longer hug.

"Hey, I'll be right outside," Lyssa said, getting up.

"No, stay," Callie said, letting Brian go and explaining, "Lyssa was going to tell me about the police. But first, how is Ben?" She'd last seen the nine-year-old being carried out of the ambulance that took them both to the hospital. With all the medical people bustling around, she hadn't had much chance to talk to him.

"I just left him. Annie and Mike are with him, and Justin too, of course. He's okay. Shaken, but no physical harm. They'll be setting up counseling."

"And Annie and Mike?"

"A flood of emotions to work through, but mostly relief that Ben's unhurt. At least they didn't have to go through fear and panic. The first they knew he hadn't made it to school was when the police called to say they had him and he was fine."

"How did Duane manage to get him?" Lyssa asked.

"Duane was careful to dress in his shopkeeper's clothes, not in sweats like he wore that night in front of the house," Brian explained. "It was a risk, but since Ben hadn't really gotten a clear look at him that night, it worked. Then Duane gave him a story about the bus breaking down and Annie asking him to pick Ben up. He claimed he'd be picking up more kids at the next bus stop. Ben's young enough that he never questioned it. Nor did he recognize Callie's car, which he's barely seen. Before he knew it, he was tied up in the back seat and probably scared out of his wits."

"Poor kid."

"So, how did the police know where to find me?" Callie asked Lyssa again.

"Okay, first of all, I picked up your voicemail a few minutes after you left it." Lyssa grimaced. "I was in the middle of working out a plot twist when you called. If only I'd answered right away!"

"You couldn't know," Callie said.

"But as soon as I heard your message, I figured no problem, I could catch up with you at that pub. So I hopped in the car. The place was jammed! I had to push my way in, then inch around to find you. I'm not that tall, you know, so it was hard to see over heads. I did text you to let you know I was there, but the place was so noisy I guess you didn't hear."

"No, I didn't. I wish I'd checked my phone."

"Me too. Anyway, I caught a glimpse of you when you were going out the door with Duane. I tried to catch up, but a couple of idiots thought it was cute to block my way. By the time I got to the door, I saw Duane driving off with you in the passenger seat. Nothing about that looked right, especially the glimpse I got of you. So I dashed over to my car to follow. But I couldn't get out on the road in time. He'd disappeared. I tried texting again. This time I knew you should have heard it, so when you didn't answer, I went straight to the police."

"But how did you convince them she was in trouble?" Brian asked.

"Well ..." Lyssa shifted in her chair with a guilty grin. "I kind of embellished what I saw. Like, maybe I threw in a bit of a struggle, and I might have suggested a gun. Hey! I'm a fiction writer, right? But it got them moving."

"I'm glad you did! But," Callie said, "they still had to find me. That shed seemed to be in the middle of nowhere!"

"It is," Lyssa agreed. "But after they didn't find Duane at his house or shop, they did some digging and learned that he owned that property. It's several acres of wilderness, but they saw from overhead photos, I think, that there was a structure of some kind on it. They were on their way to check it out when they spotted someone turning onto the property. Duane was driving your car, which is how he'd managed to evade getting caught sooner. They had a lookout for his SUV."

"He must have gone back to the pub to get my car," Callie said. "I think he was planning to kill Ben and me in a way that looked like a car accident."

Lyssa nodded, wincing. "Anyway, once they called in the license number and realized it was your car, they took action."

"It was their siren and flashing lights that probably saved my life." Callie remembered the feeling of helplessness as Duane pinned her against the tree. Would she have been able to fight him off? The shop owner wasn't an athletic man, but he was surprisingly agile despite his injuries, and though not tall, he definitely outweighed her. Her odds hadn't been good. She shivered, and Brian put a comforting arm around her.

Just then Annie and Mike came in, full of tears and gratitude that Callie deflected to Lyssa. "She's the one that deserves the credit."

"Well, the police played a part too," Lyssa added modestly, gathering up her things.

"We're getting Ben a cell phone," Annie said, "which he's promised he'll use in the future to check anyone's claims about broken-down buses or messages from me or anything else sketchy."

"It's something he's been begging us for," Mike said. "We held off on it, believing he had no need for one at his age." He shook his head.

"Who could imagine anything like this happening around here?" Annie stroked Mike's arm. "But this phone will be very limited. No game-playing or endless texting."

Mike nodded, still looking regretful, and Callie guessed that he had been the original holdout on the cell phone question. But as Annie pointed out, who could have guessed?

"We'd better get the boys home," Mike said. He stepped forward to give both Callie and Lyssa a heartfelt hug, and Annie followed suit. They left amid promises to talk more once all had recovered.

✑

Callie spent the rest of the day and that night at Lyssa's and allowed herself to be fussed over—it wasn't to Delia's level, of course, but who could match that? She also checked in with Tabitha, but not before calling Hank with the good news, which, it turned out, his lawyer had already beaten her to.

"Yeah, Allard's here," Hank said. "He'll be taking me out of this place any minute. Hallelujah! I'm more than ready. So it was the guy who organized the festival, huh?"

Hank didn't seem to know how Duane's crimes had come to light, and Callie skipped sharing those details right then. "It was a shock to us all," she said. "But I'm so glad you're cleared."

"Yeah, me too. Hey, thanks for the support. It meant a lot." Callie heard another voice in the background. "Gotta go," Hank said. "I'll catch up with you later, soon as I can, okay?"

She was glad to hear him sound more like his old self. It had been rough … on both of them. But the worst was over. Hallelujah, indeed.

✑

As much as she enjoyed her rest time at Lyssa's—and the hot shower—the next morning Callie announced her intention to return home. "I have to fly out to Oregon tomorrow night, and there's a bunch of things to get done before that," she explained when Lyssa protested.

"You're still going?"

"I promised, and Mom's expecting me."

"Going to tell her what happened?"

"An edited version. Mom will have enough on her mind with her surgery coming up."

With nothing to pack at Lyssa's, Callie was ready to go as soon as the breakfast dishes were cleared. As they climbed into the Corvette, Lyssa said, "You know that Duane probably set that fire at your cottage, right?"

"I figured, once I learned everything else he'd been up to. He was probably expecting to throw me off track."

"Didn't know you very well, did he?" Lyssa grinned and started her engine.

"Or you," Callie added.

"Well, they can add arson to his list of crimes. It'll be the least of his worries, though the more they pile on him the better, I say."

When they reached Keepsake Cove, Lyssa detoured slightly to drive past Duane's glass collectibles shop. It was closed and dark, with no sign that its owner was currently locked up in jail. No curiosity seekers peeking in or angry graffiti on the windows. It was as if the Cove had quietly but firmly turned its back on both the shop and its owner. What would become of the shop, Callie wondered. Hopefully it would be taken over by someone who would erase all the bad memories associated with the place.

Lyssa pulled up in front of *House of Melody*, and they hugged before Callie climbed out. She headed down the side path to her cottage, feeling as though it had been months since she'd left it. Jagger apparently felt the same, as he greeted her with an agitated mix of joy and scolding. Delia had, of course, taken over his care and feeding as soon as she'd learned Callie was in the hospital. But to hear Jagger, he'd been starved and abandoned for ages.

Her neighbor had also apparently been watching for her and soon appeared at her door, full of many of the same emotions as Jagger, which included an affectionate scolding. Duane took a well-deserved hit as Delia expressed her horror and anger over everything he'd done, seeming to feel much better once she got it all out. She then moved on, saying, "I have some good news. Jill got a job."

"Wonderful! Is it something she'll be happy with?"

Delia smiled knowingly. "We'll see. But it'll allow her to be independent again, a major concern. She'll be working with a school photographer, one of those guys who takes yearbook photos."

"At least it's in her field. I'm very glad for her." Callie hesitated. "You know, I was suspicious of Jill concerning the murder. But I'm more than happy to be proven wrong."

"I knew you had your doubts about her, and though I didn't agree, I could understand why. Jill's been so angry and defensive. But a lot of that, I'm sure, was due to unhappiness with her own life." Delia smiled again, this time with a little sparkle in her eyes. "But that might be changing."

"You mean with the job?"

"I mean with a little romance. Jill and Gavin have been talking. She's starting to realize how much she's meant to him all these years. So much so that he actually relocated a few times just to be near her and make sure she was okay. She told me she's had difficulty for years believing that she was worth anyone's love. But she's starting to come around."

Callie thought that Jill's time with Delia probably played a big role in helping her turn things around. She remembered Brian's comment some days earlier about Delia being protective of her friend. At the time, she'd worried that Delia might be overly protective and naively shielding a criminal. But it was likely that Delia was just what Jill needed at a particularly low time in her life.

So it appeared things were getting back on track for the photographer; now Callie needed to do the same for herself. With that thought, she promised to check with Delia later, and bustled up the stairs to cover her scrapes and bruises and generally make herself presentable for that day's music box shoppers.

Thirty-Nine

*C*allie had barely opened her still-dim shop when a woman walked in who looked vaguely familiar, though Callie couldn't place her. That was explained when she introduced herself as Jamie Brooks, daughter of Rhonda Furman, who she resembled strongly.

"I came down yesterday for a little visit with Mom and Dad," she said.

Callie welcomed her, and they chatted a bit about the clock shop and the new baby in the family—Jamie's nephew—who Callie remembered Rhonda mentioning. Then Jamie turned serious.

"I heard about the arrest of that glass shop owner for the murders."

Callie nodded.

"You know, when Mom told me about Bobby Linville's murder, I hate to say it, but I was almost glad."

"Oh?"

"Terrible of me, I suppose, but he was an awful person. And he hurt someone I cared about very much." Jamie's expression was a mixture of anger and sadness. "Tiffany Cobb."

"Krystal's daughter."

"Uh-huh. I'm sorry about my mother misleading you."

Callie's eyebrows went up, questioning.

"Mom told me about that crazy story she made up."

"You mean about buying a car from Bobby?"

"She was trying to protect Krystal from unnecessary and hurtful questions," Jamie said. "Krystal still struggles with Tiffany's death, which wouldn't have happened if Tiffany never met Bobby. While Krystal despised the man, as we all did, she never would have acted violently against him. Mom knew that."

"What happened to Tiffany?" Callie asked softly.

Jamie sighed. She picked up a musical snow globe and rocked it back and forth, watching the gentle snowfall before putting it down. "They met at Clayton Daniel during our first year there. Bobby was a year older and seemed very man-of-the-world. He was also a big drinker, a party guy, and I blame him for drawing Tiffany into that too. Once she started drinking, she couldn't seem to stop. She got pregnant and dropped out of school. Bobby, of course, disappeared. The baby was born with major problems and didn't survive, which Tiffany blamed herself for, and she fell into a deep depression. Her folks tried their best to get her help, but nothing worked. She died a few years later in a horrible accident while driving under the influence."

"How sad."

Jamie nodded. "It was. I don't know how Krystal got through it all. But she's pretty amazing. I just wanted you to know that, and to understand why my Mom spun that tale, in case it happens to come out. That kind of thing isn't like her at all. But it came from good intentions."

Jamie picked up the snow globe again and turned the key under its base. "Let It Snow" began to play as the figures of two children skated in circles inside the glass ball. She smiled.

"This reminds me of when Tiffany and I were kids. We had such fun together, growing up. Happier memories."

She reached into her purse for a credit card, saying she wanted to buy it, but Callie stopped her. "Please. I'd like you to have it. It was good of you to come and tell me this."

Callie's heart ached for Krystal, who had endured some of the worst pain a mother could have and continued to suffer, never letting on to her new friends in Keepsake Cove. The small room in Krystal's home with the collection of what were probably Tiffany's dolls, and its single chair facing them, must have given her some comfort. But running into Bobby Linville so unexpectedly had surely brought back all the pain. And the revelations about Duane Fletcher, a man Krystal had worked with and trusted, could only have increased it.

Thankfully, Krystal had her good friend Rhonda nearby to help. Callie intended to do what she could while also respecting the older woman's privacy. If, in time, Krystal felt inclined to talk about her daughter, Callie vowed to be there to listen. And if anyone raised the slightest criticism against Krystal as association president or anything else, she would be her staunchest defender.

⚛

Callie and Brian walked through the airport after she'd checked in. Brian toted her carry-on, which she appreciated since she'd stuffed far too much in it, as she always seemed to do. She was glad he'd come in with her, despite her urging him to simply drop her off. He'd seemed to read her mind and suggested they stop for a meal before she went through security, since all she'd likely receive on the plane was crackers or peanuts. No nonstop flight to Oregon for her, unfortunately.

"Pizza? Soup and sandwich? Tacos?" he asked as they strolled.

Most of those places looked super crowded. Callie pointed out a cocktail lounge that offered food and, for the moment, at least was quieter.

"Excellent choice."

They grabbed a table and got their food, which included a glass of wine for each, which Brian added without asking, making the dinner much less of a hurry-up-and-eat event and more sit back, catch your breath, and enjoy.

Callie started to do so, and as they ate she told Brian about her siding having been unexpectedly repaired that afternoon. "Bob Hawkins managed to scrounge up enough pieces of siding in my particular color. The power company promised to come out now that it's fixed. That'll make things so much better for Tabitha while I'm gone." She started to reach for her wine glass, then stopped. Somebody had called her name.

"Callie! Hey, Callie! Wow, I can't believe this. What luck!"

She looked toward the outer walkway to see a tall man in denims, cowboy hat, and boots. *Snakeskin* boots. She sighed.

"Wow, who'd a' guessed we'd run into each other here." Hank swung his duffle over one shoulder and bumped his way toward their table.

She had thought they'd made their final goodbyes over the phone. "Hey, sorry to do it like this," Hank had said the day before. "But I got tied up a lot more than I expected, and now I have to grab a flight to catch up with the band." Callie had been perfectly fine with that and told him so, happily wishing him all the best. And now he was here.

"My flight got canceled," Hank explained, scraping a chair over to sit with them and nodding cheerfully to Brian. "Thunderstorms or something. Spent the whole night here trying to get rescheduled. Pain in the you-know-what! But, hey! It must have been meant to be 'cause now I get to see you before I go."

"What flight did you get?" Callie asked. On hearing it wasn't hers, she relaxed.

Hank sobered. "Babe, I heard about what you went through. You never said a word about it! If it wasn't for Allard, I never woulda known."

Callie shrugged. "It turned out okay. No lasting effects."

He covered her hand, ready to say more, at which point Brian popped up. "Excuse me. I'll be right back." Before Callie could say a word, he was gone.

Hank leaned in closer. "If I ever thought anything like that would happen…" He choked, clearing his throat. "Believe me, I never wanted you to be hurt in any way."

"I know, Hank. The important thing is, I'm fine, Ben is fine, and you've been cleared. This horrible mess is over, and we can get back to our own lives again."

Hank brightened at that. "Yes, we can! The band kept up with the gigs that were already scheduled, they held my spot open for me, and…" He paused dramatically. "I came up with a new song while I was in detention!"

Callie grinned. All was right with Hank's world. "I'm glad for you, Hank."

They heard a final-call flight announcement. "Hey, that's me! I gotta run!"

As he pushed his chair back, Callie stood to give him a farewell hug. "I'll be looking to hear that new song on the radio someday."

"This might be the big one!" Hank dashed off, his duffle coming close to sweeping a table or two, and Callie resumed her seat. She'd finished her wine when Brian returned and slipped back into his chair.

"Want another?" He indicated the empty glass.

"I'm good. Sorry if you felt run off."

"Not at all." Brian picked up his fork.

"You've been wonderfully understanding and helpful during this whole ordeal, Brian. I want you to know how much that means to me." Callie reached out her hand.

Brian took it with both of his, saying, "Just so we're clear, I did it because of what *you* mean to me."

It was Callie's turn to get emotional. When she had her voice back, she said, "Right now, I wish that woman with the big hat who's sitting behind you wasn't watching us like a hawk."

Brian smiled. "We could give her something to really watch."

"Or give her a heart attack. I also wish I didn't have to fly off for several days."

"You'll be back. And we can get back to our lives again," Brian said, unwittingly echoing what Callie had just said to Hank, which made her grin.

"And will you write a song for me while I'm gone?"

"Huh?"

"Never mind. Just be you." Callie pushed back her chair. It was time to leave. "That's all I want."

While other passengers loaded carry-ons into overheads and settled into place, Callie gazed out at the tarmac from her window seat. Her phone rang and she smiled, instantly recognizing the ringtone.

"Hi, Delia. What's up?"

"Good news! Your new electric meter has been installed. You have power!"

"Fantastic! Thanks for letting me know." They chatted briefly, Delia wishing her a safe trip, and then said their goodbyes.

As Callie put her phone away, she thought of how it had rung when she'd been bound so helplessly in Duane's storage shed. The idea that she had a way to call for help had urged her on. And then she'd found the phone useless.

She'd forgotten this part of her ordeal, what with everything that had followed, but now she had to wonder. If she hadn't had cell phone access in that shed, why did her phone ring, and who had called? Her phone hadn't shown any missed calls.

Just now, she'd recognized the personalized ringtone she'd set for Delia. And she had ones for Brian, Tabitha, and Lyssa. It hadn't been any of those. Callie pulled up her contacts list and scrolled down, thinking. Then it came to her.

Over a year earlier, when she and Aunt Mel had chatted before Callie's visit to Keepsake Cove, she'd chosen a special ringtone for her aunt. It was the first few notes of a song that fit with what those conversations with her aunt meant to her. With her aunt's death, of course, the calls had ended.

Or had they?

It was shortly after Aunt Mel died that Grandpa Reed's music box, treasured by Mel and Callie alike, had begun to play unexpectedly, often at crucial moments. Coincidence? Callie never knew for sure.

There was no music box in that storage shed. But her phone had rung unexpectedly, and at a crucial time—when she was about to give up. Hearing the phone had spurred her on.

She pressed the ringtone she'd set up long ago for her aunt, and which she now knew was what she'd heard in the shed. The familiar notes of "You Raise Me Up" played.

The man who'd just buckled himself into the seat next to her looked over. "Nice song." He smiled a grandfatherly smile. "Must be for someone special."

Callie smiled back and nodded, then looked out of her window.

Yes, it was.

The End

Acknowledgments

I'm very grateful to my husband, Terry Hughes, who has been endlessly supportive and patient, especially when a deadline looms and there's no food in the house. The long-running Annapolis Critique Group has, as always, been invaluable in the development of this book. Thank you Becky Hutchison, Bonnie Settle, Debbi Mack, Penny Clover Petersen, Marcia Talley, and particularly Sherriel Mattingly, who saved me from wasting a major plot point.

I'm also grateful to the Midnight Ink team, especially my excellent editor Sandy Sullivan, amazing cover illustrator Mary Ann Lasher-Dodge, and the person who oversaw and kept it all together so well, Terri Bischoff.

Many thanks, once again, to agent extraordinaire Kim Lionetti, and to all the wonderful readers who let me know, one way or another, that it's all really worth it.

© Angela Powell Woulfe

About the Author

Mary Ellen Hughes is the bestselling author of the Pickled and Preserved Mysteries (Penguin), the Craft Corner Mysteries (Penguin), and the Maggie Olenski Mysteries (Avalon), along with several short stories. *A Curio Killing* continues her Keepsake Cove mystery series with Midnight Ink, which also includes *A Fatal Collection* and *A Vintage Death*. A Wisconsin native, Hughes has lived most of her adult life in Maryland, where she's set many of her stories. Visit her online at www.MaryEllenHughes.com.